Praise for

Down Under

"A sly, subversive take on the familiar boy-meets-girl, boy-loses-girl, boy-becomes-a-world-famous-movie-star-and-tries-to-win-girl-back story, *Down Under* is a sheer delight. Sonia Taitz has written a fast-paced, quick-witted novel filled with trenchant observations about celebrity, aging, culture wars, and the search for true love. I raced through this witty and insightful book, anxious to reach the end. It came not with a whimper but a bang."
—JILLIAN MEDOFF, bestselling author of *I Couldn't Love You More* and *Hunger Point*

"*Down Under* is a beautifully constructed farce that reaches out in many directions—some amusing, some disturbing. The novel portrays a young boy's thrillingly brave and heroic struggle with his domineering father. We are hooked on the character of Collum Whitsun, and on his girlfriend Jude's obsession with this young, courageous boy. The writing is at all times so subtle and so right. When the middle-aged Collum sees himself become his father, the author brings a tragic dimension to her tale, even as the hero begins to go kablooey. It is all very enticing to follow her intelligent lead.

While very much of the moment, and no less than a witty take on the zeitgeist, this novel is at the same time imbued with deep, dark truths and a sense of warped wisdom. Sonia Taitz is able to segue from an arch scene or grotesque moment to a heartfelt observation or smart insight with ease, finesse, and an unerring sense of literary mischief. A bravado performance, full of truth."
—WESLEY STRICK, screenwriter of *True Believer, Cape Fear,* and *Final Analysis*

"Boy meets girl, boy gets girl, boy loses girl, boy finds girl again. Sound familiar? Not in the deft hands of Sonia Taitz, whose funny, tender, big-hearted novel about love, loss, and the one that got away is a pure delight from start to finish."
—YONA ZELDIS McDONOUGH, author of *You Were Meant for Me* and *Two of a Kind*

"*Down Under* is a sharp, sad, and funny trip to the emotional antipodes. Weaving a story that's based, in part, on the broken soul of one of the world's erstwhile heroes, the author takes us from the northern exurbs of New York to Australia and back. Love, madness, and the meaning of loyalty form the backbone of this fabulous (in every sense) yarn. Sonia Taitz combines depth, pathos, and hilarity, creating a love story that is part legend, part cautionary tale, and entirely delicious."
—SUZANNE FINNAMORE, bestselling author of *Otherwise Engaged* and *Split*

Praise for
The Watchmaker's Daughter

NAMED A BEST MEMOIR OF THE YEAR BY
FOREWORD MAGAZINE

NOMINATED FOR THE SOPHIE BRODY MEDAL BY
THE AMERICAN LIBRARY ASSOCIATION

"Not your typical coming-of-age story ... American Sonia Taitz, born to survivors of the Holocaust, lives under its long shadow in *The Watchmaker's Daughter*." —*Vanity Fair*

"Funny and heartwrenching." —*People*

"One of the year's best reads. This poignant memoir is a beautiful and heartfelt tribute to the author's parents. Funny, yet moving, *The Watchmaker's Daughter* illuminates Sonia's Taitz's life growing up in New York City, the daughter of Holocaust survivors . . . It is the story of an ambitious and gifted daughter whose aspirations and goals collide with those of her parents." —*The Jewish Journal*

"Taitz writes beautifully about religious roots, generational culture clashes, and a family's abiding love."
—DAWN RAFFEL, *Reader's Digest*

"An invigorating memoir . . . especially noteworthy for its essential optimism and accomplished turns of phrase." —*Kirkus Reviews*

"Sonia Taitz, born to survivors of the Holocaust, lives under its long shadow in *The Watchmaker's Daughter*."
—ELISSA SCHAPPELL, *Vanity Fair*

"Even now, as the last Holocaust survivors pass away, wrenching reverberations run through Taitz's poignant, poetic memoir."
—*Booklist*

"A heartbreaking memoir of healing power and redeeming devotion, Sonia Taitz's *The Watchmaker's Daughter* has the dovish beauty and levitating spirit of a psalm . . . A past is here reborn and tenderly restored with the love and absorption of a daughter with a final duty to perform a last act of fidelity."
—JAMES WOLCOTT, *Vanity Fair* columnist and author of *Lucking Out*

"Sonia Taitz's memoir of growing up the daughter of a master watch repairman who survived the Holocaust is also a haunting meditation on time itself. Taitz writes with a painter's eye and a poet's voice." —MARK WHITAKER, author of *My Long Trip Home*

Praise for
In the King's Arms

"Beguiling . . . Taitz zigzags among her culturally disparate characters, zooming in on their foibles with elegance and astringency." —*The New York Times Book Review*

"A witty, literate, and heartfelt story, filled with engaging characters and relationships." —*Jewish Book World*

"Evelyn Waugh, move over."
—JESSE KORNBLUTH, *Vanity Fair* essayist and curator of HeadButler.com

"In her gloriously rendered novel, *In the King's Arms*, Sonia Taitz writes passionately and wisely about outsiders, and what happens when worlds apart slam into each other."
—BETSY CARTER, author of *The Puzzle King* and *Nothing to Fall Back On*

Down Under

Also by Sonia Taitz

Fiction
In the King's Arms

Nonfiction
Mothering Heights
The Watchmaker's Daughter

Plays
Whispered Results
Couch Tandem
The Limbo Limbo
Darkroom
Domestics
Cut Paste Delete Restore
The Day Starts in the Night

Down Under

Sonia Taitz

McWitty Press   New York

For information, address McWitty Press, 110 Riverside Drive,
New York, NY 10024.

www.mcwittypress.com

Cover design by Jennifer Carrow
Interior design by Abby Kagan

Library of Congress Cataloging-in-Publication Data
Taitz, Sonia
Down Under: a novel / Sonia Taitz.—1st ed.
p.cm.
ISBN: 978-0-9852227-4-1

This is a work of fiction and the usual creative rules apply. None of the
characters are real. None of the events ever happened.

In memory of Neil F.K.B.K. Boyle,

1953–1990

The advantage of the emotions is that they lead us astray.
—Oscar Wilde

For the sword outwears its sheath,
    And the soul wears out the breast,
And the heart must pause to breathe,
    And love itself have rest.
—Lord Byron

Down Under

Prologue
The Middle, or the Muddle

n the middle of the journey of her life, Jude Ewington realizes that she is starting to see real lapses in the looks department. For a once-handsome woman, these downturns hurt, the losses as portentous as a rich man's failing fortune. Some small restitution might be made—the equivalent of cents on the dollar—and rather than bemoaning this fractional comfort, Jude tries to embrace it. Products are available and she buys them; they promise to restore the appearance of a viable sexual allure. And buying them is action. It is dynamic, almost lusty, to care this much. At this particular moment (the eve of another birthday whose number insults her), Jude stands gamely in front of her mirror, wrangling the hooks and eyes of a waist-cincher. Her face reddens in a tug of war against time, that flesh-destroyer. She could rage against the dying of allure—or buy the right foundation garment.

A feminist, a reader, intelligent and educated, Jude has to laugh at the irony. Having started her life on a par with any male, she now willingly tortures herself in ways they rarely would. It is the early twenty-first century, and yet the boned garment with which she wrestles resembles one forced upon the females of a more

3

benighted time. Worse still are her anatomically incorrect shoes—
too tight, too high, too pointy. Modern women bought such dag-
gered monstrosities in order to follow the fiat: Seduce. This kind
of self-inflicted pain—so female—was now oddly deemed macho,
not masochistic. But no settled soul would stand it.

Jude had come of age in the heyday of sexual and gender revo-
lutions. She knows that men no longer bestow identity, status, or
joy. She accepts that women can and should attain bliss on their
own shoe leather (however pointy). She has her accomplish-
ments; she has had great moments independent of male company or opinion. Most, however, occurred before desire had swept
her away, weightless, into its arms. She'd been an eager, curious
girl until boys entered the picture. Then her life had tilted as she
leaned, eagerly, curiously, toward love. After that came marriage,
home, and children. Yes, she worked (sporadically), but passion
remained her narrative focus. Somehow, she'd been cast out as the
lead. She'd had twin boys, which meant that three males circled
her hearth, running toward or away from it just as they pleased.
So much of Jude's life was conditional, vicarious.

She knows it all. But knowledge is not wisdom, and neither
will temper a true desire. Nothing had ever felt as good as that
first sweep of erotica, the brief touch of immortality that romance
had once brought her. Jude is no pioneer anymore; she wants
to be a paramour. Like a courtesan, she needs to adore and be
adored. After all these years, her dearest wish is still to buckle
up and rocket to the stars. Wasn't love still the deepest source
of truth? She wants to shudder with love and relief as the truth
reveals itself, crashing. What, she thinks, did these clomping
years have to do with passion? They'd buried it. But wasn't truth
supposed to be timeless?

Jude still feels that love *is* the deepest source of truth. She will
excavate and find it once again. Even as her husband's hair has

grayed and his stomach softened, Sam has remained the focus of her days. Which is unfortunate, because over the same decades, Jude seems to have become less and less the center of Sam's own, increasingly busy, calendar. And passion unreciprocated is—no, she couldn't think of it. She could not grow bitter, a wire-haired harridan, or resign herself to the portly eunuch's corner, consoled by a torsade of shiny pearls. There are ways of getting to men, and Jude is doing what she can to learn, buy, and apply those ways.

On this night, she colors her lips with a deep pinot stain and glistens them with a sweep of an oily foam wand. She lights scented candles—how like love they seem, hot and flickering, then sputtering in a death-crackle, followed by a pool of velvet darkness. She lies down on the bed and arranges her garters. Her black-stockinged toes point prettily, she thinks. Ten ninety-nine a pair, and they'll probably rip five minutes after he gets here. She yawns loud and long, her jaw cracking. It is 11:20 now. What an embarrassment, she thinks, if she were to fall asleep before her husband comes home, an effigy of waiting and wanting.

Jude falls deeply asleep, which actually gives her more pleasure than the best coitus she (or anyone) has ever had. She is tired; her life as a disengaged wife makes her very, very tired.

The telephone jars her. Jude leaps, wipes her mouth, rummages for the phone, swipes it toward herself.

"Heh—?" Not even a word. She's made a sound, a cut-off syllable. For an oddly pleasant moment, Jude doesn't know who she is or where she is. There are possibilities in this waking haze. She'd been dreaming, and she can remember some retrieved sense of her actual self. Her "look" has blurred now: the gloss is smeared, an indignity she herself can't see, just as she can't see that her two coats of extra-rich mascara have turned into smuts of sorrow under her eyes. In her dream, there had been no sorrow, no husband, and no smuts.

"It's me." Sam Ewington's voice is hard and harsh for this hour of night. It is the voice of a man in a good suit and tie, rushing relentlessly in the world. Male energy is like that—brisk and cold. You had to warm it up with your stockinged feet. Jude feels a tug of habitual longing. Always so far away these days, which makes her wish him closer.

"Can you believe it?" he continues rapidly. "The plane was late. I only just got into the airport. Don't wait up. It's gonna be baggage claim and customs and the whole damn rigmarole."

"What time is it?"

"Just after midnight. Happy birthday—got you some great stuff! When you wake up, you'll see. Get some sleep, sweetie."

Sweetie. That word, which lately replaced her name, had never sounded sincere. Jude sinks back down into unconsciousness. She dreams a new dream.

In her dream, she encounters a boy whose passion never wavers, no matter how many years go by, how old they become, or how far he has flown from her side. He shows this constancy in the way he holds her, looking into her eyes, his own eyes shining with deep recognition. In her dreams, Jude stirs him in a way that cannot die. She doesn't need to stuff herself into outfits; she doesn't need to set the mood. It's there. It's set. She can enter it herself.

You Can't Touch This

Collum Whitsun's life is all about distances. Once he was poor, and now he is rich. Once he was shunned and hurt, but for years after that he was worshipped—he's been famous. As a boy, he had to move from New York State to New South Wales—a jarring change of continents and climates. That was his father's doing. Then, his meteoric rise as an actor took him all over the world, from dripping Aztec jungles to the golden hills of Jerusalem. But none of that travel was real, he thinks; he's been sent like a package, tied, stamped, and flung.

Or like a yo-yo, maybe. Out into the transcendent, and back to his small, real self. It's all been rather polar.

He is traveling on his own now, a hero's sort of quest. This is not a boy uprooted by his father's crazy mandates, or a star driven by the exotic demands of blockbuster filmmaking. This journey is as real as life can get. That makes it harder. That makes it frightening. No father, mother, brothers, wifey, passel of kids; no crew, no doubles, script girls, fluffers. Collum will have to be brave now, alone—but not so brave that he breaks. In the last few years, he's noticed a wear and tear on his sanity, the presence of black rages and blazing pangs of sorrow that increasingly unnerve him.

Sometimes that has meant drinking. An old fallback, yes, like stepping into another language, costume, wig. There's no shame in a bit of self-preservation. Buffers stave off madness. A man might need such props from time to time. Collum's nervous system jangles and twangs more than most. It's the core of his appeal and his undoing. But finally, at least, he is going where he wants, and going *for* what he wants.

What does he want? What everyone seems to want: love. The man is alone wherever he goes. He'd love to be embraced and understood.

Collum, like Jude, is getting older. It's inevitable, insulting; it's unbearable. All of his life's efforts have begun to taunt him. Nothing lasts, not even world fame. His star is falling, and people have stopped paying to see him on the big screen, where he thought he'd be immortal.

So what, he thinks, because (as he now grasps) their "love" has never been real. Fortune is fickle, isn't that what they say? Real love, he now knows—*that's* permanent. As a boy, Collum had tasted it briefly—a pure and giving grace. The girl who had offered that brief shelter would remember him. He's never forgotten her. Well, maybe for a while, when he'd been distracted by hellish illusions. There had been an increasingly disgruntled wife, and many insufficient lovers full of lies. Users, tossers. None of them had been true. Not one. The proof was in his solitude.

Collum's traveled a long way to get back to his girl. He's getting there now, and he's nervous. What if she doesn't want him anymore? What if she really hurts him? Time, then, for a drink.

Collum's head lies heavy on a pub counter. The establishment is located about an hour or so north of New York City. The actor's cheek sags on a carpety beer-cloth, stiff with hoppy, old spills. Alone as he feels, he's in public, and the folks around him begin to notice his hair, too yellow to be real. Baby-chick yellow. Technicolor blond. They take in the broad shoulders under his distressed leather jacket. Ordinary men don't often have shoulders like that. Collum works out, though to less and less effect. They gossip and wonder who he is. Their curiosity is almost aggressive. Famous people are not like the rest of us. They seem dangerous, like game. You want to tame them.

"It's not him. He's taller."

"I read somewhere that he's shooting a movie in Costa Rica!"

"No—I think they said Upper Westchester!"

"Boston. Back Bay. He's great with those accents."

"You know what? It's one of those professional look-a-likes," says a woman, pensively chewing on the straw in her cocktail.

"Love to have one of those at my bachelorette party," says her friend, tossing her extensions, which boast permanent banana curls. "Do you think he really looks like him?"

"Nah. This one's too old to strip," says another woman, licking margarita salt off her upper lip. An astute observation. Good shoulders, yes; but the hips and legs are wider than desired. Despite the hair, they give away his age.

"Too old and too damn drunk," says a man in a seersucker blazer, jealous of the lug on the barstool. His comment is sustained by a wave of nasty male laughter.

Collum is stirred by these noises. He mutters. His large head rises, peers around briefly, then sinks down again, calling to mind a Disney animatron.

"Don't touch me," he growls, though no one's touching him. "You'd drink, too," he slurs, sitting himself up almost straight. "Been through what I been through? Be drunk like me. If I was drunk . . . which I'm not."

"Wow! You're so beautiful . . . *Colm Eriksen*? It's really you?"

He's always hated his movie name: "Colm"—like a coxcomb.

A hair comb. One syllable, a silent "l." His real name is Collum. Like a column of soldiers. A column of fire before them by night, a pillar of cloud in the day.

A woman bends over, breathing what feels like steam in his ear. Collum smells something juicy, like peaches, mixed with the musk of a tropical bloom. Warm female, closer than before. Flowers and overripe fruit.

He arches his head away and peers at her. The woman gets a blast of his blueberry eyes, bloodshot but still dazzling. Collum notes that hers are dark from pupil to iris, black-widowed with stiff mascara. Her breasts push into his face, proffered like a summer basket.

"Hello, me Sheila," he says kindly. She's wearing a V-necked leotard and pencil-thin pants. She's worn them to be wanted and is now delighted to be seen, finally, by no less than Colm Eriksen.

"I know," he murmurs considerately, acknowledging the awe in her face. She looks enraptured, lost, and loving it. Collum is familiar with the way such star-fan meetings go, has been ever since his image was first projected onto big screens in the dark, making it iconic. If only they knew how heartsick he is, how he, too, longs for what's holy.

"*What* do you know?" she whispers, touching her own long neck. Other than the immoderate breasts, she has a dancer's body, legs long in proportion to the torso. She should leap, he thinks; she should run far away. He has nothing for her. A cock without love is a weapon, he knows, even as he feels himself stir. Here we go again, he thinks. To the dungeon. Down to hell. He's been there many, many times.

Collum's words come quickly, but his voice remains soft: "I know what you all tell me: 'you're great, you're handsome, you're—sexy.'" He spits the word out.

"You don't—I don't understand . . ." she says. "I never met you before."

"Oh, but you did," he says. "You're a fury and a succubus; we're very well acquainted. Let's see what happens."

"OK," she says, nodding without understanding, the way they all did when stung by the toxins in his heart. *Aw keh.* He hears a trace of an accent. Albanian? Persian? Slav? He's sad to think that he's had most of them.

"My name—it's not really Sheila—but I love your crazy words. Like in that film where you were so mad and had to take revenge?"

"Be more specific," he growls, smiling at his own harsh wit. All his movies were like that. His life was like that. "Anyway, I'm still quite mad."

"Stop joking," the woman says. "I'm sure you're very nice person. Oh, God—" she interrupts herself, "I have to take this."

She reaches into her purse and pulls out her phone, aiming it at Collum's drunken face, his red eyes and sad mouth.

"Take that snap and I'll break your honker."

The woman freezes.

"Don't be so bloody frightened, Sheila," says Collum, laughing gently now that he's frightened her. "When I was a lad, I got my nose broken many times."

He continues as though on autopilot. He often tells this tale to the magazines.

"Nothing like the feel of a man's fist, coming at your face, all knuckles and hate. 'Now you're not so pretty, pal,' said a thug called Tim. 'Oh, but you're rugged now,' said a lass called Briony, kissing the broken path of my airway."

"You talk like artist. You have poems inside you?" The lunatic words and the veins in his eyes confirm that for her.

"Oh, that I do," he responds, scanning her so intently that he seems to care. "I'm an artist and a poet and a pirate."

She nods in sincere harmony. "But tell me, who is this Brian?"

"Not *Brian*. I'm not a bender, darling. *Briony*. Tahiti, location. Hair, makeup, shag. Dead to me now, all lost and cold, but the one that I can't kill off."

"You are talking zombie movies now?"

"In movies, I do pulverize them all. But this one. Crikey. She just won't die, will she?" His face turns downward, and a little sob escapes.

"Wait. I know. Your wife of many years," says his new friend. "I read about divorce. And after all that history," she adds, as though it were a shame rather than a wonderful opportunity.

"Like the blossoms of Kyoto. Such delicate perfection. They all fall down to dirt, you see. But one small bloom remains."

"You are single now?" the woman tries to clarify. Has he been in love with an Asian woman? She's read nothing like that in the tabloids.

"One little cherry bud stubbornly remains," he repeats sternly, "but I guess I must *spell out* that I am using metaphor, my darling."

"Heh?"

"I'm talking about a GIRL, for Christ's sake!"

"Oh. What girl?"

"Yes, that's right, there are so many girls. You, for instance. You're a girl."

"OK."

Aw keh. Collum was great with dialects, a skill that had served him well in his acting career. Turkish, perhaps? He'd never been with a Turk. Might be wild. He made a tiny gesture with his hand, and the bartender sped over.

"Same again?"

"Lots more," says Collum. "Here's what I do with girls," he continues, rising to his subject. "I make 'em wait while I have my smoke."

Gazing at her breasts, Collum pulls out a cigarette. He doesn't light it; he just rolls it in his fingers. "She waits for me . . ." he continues. "Such patience."

"Who? The blossom? Your many-years wife?"

"Yes and yes and yes. She watches me take a long, deep drag." He mimes with the unlit cigarette. He *is* good actor, she thinks, breathing like that, inhaling as though he were really getting buzzed. When he lets go, he emits a long, shuddering sigh that thrills her.

"The whole process looks as though I'm thinking, yeh? It makes *her* think exciting thoughts of how I'll do her, later. In my own good time." With great care, Collum puts the cigarette back. He lets his eyes meet her eager eyes again.

"You w— you will really 'do' me?"

The drink appears and he downs it quickly, his face slightly pinched.

"All night long," he says, pushing the empty glass away, exhausted. He really must be on his way, on his journey, but now his legs don't move. He wants to fall on his knees; he wants to cry long and hard until the waters finally dry.

"Oh, my God, you're incredible hot!" says the woman, taking his head into her hands. Suddenly she's kissing him. Collum notices and pushes her off.

"The lads of my youth, *they* weren't hot. Cold-blooded, they were. Don't move to Oz as a teen, my dear. Ozzies don't like it when you don't talk right."

"I am also immigrant, so I—"

"Good on you! Try being new in the never-never, back when the bush was kinkier, when sprinklers weren't hissing and lawns didn't cover up the dingo-bone truth. I was the abo, the wog, the wretched Yid of Yids. My fish-belly face broiled in the sun; I didn't belong; I was mocked and jeered. Only the horses understood me, and I broke those brumbies hard as I could, 'til they couldn't run away. But I had to run, broken or not. Had to run, run, run . . ."

This is another set piece for the press. Collum pauses and takes a breath. "I'm running now," he admits, now honest. "And I don't know who I am."

"Oh, let me help you," she says, with that tinge of an Eastern European accent. "My name is Ada," she adds, scrabbling deep into her shoulder bag. "Here is card. I am artist like you. Pianist. Powerful fingers. Also good massage."

Collum lets Ada tuck her card into the back pocket of his jeans. She takes her time with that, then kisses him again. Slowly, he becomes aware of the genius in her tongue. She's not so much sexy as talented, like a dog that can do acrobatics. And not only her tongue but her teeth, too, little jolts of surprise. Hind limbs and fore. Not only the dance, but a wave of the paw.

Collum unlocks his mouth from hers. He can't think when women play him like that. Why was life push-pull? Why no peace? Why this constant boring pain?

"Please, Sheila. I just wanna please, please God come home." His head feels heavy, and he needs to rest it. Just briefly. To momentarily regroup.

"You are very sad man," says Ada, sheltering him in her thin, strong arms.

Tied Up and Run Down

J ude Ewington lives in the village of Plum Grove, about an
hour north of New York City. Most of the time she is not
a vamp in bustier and garters, akimbo on the marital bed.
She's like that, with less and less effect, only on her birthdays
or on Sam's. She's really just a part-time teacher, mother of two
boys. Her energy is waning; life has taken a few turns downward
in recent years.

A decade ago, Jude's husband, a successful management consultant, lost his job. During the economic tailspin, every firm Sam
tried to manage or consult with disappeared into the ashes of bad
accountancy and global shrinkage. So the worst fate in America had
occurred to this family—it had slipped and skittered downward.
For instance, the family no longer found seasonal respite in the
country club to which Sam had once belonged, with its clay courts
and fantastic cocktail service. Nor did they take off to Europe or
Wyoming for cultural experiences. They had reined all that in.

It is August, and all the summer holds for Jude is searing heat,
relieved by paddling in a plastic pool, four-feet deep and seven in
diameter.

Money was meaningless, said the sages. Except when you didn't have it. If you had it, it was meaningless until you lost it. Both ways, money could make you feel slighted or bruised, as though fate itself were snubbing you, running ahead and letting a big door slam on your toes as you tried to catch up.

After the downturn, Mr. and Mrs. Ewington and their boys had moved. They moved out of the glass-and-marble house with the natural pool and koi-stocked pond and into the repurposed farmhouse with parklike garden and wide-beamed floorboards. Then they moved again, into a "charming" cottage in Plum Grove, a house so small and nondescript that the broker touted no hyphenated features. Still, the community boasted a lake, a clubhouse, and a sandy little beach where toddlers ran around in waterlogged swim diapers.

Jude's husband is now finding the ground under his feet—metaphorically, that is. In truth, he's in the air more and more, flying to Europe and back for his new business. He works for himself now and calls himself "a food entrepreneur." It's wartime, the time when the tough get going. Sam is grimly excited. He's going to make it all back on his own ingenuity.

Jude, recovering less masterfully, is still recalibrating her life.

She had grown up comfortably in a nearby town, so living in Plum Grove as opposed to, say, Bedford, Pound Ridge, or Greenwich, is actually no great shock. In fact, at times it's familiar and cozy to live in the little cottage. Her parents had been middle-class, upper-middle at best, not wealthy. The only sad part was that the chutes and ladders tumble had made her husband tense, almost fierce, about recouping his losses. And with that new passion, something in their bond had been displaced. These are lean times, his eyes seem to say, cutting off Jude like a dog who has gotten all the treats he (she) is going to get. No more Milk-Bone—and not even a scratch behind the ears.

Their money was gone, and that could be restored. But where has her marriage gone? Where is the love of the groom and the bride, promised and somehow unmissed? Most men, Jude realizes, are not crazy for love the way she increasingly is (just as it's fading). "Eros" (like studying Byron in college) was a phase many of them simply endured, a toll they paid to achieve what they called adulthood. When they paired off with a mate, they were done. Most men, she realizes, are relieved to go back to "normal," to seal the marital deal and move along. Parenthood often replaced romantic passion, but even her children, who'd worshipped her once, were teenagers now. Jude's little nest was lightening; it swayed up on the bough without ballast.

For now, she could play the thrifty housewife. And more— she could go out into the world. While Sam struggled to restore his tail feathers, Jude had increased her hours as a teacher. Luckily, she'd majored in English at the State University of New York, at New Paltz, and now taught creative writing at the local high school. Long, languorous summers were one perk of this profession. But they left her wistful, and the sultry heat didn't help the mood.

Jude's pool was purchased at Toys*B-R*Joys, an emporium at the nearby mall that sold everything from cardboard, glue sticks, and glitter to bad bicycles and short-lived summer hats. The boys had fallen in love with it when they'd been much younger, and now it still served Jude well. In any case, Sam would never surrender to the indignity of an above-ground pool, which—though perfectly serviceable—told the world you couldn't pay for excavation. But it was all right to have a little something for the kids.

And Jude took comfort in it. If you looked at it with the right attitude (one of someone who had never had an inground pool, much less one hewn out of rock with dove-gray tiles and a lovely heater), the little pool was actually no "toy" but a nicely cooling body of blue water. Once Jude's boys got in they could frog kick a bit and feel refreshed. The plastic cover that kept the bugs out was bright and cheerful, a button on Jude's tidy backyard. This summer, the boys seemed to have outgrown the pool.

Though they are gone, their mother still floats in its sweet little circle, curling a foam tube under her arms and kicking with her feet, slow and pensive. As the water caresses her body, she broods. Summer is almost over. Summer, when the air was hot and pools were cool, and women were, perhaps, entertaining little shivers of sheer, imagined joy. The way they used to do when their cycles first began. Even if they were now middle-aged, nearing the end of the hormonal ride, even if they were tied-up and run down. Their minds still wandered free and ageless. Jude's did, and still does. Especially when she rides the versatile tube like a horse, a loyal and intelligent steed that could carry her anywhere in the world on a lover's journey . . .

More and more, she finds herself thinking beyond this marriage, backward in time to the first and strongest love of her life. That boy is of course a man now, no longer young. He has married, divorced, raised kids, burned out—but Jude knew him once, before any of these diminishing events had ever happened. These days, she knows about his life the way everyone does—through the tabloids, TV, the Internet. She can follow his life more closely than she ever had, even when they lived right near each other and went to the same school. Everyone can.

But being lonely, picking up a magazine at the supermarket is dangerous. There he is, her first love. His face has changed—there are wrinkles and sags—but the hurt, unsettled eyes are still the same. They drew her then, and they draw her now, more deeply than before. This is someone, she is certain, with a soul as hungry as her own. Underneath all the accretions of their lives—and time was one of these—something absolute remained. At first, it had been enough to know this, to hold the past as a shield against the losses of the present. But soon, Jude had felt a compulsion to reach out. It is so easy to go from voyeur to participant these days.

Perhaps it was not the wisest idea in the world to have opened a Facebook account on her birthday, only to request him as her first "friend." Not after all those years and the harsh way it had ended. But what harm could really come of it? "Colm Eriksen" had a fan page with thousands of "friends." His profile photos were a gallery of him in endless movie getups—brooding, handsome, and heroic stills from his artificial life. The Indian, the Zulu, the monk, and the rogue. The Viking berserker, the widowed philanthropist. Jude studied these obsessively, and one day, when scouring through the list of his fans (and their own friend lists), she had noticed his original name. "Collum Whitsun" had a profile of his own, one with only about twenty "friends"— Collum's children (all with the Eriksen surname, most still in Australia), and some of their pals. His brothers, their wives, some nephews and nieces.

Jude had then contacted Collum with a new profile that used her own "real" name—the maiden name of Pincus. A little map located her somewhere in the suburbs of New York. In her message to him, she'd written, "Another birthday, but my heart hasn't aged." To her delight, Collum had accepted her "friendship" immediately. The quick response felt like a huge squeeze around her, a confirming hug that warmed her, head to toe and everywhere in between.

"Hey Mom!" David still calls her Mommy, but Joe has taken to this cooler "hey Mom" locution. Either way, they often drive her mad (Jude takes pride in how well she controls this moodiness). These "kids" are fourteen now, and one is approaching the word "hulking"—couldn't they get their own snacks?

Joe was off in boarding school during the academic months, but in the summer Jude gets to remember how loud, insatiable, and demanding he can be, and even the shy David, who stays home all year long, echoes his brother's boisterousness after a few weeks together.

In the spirit of good grace, "Mom" would do just as they wished. "Mommy" would haul herself out of the cool waters and out of her reveries. Up the pool's shaky little metal stairs and down the other side, she will pad across the lawn, up the deck stairs, and into the kitchen. By the time she gets inside, overwhelmed by artificial light and the packed, humming fridge, the water spell would certainly have broken. Not only might Jude end up not going back into her pool, but she would probably drive the boys somewhere, to that mall, for instance, to buy them shoes for the new term. From fridge to car to mall, anti-sensual and almost cruelly banal.

But they were boys in summer, so brief a season, playing Ultimate Frisbee and beating each other up, laughing at nothing at all. That was their fun; they should have it. But what was her fun to be? Was pleasure merely a thing of the past? That seemed too cruel and Darwinian—that she had fulfilled her biological purpose and could now be ignored, except for drudge's duties.

The twins rarely let her touch them, much less hug them, anymore. In the past, they had been her puppies, her cubs—tumbling with her, allowing her to tussle their hair. At night, she would read to them, their heads on her shoulders, right and left; she would kiss them and smell their yeasty smells. Now, getting their ice pops was one of the only ways Jude still experienced the fleeting perception but still undeniable fact that she loves them and that they love her. It wasn't their job to show it; that would increasingly be the job of her husband. And he did, at times: he had surprised her with the pool. What is more, he had set it up, refraining from cursing when the byzantine instructions had, here and there, frustrated his sense of mastery.

The ice pops' colors are so fake that Jude often worries if she really ought to be buying them. Was she showing love to her boys, or perhaps contributing to a future disease, the sort that would strike at about her current age? But she gets them anyway, running to the enormous fridge.

How she'd loved tending to her children's needs when they were born, when she could hold each like a football and nourish them from her own breasts. Her body had magic then; it could create life and nourish it. Every biological step had been sensuous and rewarding. The seeds inside her growing into people she would love forever. The round tummy, a pool itself, heated and protective. An ocean, in fact, salt-rich and sustaining; in it, they swam and grew. Her voice must have been fascinating to them then, muted and mysterious, a sea-mother calling from a larger sphere.

The births were hard, but then again it was a war that is won and ends in glory, a parade, and that fountain of victory— mother's milk. Their eyes had met hers in recognition, old soldiers who share undying memories. But now they had forgotten all that, and that was . . . that was good. That was what the world wanted: that a man leave his mother and father and cleave to his wife.

But what should the mother then cleave to?

Phrases from the Bible often echoed in Jude's ears. The boys' names were biblical, too. David and Joseph. Jude's parents were Jewish; her father quite traditional. Jude's own name was originally Judith, but how could she keep the name of a woman best known to the world for chopping off a man's head? (Jude's father had had the female form of Judah in mind, not the decapitator.) As Judith grew up, in any case, the name had diminished into "Judy," and later "Jude" began to fit her better. That was a name she would keep, a brand she treasured, evoking, as it did, both the darkness suggested by Thomas Hardy and the Beatles' comforting tune. "Take a sad song and make it better," they had cajoled. She was trying. In fact, she had been doing so for years.

Jude's name helps her now when she wants to be more than a fecund farm animal. It helps her when she's the wife of a man who is always in Italy, exporting special pasta from Rome. The pasta is shaped like spaghetti, but significantly thicker and more expensive, and empty in the middle, like a drinking straw or a pipe that has run dry.

She doles out the ice pops and grabs a red one for herself. Later, after showering, I'll check my Facebook account, she thinks with a little shiver.

She has not been able, after all, to resist opening up to Collum. She didn't stop with the first little greeting. No, she's come forward, she's been honest, and told him that she missed him. It was out in the open: she was married and she had children, but no one had ever known her, never needed her, the way he had.

Collum had responded to this honesty with heat. *His* life, he said, had been one big lie since they'd parted. Everything he'd done had been false. Every step away from her an agony of exile.

Jude had been delighted by this intensity. She remembered the boy she knew, lost and lonely. She'd found him and he'd clung to her, become her own soul to tend to. How amazing that after being lauded as the biggest star in the world, and all that fame and money, he still felt that way and needed her. She needed him, too. His longings were linked to her heart, soul, and groin. His need summoned hers. It made her body hot and willing. All the water in her little above-ground pool couldn't cool her off these days. There was a man in the world who might claim her now—a man whom every woman wanted, but who wanted only her. A man who knew her without age and time and trouble.

If he were to stand in front of her now, she'd jump on him, wrap her legs around his waist, bite him on the shoulder, mash his mouth. They'd drop down to the ground and he'd cover her with his body. You wouldn't be able to see her; she'd be down, under. Lost and found at the same time. This was the kind of sex people wrote volumes about. Byron had composed poetry in honor of it. And maybe Jude could have it. She could have it and have it and have it. Sometimes him on top and sometimes her.

On the other hand, it was all too real, and it was crazy, rotten, wrong. Jude had never done anything in her life that was so clearly sleazy. She had never deliberately hurt anyone. She had never committed that harsh word, adultery. Some had. There were affairs going on all around her in Plum Grove, and people accepted it. It was a way of getting on, surviving—something like a cocktail, an Ativan, a joint. But with Collum, it would be much more than that. It would be a revolution. A mutiny. It could rip hearts out and unseat thrones.

Jude had always prided herself on being not only a good girl, but a superlative one. Her father had once called her "the one you can always count on." In fact, the only horrible thing she'd ever done was hurt Collum in the breakup long ago. And even that had not really been her fault.

Should she let him count on her again?

A month after they'd started reconnecting, Jude told Collum that they should stop, that their exchanges might be dangerous.

How could this end well, whichever way it ended? She was committed to her marriage and her children.

He had answered:

I don't care! You're the one who really knew me.
You're the one who really loved me.
You're the one I'll always love.

These three sentences—sentences she deeply wanted to hear, sentences she couldn't deal with, sentences that saved and ruined her—had stopped the game. Jude had not been able to write to him again for days. Collum had re-sent his message, but then, to her consternation, had written no more.

So even if he'd "always loved" her, he could still cut her off? Love was funny like that. Love was awful like that.

Jude is worried now. She does not want to answer, or be answerable, but she certainly does not want Collum to disappear. Not now, when her boys are taller than she is, when her husband is away more than he's home. And sometimes away even when he is at home. Preoccupied. And not with her.

She goes upstairs and gets out of her bathing suit. She showers, dries off, wraps a towel around her body. She checks her computer for input. There is still no new message, so Jude composes one herself:

I have been swimming, round and round like a fish in a bowl.
Every circuit leads to you.
I had an ice pop earlier. Red,
like my lips would be if we kissed for a very long time.
It would be chaste. It would be honest. Just kisses forever and
nothing else. Or everything else, but so pure and so true.
Of course I love you. I always have. Come here and get in my pool.

Her heart beats wildly as she presses "send." The words instantly come to Collum and he reads them. Her words pierce his heart just as his words pierced hers. His heart beats wildly, and he tries to calm himself down.

What a tease, he thinks, hoping his cynicism can save him from pain. Just when I think she's there, she's nowhere. "*It would be honest,*" she says, and I don't even know her married name. "*Come here and get in my pool,*" she says, and she's playing house somewhere with some lucky bloke, but I don't have a proper address.

Slam

Jude's husband was nicknamed "Slam." His real name is Samuel T. Ewington, but he's such an incredible tennis player that his friends, and there have been great crowds of them, dubbed him "Sam the Slam," which led to plain old "Slam." Men now greeted him like this:

"*Hey Slam!* How's it *goin'*?"

Possibly this brash camaraderie hid their fear. Slam could be formidable. He tended to be first on line in life's proverbial banquet. He won all tennis games. He still made good money. He'd have to be tall (lucky for him, he was towering). He'd have to have sons; he had two, born efficiently at once. He'd have to have the sleekest, darkest mane in all the jungle, that is, the world of business in which he operated. And he did: thick, abundant, sleek, and shiny hair, the coif equivalent of the Cadillac Escalade SUV. Now that he was no longer in the formal business of consulting, he wore his hair long and wavy; its touches of silver only enhanced it. Sam's height and his locks and his tennis and his cash had to exceed that of everyone in his circle, including his two growing sons, which for now they still did.

You could laugh about the new pasta importation career, but it was neither funny nor ridiculous, because, after a period of struggle, Slam was beginning to make a nice living with it. People really went for the thick spaghetti, especially the tubular whole-grain. People took food seriously.

Before his downturn in fortune, Slam had made good at his more traditional job. A management consultant, he had specialized in multinational food corporations. He had been able to make a few million, most of which he had lost in the crash, but he had invested a serious portion in the noodle world. Now he produced handmade pastas that, like the most precious matzoh cracker (Jude had described this bit of Judaica to him), is watched from the time the little seeds are planted, grow, are harvested, baked, shaped, patted, pricked, and marked with an "S" for Sam, Slam, or Success. No, not literally marked—metaphorically. In short, the man had discovered, as he liked to put it, that "there is dough in dough."

You also could not laugh because Sam's business allowed him to—no, *demanded* that he—travel to Italy for "quality control." Slam liked to be in control of quality, and in this world there are few places where you can control anything. Or anyone.

For instance, teenage boys could sometimes be insubordinate. They spent their lives playing with their thumbs on little buttons, or watching beeps go by on pixilated screens. One of your boys could be flighty, and get such rotten grades on easy tests that his boarding school threatened to expel him, even though his father had been a distinguished alum. The other could be lanky, shy, and bookish, making you wonder if you had played enough ball with him (not that this boy had wanted to). That one could go to boarding school and return within a month with a nervous condition. The pediatrician had suggested the occasional use of anti-anxiety medication, but Jude had refused to give her son those pills. She felt that time itself would help her shaky boy.

Wives, thought Slam, were even harder to control. Wives could be moody, and sometimes they looked as though they weren't taking as much care of themselves as they should. (Bustiers and heels and whatnot could not replace hard cardio time at the gym.) No matter what you did for them, they seemed always to be muttering to themselves "Eh! Not good enough." (And that "eh" delivered with a tiresome, Abrahamic sense of moral judgment.)

And then, all of sudden, they would be all sweetness and scented candles; what was the angle with all these moods? Probably that was the perimenopause, which was another thing you couldn't control. Mother Nature, and her slight (but noticeable) loss of skin tone.

Slam himself was feeling a bit older lately—despite his vigorous exercise, both at home and abroad (at home, the recumbent bicycle; abroad, the sporadic skirt-chasing). His sense of time moving on was getting harder and harder to ignore. But the pasta, unlike Dorian Gray, Ozymandias, or Drexel, *that* was eternal and ever-renewing. So was the travel to Europe, that long glide through the air, away from cloudy Putnam County, across the amnesiac ocean, and into *la bella Italia*. There, they treated Slam like a prince of the Medici (whose coat of arms boasted three bold rock-hewn balls). There, he could sit in the velvety lounge of a hotel with tapestries hung on the walls. A man of the world, he could perch on a throne-like wooden seat with rolled armrests and stare at grapes, nipples, and laurels atop the immortalized heads of the victorious.

Breaking Horses

Collum Whitsun's closing in. He's lying low in the bush and creeping forward toward Jude. More than sober in the daytime, he is alert and purposeful. He's figured out approximately where she is, so he'll need a low-profile base in upper Westchester or lower Putnam counties. Working at a stable seems an optimal idea, good cover. These are abundant, as wealthy women liked to ride, and more than that, liked to see their children—particularly their daughters—in full gear, sitting atop handsome, trotting horses. In Australia, where Collum had spent his teen years, riding was sweat work, hard on a bloke's body. Here, it seemed to be poofter-oriented. Still, horse-wrangling was the sort of work at which one could be anonymous as he searched for his girl.

Before his fateful face had led him to playacting, Collum had been best at manly labors, and what could be manlier than the handling of large beasts? After moving the family, his father had found even Perth too cosmopolitan. Ignoring his poor wife's protests, Neil Whitsun had taken Collum and his two older brothers to a cattle station miles away from any civilized town. There, under a crazy, yellowish sky, the boys had learned to break horses. The trick was to be mean and nasty, while making quite sure (by use of ropes, whips, and spurs) that there could be no form of retaliation.

Once subdued, horses would work all day in the dust, ridden by hostile men, leading and pursuing even-more-subordinated cows into orderly lines and columns. Young Collum often felt like those horses, wild and bad, broken and good, hated more than he was loved. He even felt like the cows, hounded—there were literally hounds who chased the cattle—along with the horses. These hellhounds were wild, ankle- and shin-biters, mouths open, baying, toothy and hysterical. At home, they were confined to a shed and given no affection.

Collum could be gentle, though. His hands possessed a genius touch, and he could breathe peace into an equine beast in seconds. His strong legs gripped these animals with a message that reassured them: Stay put and do as I say. We'll both like the ride. When he learned this, he learned that love could be as big a bully, as harsh a sadist, as power. He was happy to have this knowledge in his arsenal of tricks.

Neil Whitsun was a deeply religious man, so this ordinal dominion did not trouble him; these rankings, to him, were sacred and immutable.

"It was Adam, was it not, who named all the beasts of the field?"

If you say so, Dad, thought Collum, whose own name, no matter where he had lived (American suburbs, Aussie savannahs) brought him only teasing. "Column A or Column B?" people would pipe, laughing in his face. And his last name, Whitsun? That was witticized into "witless."

"Be proud of your name," his father had said, when Collum had complained. "Collum is a Saint. He bore more suffering than you will ever know. And Whitsuntide is God's own fair season."

Whatever that means, Collum thought.

"Thanks, Dad," he said dully.

Thanks a lot, for nothing. Worse than nothing. Something sulfurous. Collum thought of his father himself as God, not the good God but rather God the punisher, God the burner of villages and instant slayer of sinner-men. God of the permanently unfair season. He vowed to find a way to escape this primal netherworld. He had tried once before, and failed. Now, the very heat he lived in seemed like Hades, invented by his father to stun the boys into submission.

Meanwhile, his mother served meat up every day. Three times a day, she plopped it on plates, red and sizzling, wet and quivering. Three times a day, and the boys chewed it in both sorrow and anger, chasing it down with hurlings of fresh, frothing milk.

Collum's older brothers, Ryan and Rob, were tall and strong, but Collum was tallest of the three. By the time he reached his eighteenth year, he was long, lean, and hardened, inside and out. His hair, on the other hand, was a swirling blond, the hair of a Renaissance angel. Collum's face, moreover, conveyed the sweetness of youth, a kind of pained but faithful longing. This expression, conflict balanced in poignant equipoise, helped him flee his world. Women had only to look at him and they would fall into a dreamy trance.

That Collum became a brawler from the time he discovered drink only made him more appealing. Drink made him angry enough to run from the ranch. He wanted out, and tried to get there, mostly with his fists. His nose was broken a time or two, and often a girl, impressed by these melees, gave him exit and peace through her body. One of those girls, an aspiring actress called Lyndee, thought he ought to try out for a small film she'd read about. She showed him an advert in the paper: "NO EXPERI- ENCE NEEDED. CALLOUSES AND TOUGH MUGS A PLUS."

"Well," said Collum. "There's no shortage of those in the land of Oz."

"Come along," she needled. "I'm trying out for the girlfriend of the lead."

"I'm not a bender," he objected, "and I won't hold your bag."

Still, a few days later, he went along, just for a laugh. A cast- ing director saw him and summoned him inward. In a simple room with a scuffed wooden floor, dirty windows, and dusty sills, heads nodded all around.

Collum was surprised to win the role in a small Australian film of a drunk, poignantly conflicted young man. He had come to Lyndee's audition straight from a brawl, blood trickling from his golden hair, matting the strands on his tanned forehead. His gaze, below, was blue and clear—a steady, daring gaze that seemed to say: "You can fall in love with me. Go ahead."

The casting director, female, took in his long frame, decked out in scruffy jeans, black T-shirt, and manure-caked work boots. In front of all the others, and long after Lyndee had dejectedly gone home in habitual defeat, she asked the young man only a few questions:

Name:

Collum Christian Whitsun.

That your real name?

Hmmm? Yeh.

Collum is real and Whitsun is real?

Yeh. And Christian is real, too, if you're asking.

Experience?

The advert says I don't need it.

Life experience, then?

All the bloody badness of life, and I love every minute of it.

Sometimes this kind of thing—cockiness, cursing—gets you thrown out of a meeting. In Collum's case, he won the part—a terse five minutes of screen time, true, but enough to be noticed. As a lad in Putnam County, he had been mealy faced and spotty, but in Australia, his skin had burnished to the color of caramel, and his blazing eyes echoed blue skies. In the coming years, the saturated colors of Hollywood films would flatter him more, but even in the dusty, drab sepia tones of the Australian product of the time, Collum Whitsun glowed. He was juicy and tactile. You could live between the bristles of his strong unshaven chin, and live happily.

In his next movie, Collum played a wild man who hated his abuser father. Was life getting easier or what? This time they gave him a cheap prop gun to act with. He loved to shoot people, staring at them with that angel's clear gaze as he took their lives. He seemed bravely moral. A man more sinned against than sinning, but definitely, forgivably, vicariously sinning. Men started to like his movies as much as women did, particularly when the guns got realer and bigger and the costumes more leathery and steel-studded, down to the heavy boots. Collum played this role over and over, the avenger, the punisher, the martyr who, shouting at epic volume, topples the pillars of the world. He became a star in New Zealand and Australia.

In his last role before his fame exploded, Collum took his vendettas to a new level. He was not a victim, not an avenger of past wrongs. He was no longer coming from below, from down under. No, he was flying at his prey from above, from the top of a sailing ship with a maiden at the prow. Collum was now a Viking without conscience or reason. He was a wild man, a victor, a pitiless marauder with flying yellow hair. Only a woman could tame his crazy Wagnerian heart.

And if she did not, she would be his prey—just like the men.

Vikings had no time for the middle ground. Something in the pink roots of their hair, the blood-tinged scalps suggesting the hide of a boar, was utterly berserk and feral.

Collum could access that part of himself very well. He could access a murderer's heart. There was no getting even, only going beyond.

In these films, of course, there were many beautiful women, all of them with heaving bosoms, all spirited as mustangs, nostrils flaring as their hair tossed in the wind. And Collum (and the hero he played) did seem tamed, from time to time. But no woman would ever fully capture him. By the end of the movie, back he would go, restlessly, to maraud some more. He would remember her, but—no, maybe he would not even remember her. Her breasts were but bubbles, her locks a flick of foam, hissing on the shore; gone. And on he would tread, a hero, a man alone.

This passionate coldness, perfectly enacted for celluloid, made Collum a movie star all over the world. The archetype translated universally. He was a man without the burden of doubt. A creature, a force of conscience-free chaos. He changed his name from Collum to Colm and from Whitsun to Eriksen, the name of a true Norseman. The sound of the "X" in the middle of his name was the snap of Thor's thunder.

Whether or not they admitted it, women loved this persona. In the darkness of the world's cinemas, they dreamed they alone could change this rogue with the cold blue eyes. Change him for good. Take him home and lock him up. Un-wild him, declaw him, keep him in a jar. Break him like a wild horse that would never run away.

The Faithful Wife

The one who succeeded longest in taming Collum was Gingerean O'Haire, a student nurse he had met when both were no older than twenty. Her pale skin and thin red hair (really countable hairs) had somehow touched his heart. Collum had been dating her much sexier roommate, Kiki, who knew how to wear three colors of eye makeup, who lined her lips with black. But one morning, Kiki (who was an ill-mannered slag) had remained in bed well past lunchtime, and Collum had trodden into the kitchen looking for food.

Gingerean was cleaning up a mess in the sink. She was scrubbing a sticky spot with a coarse sponge. Her tiny bum jiggled as she labored virtuously.

Collum slid next to her to open a cupboard and look for vanilla cream biscuits or a packet of digestives.

"Oh, I'll make you something," Gingerean had chirped helpfully, as he stared into a gallery of tins, looking doubtful. She put down the sponge, wiped her hands on a flowered tea towel, and proceeded to serve him.

It was only Vegemite and toasted white bread, but Gingerean's little freckled hands had set the table with a pretty orange plate and a paper napkin with daisies on it. Collum had especially liked that touch of domesticity.

"So nice," he commented, sighing between hungry bites. Vegemite was a yeasty brown spread that Australian people loved. It had taken Collum years to stomach it (it was salty and concentrated, like beef bouillon), but as he approached the adult age of twenty-one it became a staple of his diet and a sign, to him, of a well-stocked life.

Gingerean sat shyly, watching him gulp down the offering of her food. She liked how quickly he ate, how hungry and needy he seemed to be.

"There's more where that came from," she said, blushing when he lifted his brow in an almost suggestive fashion.

"*More*, Gingerean? Whatever do you mean?"

"Oh, no, I meant more tucker, Vegemite and that, I didn't mean—"

Her blush was a true redhead's blush and it overtook her totally, down to the top of her blouse. Though she was sitting stiffly next to Collum, drinking milky tea, her face had the look of a woman after vigorous, life-changing sex. It was very clear that this girl was a virgin, untouched and innocent. Eve before the apple, his father would have said.

Collum was surprised to find himself blushing as well.

"What's your name, again?" he said, feeling unusually tender.

"Gingerean. I know. It's unusual. My parents—they were going to call me Gillian, which I think is much, much nicer, isn't it, but they took one look at my gingery hair when I was born, and—"

"And fell in love straightway?" said Collum, for once not glib. This girl was no Kiki, selfish and difficult and hard. She had the nurturing heart of a mother. And he loved her name, a name as sweetly vulnerable as she was. Gillian was a competent, closed door of a name. Gingerean was an invitation, an open palm that you took in your hand and accepted.

As for Gingerean, something in Collum—an unconscious goodness, a remnant of innocence—touched her so much that she could overlook his handsomeness. His aggressive beauty was not his fault, and it was a shame that they attracted mean people like Kiki, who didn't know what he needed.

Before long, they were going steady. Collum grew to love Gingerean's sweet, chaste kisses. He loved her cotton bras with the embroidered little flowers, the white Christian underpants. He loved the modest skirts she wore, loose and long, when all the other girls wore hip-huggers and showed off the obscene troughs of their navels. Most of all, he was moved by the way Gingerean eventually made love—with a frown of concentration on her face and a wish only to please and gladden. He knew she would not have given her body to him if she had not loved him. And he loved her generous heart in return.

Gingerean was not only motherly in heart; she was blessed with an excess of fertility. Before he knew much more than the comforting feel her body gave him, Collum had impregnated the girl.

"I'm—I'm carrying our baby," she told him, standing in the doorway, arms reaching up to kiss him when he came home to her. In between small movies, he'd joined a local theatre company.

"Oh! Oh, my darling," said Collum, using the most tender, grown-up word he knew. As soon as he called her that, and despite the constant temptations of humid actresses, he knew that Gingerean would be his own precious wife. Catholic born and raised, Collum would let no child of his be snuffed, or born a bastard. Not while his father was alive. In any case, he cared about Gingerean. She was tender and loyal, more tender and far more loyal than any other girl had ever been. And if she now needed him, he was glad to step up and be her hero.

This first child was a boy, and he was bonny and healthy. Despite his youth, Collum took eagerly to his new family, even as his acting roles got bigger. He felt snug and proud, thinking of the good mother he had in Gingerean. At the same time, and to his surprise, Gingerean grew into being his equal in bed. Over the years, as her hips spread and her breasts expanded, she became a hearty-hearted wench when he'd return from a theatre tour or film set. She'd leap at him, kisses all over, take him in all the way, welcome back, and here's your home. All the way, with bouncing enthusiasm and no end of willingness. Like their firstborn son, she made Collum laugh with a deep delight he had never known before.

During those years of joyous lovemaking came one child after the other, in the old-fashioned way. Boys and girls, redheads and blonds—hugs and piggyback-rides and shrieks of delight and discovery. Collum was truly happy for the first time in his life. He had a nest; there was a brood; it was all honest and kind and cozy and warm and hot.

Collum's career expanded alongside his family. Eventually, a husband and father called Collum Whitsun became the gargantuan star called Colm Eriksen. A war—first internal and then external—began to brew, as the star became more and more famous. His American manager, Sydney Koplin, took him all the way to the top. There, Collum found temptations of all kinds—salaries, luxuries, perks, and veneries. Collum tried to keep a level head, but no man can forever resist the luscious comforts of vanity. He dampened his guilt by buying bigger and bigger properties for his family ("Suitable for a star of your magnitude," the estate agents had said), and hiring more help to take care of them (the family and the mansions).

At first, Collum battled only with his own conscience, lying to protect his innocent wife. But then Gingerean, growing ever more knowing, would start shoveling for answers. A whinging note had entered her voice, turning her questions into complaints that annoyed him.

"Why are you re-shooting? I thought you said it was a wrap!"

"Why is she there? She's not in your scenes!"

"I thought you were done looping yesterday!"

"Can't we meet you somewhere on the weekend?"

"Don't you love me anymore?"

It was just maddening. Was it not enough that he told her to spend as much money as she wanted? (But she never even wore high heels; cheap and sturdy sandals were good enough for her.) That she lived on the biggest estate in Bondi Beach? (She'd slipped on the marble too many times, and one of the little ones, toppled by jets of water, had almost drowned in the eight-seat Jacuzzi.) That he pounded her in much the same way when they lay together? That he tried to please her as often as she wanted, forcing himself to groan and moan as he summoned thoughts of studio-paid, subservient Asian call girls and delicious black stuntwomen? (He had never been stupid enough to actually fall in love with a film co-star, or even to seduce one; that way lay diva madness and tabloid hell.)

But he should not have done that, Gingerean secretly thought. Not the whoring; he was a man, and men did that. But he should not have pretended to love her as he did, when he didn't. Her own husband didn't seem to care that their special bond was dying. Collum still made love to her as though he were the same man who had loved her and only her. That was a lie: he was not the same person—but he would not admit it. She could see in his eyes that she was not the girl who had once touched his heart. To him, she was no longer Gingerean, a young and innocent being whom he had once loved enough to bed, impregnate, marry. But begging him to see that she was still Gingerean would only come across as one more complaint.

"'Course I know who you are!" he'd bellow. "How could I bloody *forget?*"

Collum began to resent his wife's encroachment on his own desires, which had grown and grown. Like so many married men before him, he was forced to reckon with the stringent emotional needs of the female. His appetites were satiable; hers were not. She wanted the past back, and that was impossible. She was screaming at him now, full-throated screams that reminded him of his crazy father's fury. Another Neil Whitsun to poison his days?

"Cut!" as they say in the movies.

For the next few years, apart from child-rearing logistics and updates, they barely spoke. Collum and Gingerean were simply the management team of the Eriksen firm. Still, once in a while they lay together. Gingerean would be passionate sometimes; she would get pregnant again and seem proud to tell him that he had once more filled her with life.

After the twenty-fifth year and twelfth child, Collum and Gingerean stopped sharing a bedroom. Gingerean, at last, could no longer endure another round of childbirth. Collum retreated to one of the better guestrooms, which had its own rainforest shower and two-tiered sauna. He had been finding it harder and harder to feign any desire for his wife. He collapsed at home after long flights (he was shooting in the States now, a real star); he had no energy for her or the boisterous kids. The children were shushed by their mother, whom they took for granted and even resented. Daddy was different. The younger ones squealed when he tossed them in the air between naps. The older ones admired him—he was the special visitor who made their lives shine again. They had learned to see him from afar, and from that distance, he was always perfect.

In this retreat, Collum became more and more lonely. No one could see the real him anymore, and those that did just complained and complained. His very looks—*People* called him "the Sexiest Man Alive"—now offended his wife of decades. Why had she aged so much faster than he?

It was simple. In the real world, spring and summer had turned to autumn. Gingerean was tired, heavy, worn-out despite the horde of servants—nannies, tutors, cooks, chauffeurs, and laundry women—they could now afford. No naps could restore her. The sexiest man alive had used her up good and proper. She had formed and carried twelve healthy, strong babies, nursing each one for over a year. Her stomach had loosened, and although her tidy breasts did not exactly sag, they flapped emptily, envelopes whose contents had been skimmed and tossed away. And there was still hard work to do.

While "Colm Eriksen" flew off to location, often more than a dozen hours away, Mrs. Whitsun remained down under, shadowed by his jets, weighted by the mob he had bred into her and out of her and left her to raise. Yes, she loved the children, and was amazed that she and Collum had created this pack of healthy, active kids, vibrant as Kennedys. No one could ever doubt that their love had once glowed with life and shared purpose. But Gingerean herself was no longer vibrant. Heavy and slow, she plodded through her days, months, and years. Gravid with accumulated grudges.

In interviews, Collum always called Gingerean his "Rock of Gibraltar."

Gingerean felt hurt by this glib epithet, which actually compared her to a heavy piece of stone. I'm not a rock, she thought, from time to time. I'm a bloody volcano.

She finally kicked him out.

Collum was more shaken by this than he could ever admit. He was speechless, and when he talked the liquor slurred his pain and his words. There was often a grinning girl on his arm, now openly. Sometimes two, holding him up like a trophy between them. In his own hand, quite often, a bottle. After all these years, he thought. He felt homeless and hurt, and a little bit crazy. He felt hatred for all the people who had ever betrayed him. He was an orphan and an outcast and a lover too much scorned.

Jude Had a Friend

Jude had a friend in the vicinity whose name was Heidi. Despite the pleasantness of the name, which sounded like a greeting from the spruce-scented Alps, Heidi's life was in certain ways unsound. Like many a marriage (Jude's, Collum's), Heidi's had become shaky as the years and events piled on. Now, it wobbled like a too-tall column of blocks.

Over the past few months, Heidi's husband had started sporting a thin braid of straggly pewter-colored hair, the tonsorial equivalent of the pencil moustache. He was also, surreptitiously, a junk food addict. This was especially insulting to Heidi, who ran a gourmet, organic, and eco-friendly cooking service for her village and those adjacent to it. Even more insulting was the fact that Dan attempted to hide his eating vices from her. He did it ineptly—shoveling Ding Dongs down his throat and explaining the chocolate stains by claiming to have simply "tested the Valrhona."

"Valrhona" was a holy word to Heidi, and not to be taken in vain. Nevertheless, she swallowed her rage and pretended to accept these lies. It was better than fully knowing the details of her partner's revolting new life.

Though his given name was Daniel, Heidi's husband now presented himself as "Dante," without the Italianate second syllable, and thus pronounced "Dant." Earrings? Yes, of course: two on each side, studs and janglers, to show he wasn't taking it anymore, "it" being the bourgeois life and all its discontents. For no apparent reason, after a spring in which he pretended to be on vacation, Dante had gone on strike and wouldn't return to work. He was finding himself. His life, he announced, had been a masquerade and a sham. From now on, it would be authentic. In this, Dante found honor and a rare sense of reclaimed manliness.

It was now nearly September, formerly the beginning of the year, but now, for Dante, just another month in the whirling gyre others called life. What was at the center of the center of that gyre? Dante aimed to find out before existence had fully crushed his testicles.

He and his wife had a daughter. For years, Heidi had been barren, so she'd had the treatments, from acupuncture to injections, and finally resorted to donor eggs. After years of effort, months of nerves, and hours of wrenching labor, Heidi gave birth by Caesarean to a ten-pound, shrieking baby girl who now glared at her with malice. This child, Delaney, had just entered Jude's tenth-grade creative writing class, an elective to which only the most talented or troubled were drawn. Delaney, six feet tall and glowering, was of the latter camp.

Delaney idolized her teacher. Ms. Ewington truly seemed to understand Delaney's unmet needs and poetic rages. Each week, when the class was asked to compose a story, Delaney wrote about her mother. All her stories went like this:

Deena's mom is such a lying bitch. She whores around like a prostitute. She is mean to my Dad. Because she herself has eating issues, she thinks her daughter is fat and hides all the food. But the daughter finds it.

HA! HAHAHAHAHA!

Deena puts poison in her mom's special herbal tea. Her mom drinks it. So pathetic. She thinks she can taste everything so well, but she doesn't.

Slurp! Her mom drinks it all.

Her mom gets poisoned.

She dies.

Deena is happy. Then she runs to her father and says:

Dad! Dad! Dad!

We are finally free of the wicked bitchy witch!!

Delaney gave Jude stories like these, asking if they were good. She wanted to know if she should become a writer. Jude placed check marks here and there, although it was hard to find a place to show such assent. For example, near the phrase "we are finally free," Jude wrote: "Yes. The search for freedom is indeed very important in our lives!" On the bottom of the essays, she added, as mothers and teachers of our day often do: "Good work!!" She wanted Delaney to have high self-esteem.

Jude said this even though she knew that the writing was not "good," and not even the product of "work" (as the word is commonly meant, with the intimation of energy expended). It was the result, rather, of a kind of instinct, like gagging. Just as newborn babies are capable of the Babinsky reflex when the bottoms of their feet are tickled, many teenagers could spew out the sort of lines Delaney did without the slightest effort. Usually, these hostilities were tamped down and civilized. Delaney, instead, was proud of her words. She thought (at least partly because of her teacher, Ms. Ewington) they were "good," and would not write about anything but her mother, and how much she wanted her to be dead.

If the class assignment was "Write about a color," Delaney would compose an essay about her mother turning purple as her throat is relentlessly squeezed.

If the class assignment was "Write about your favorite moment in your favorite day," Delaney would respond with a view of the near future, when her mother will lie unusually still, having taken her last breath. HAHAHA!

Jude thought of talking to Delaney's mother, who was, after all, her neighbor. But Heidi seemed willfully banal—a dangerous type that was prevalent in these parts. "Think positive" was not merely a helpful cliché out here, but a fiat. Like keeping a tidy lawn. Or not having an old above-ground pool remain, like an eyesore, when your kids have outgrown it.

Jude sensed that Heidi would not react well to the implication that any aspect of her life—much less her only child—was flawed. Her lawn was not only tidy, but organically so. Like many a college-educated suburbanite, Heidi applied fierce deliberateness and intense consideration to the most mundane tasks. Soignée and petite, she was like a housewife from the fifties, or rather a show about a housewife from the fifties. In pumps and a double-row of pearls, she baked cakes and made soups from scratch (the base carefully brewed from chicken or beef bones, the vegetables cut and blanched just so). Her pots were always aboil and bubbling, and the kitchen smelled as intimate as a barn of sows and sucklings. On the sill one could find homemade kefir, to be added, later, to homemade preserves.

Heidi's full name was Heidi Dorcas Kunst, a series of clacking sounds that are hard to say. It was hard to be her acquaintance, harder to be her friend, still harder to be her husband, and hardest of all to be her mannishly tall and broad daughter. Heidi was, in fact, both the blessing and bane of striving womanhood, for anything she did was sheer perfection.

Heidi's domestic arts were proprietary; she would not trumpet her secrets to the world. She would not share her womanly arts with the common viewers of television or readers of magazines. No, Heidi's province had begun in the small and leafy town in which she lived, and was only now beginning to slowly expand. The town was West Salem, an upscale enclave ten miles from the one in which Jude lived in confusion, metamorphosis, sexual longing, and sometimes squalor. (Jude and Sam *could* live there, by the way—his income was rising—but there would be less money left over then for luxuries like Heidi's food and other suburban word-of-mouth necessities.)

To illustrate with "compare and contrast" examples:

Jude often left dishes in the sink overnight. True, she'd "presoak" the odd plate or saucepan, but . . .

Heidi washed her dishes, saucepans, blenders, cutlery, zesters, and sieves by hand, lovingly, with an organic cleanser that not only smelled like lemon, but did, in fact, contain lemons, cruelty-free lemons (not plucked, but coaxed, from the tree) that were grown especially for her, and which she added, in her spare time, to the nontoxic cleanser base.

Jude, after many years of nagging and cajoling, had let her sons quit playing the piano. Joey now played guitar, but it was the electronic kind, in which one of four buttons was pushed, each in a bright color, as badly drawn bands rocked out on the screen, and for which imaginary points were won and lost. Davey, the social misfit (piano would have helped him make friends), merely listened to music, alone in his room. Usually power ballads, sung by women.

Heidi's daughter, Delaney, had been hammering her piano for years. Not only had she gotten to a studio within Carnegie Recital Hall (with a humorless Juilliard teacher) by practicing, she was now composing her own concertos for clavier and tympanum.

Jude wore yoga pants and monotonal cotton T-shirts all the time. Her nails were short and the most she did with them was file them. Her long chestnut hair was pulled back into an efficient plastic barrette. She wore ballet-style flats whenever possible, this despite the fact that she did no barre work. In fact, Jude practiced neither aerobics nor Pilates, nor did she (or would she) "spin" on an anchored bike, pumping her fists in victory.

Heidi was fit and tight from power yoga (she did not just wear the pants). Her flowing asanas were performed in a room so hot that, had the temperature been the same outdoors, it would send sane people fleeing into an air-conditioned room. Heidi could stand her whole body on one of her hands and wave calmly at you with the other. She wore ensembles and yet was far too knowing to have them match. Instead, her color schemes harmonized and "popped," the proportions alluding to each other. Her pants, often in light colors, were made of easily wrinkled fabrics, yet were never wrinkled. She wore blouses that possessed patterns of great and subtle interest, patterns that did not break unevenly at the seams. Her shoes always had a heel, be it a high one or a wedged platform (often of cleverly woven sisal). She especially favored the delicate "kitten" heel. Many of her shoes had peep-toes, which meant that they revealed the perfection of coral-colored toenails. Heidi exercised daily on a difficult elliptical machine, weighting her ankles with blue plastic shackles. Besides the hot yoga, she did advanced ashtanga, a practice so extreme as to involve the perineum.

Jude's furniture was simple and "modern." The boys slept on single beds they'd had since they graduated from cribs. Their room was often impassible with clothes and junk, and the bathroom equally repugnant, displaying such habits as uncapped toothpaste and lidless, unflushed toilets. One could often find a pump-bottle of body cream and an assortment of balled tissues on the gritty tile floor. Jude's living room sofa was leather, and black. It faced a large, old-fashioned television set. Deep within the sofa cushions, there were crumbs, attesting to a slovenly history of eating (worse, snacking) outside the kitchen or dining room.

Heidi's home paid homage to the countryside of France. Delaney slept in a full-size bed, covered in bright Provençal prints. The duvet matched the "window treatment" (and coordinating pendant curtain ties), and both matched the cloth shower curtain in Delaney's bathroom. The toilet seat was oak, rhyming visually with her bedposts and capacious desk. That desk was covered with a blotter, although little blotting was required (Delaney used a laptop). That blotter matched the paint on the wall, artfully mottled by Heidi herself. The living room (or "sitting room," as Heidi termed it) displayed Persian rugs, brocaded chairs with curved wooden armrests and legs, and an elegant, mushroom-colored sofa. Guests might enter this room and feel the hushed graciousness that is so often missing in modernity.

Jude ate pre-cooked food, often from the supermarket's freezer section. Lately, she had begun to order Heidi-food on an almost daily basis, and not just meals, but juices and condiments. She hated to cook, and considered it a demeaningly earthy chore, like being a prostitute or charwoman. The peeling, poaching, plucking, and stuffing of bagfuls of produce and carcasses seemed endless and unnecessary. Her sons ate processed foods and many dishes seasoned with hidden MSG. The spices on her rack were far from fresh.

Entire neighborhoods dined off of Heidi's gourmet cooking. In her immaculate, professional caterer's kitchen, she prepared salads and grills, gelées and croutes, purées, potages, and dainty, peaked meringues.

Jude could be very pretty *on a daily basis* if she tried, which she didn't. She was once the cutest girl in town. Her skin shone and her eyes glowed, and to see her smile was to hear the first birds of spring.

Heidi was plainness transformed by sheer force of will to a durable and lasting attraction. She wore a full, round do of beige-blond hair like a halo around her face; she acquired this look in the 1980s, during which curls and roundness in the coiffure were last permissible. She centered her tonsorial arc with a hair band, usually grosgrain, often with stripes that recalled the boating world, in which she was comfortable.

Heidi Dorcas Kunst was, in fact, one of the West Salem Dorcases, which meant something in her part of the world. It meant that she was wealthy and well-born. But unlike most members of her class, she felt an inner distress, a constant feeling that the best one did would never be enough.

It was simply not enough for Heidi to be a good mother to her daughter, which meant packing balanced and varied lunches and snacks, with caloric and other nutritional information attached. It was not even enough to feed everyone for miles around, to make a go at a culinary business. It helped; it distracted. But it was not enough.

Nor was it enough for Heidi to keep an immaculate home, constantly upgrading its surfaces, some to make smoother (from wood to marble), and others to roughen (from latex to impasto to textured coir walls).

It was also not enough to have a white flower garden as well as a stony Japanese garden with pagoda and water features, or even to have a built-in, walk-in wardrobe that held fashionable clothes, color-organized on padded hangers and all in the proper size (zero or XS).

It was not even enough for Heidi, surrounded by foods, to eat only what kept her body small, and to exercise vigorously each day so as to keep her body hard, with little balls of muscle here and there, not to mention the taut perineum.

It was just *not* enough.

So Heidi, feeling inadequate, was never happy enough. In this way, Jude sensed, her friend was dangerous.

Collum the Cowboy

Collum, once in pursuit of a tangible goal, was not easily deterred. Here was a man who had sired a dozen children, whose face and form had conquered the world entire. In movies, he had played many roles and learned many dialects and even languages, some dead. He had learned to juggle and Jet Ski and fake a dead man's fall from a tall building. Now, all he needed was that horse job; he must have some work to do during the weekends, a cover for himself as he sought his long-lost girl. And yet, there were obstacles.

He'd costumed himself with great care as the quintessential American cowboy, with a blackened moustache that ended in handlebars, a red bandana, and a white Southwestern hat (covering his darkened hair) that tied under the chin. And yet, wherever he now went, no one seemed to appreciate how much he knew about horses. Collum had worn this very outfit in an early Australian film about the Wild West, so why were people laughing at him? Yes, he was currently in the Tame East; he understood that, but didn't they get the iconic aspects of his getup? Could they not read his intentions?

Or was there something wrong with the way he rode?

Each stable Collum-as-cowboy had visited requested that he mount a horse and show them what he could do. He had learned to ride on the Australian saddle, traveled countless acres on that virtuous armchair with poleys for the knees, could sleep on it drunk and not fall off, even if the horse broke into a gallop. And in films he had ridden Western over and again. He had always known how to hold his seat and show them who was boss.

But here, the horses wore something quite extraordinary on their backs. He'd heard of the English saddle, of course, but was *this* what the Poms had actually sat on for all these years? That explained a lot. It looked like a thin, worthless pad, something you'd find on a girl's push-bike. But OK, he'd thought—riding's riding. Park your bum on something or other—saddle, blanket, throw pillow—smack the bloody beast, get on with your day, and no worries. If these snooty toffs in the North Atlantic wanted to prance around on wee leather cowpats, so could he. No spurs? No problem. Nothing in the front to wrap your leathers and gear around? Fine. A girlish whip to tickle the geldings? Whatever you say. It's your dollar, mate, so you can call the tune.

His manager had taught him that he who pays the piper calls the tune. That was supposed to mean that those who paid you owned you. And Christ, had he been paid, thanks to Sydney, master teacher in the care and handling of the almighty shekel. But did that mean they owned me, Sydney? Collum smiled as he thought of his keeper, who was surely now wondering where the star was, and how he'd seemed to vanish off the face of the earth.

How do you find the balls to disappear? Syd would be thinking.

Because *I* call the tune, my Levantine business partner, and it ain't the hora. Because money is not everything, and I would burn it all up in a pyre to have one night alone with my girl, Judy. She

53

needs me and I need her, whether she admits it or not. We have a lot of catching up to do, a lot of scores to settle.

And if she lacked the courage—well, he had played the hero enough times. He could take the lead. And here he was, so close already! With his taste for disguises and mastery of accents, he would not be easily discovered. He could bide his time, if he could just manage to get a job and blend in.

But that was the trouble—he couldn't blend in. It was like his first days in Australia, when everything about him was wrong— his language, his taste in foods, even his Catholic practices. They had laughed at him then, and he'd never forgotten it. They were laughing right now at these ranches.

They laughed when he'd fallen off a huge gelding, trying to "post." The minute his arse (in chaps) had left the whoopee cushion they called a saddle, the minute Collum had tried to mimic the weird up-down up-down of riders (nearly all sheilas in this part of poofterland), he had slipped out of the stirrups and slid earthward. And no horn to hold onto to get you back up! He'd wanted to sling his leg over but instead fell back to the dirt. The snickers! He had almost turned and smacked one of the cheeky looky-loos who'd mocked him. But attracting notice now was not an option. At least no one recognized him for now, in his western gear. He could have the last laugh, in time.

Toward the end of the summer, his persistence finally paid off. Collum found a suitable place to work, right in the town where he needed to be, East Plum. (Thank you, Facebook.) Close enough, but not too close. A man could drive from there to Plum Grove in no time, but few could walk it in less than half a day. Perfect.

His final job interview, though, was odd (like everything else around here). He tried to impress the jackaroos with how tough he was, how wonderfully quickly he could break down the meanest horse's will. By now, he could even post; hell, if they gave him time, he could have learned the sidesaddle. But they were not impressed. The titters again! (Were they laughing at his bolo tie?)

The manager of this farm asked Gretchen, one of the hands, to take Collum over and show him the stables. And slowly, then, he began to understand the kind of place this was. It was the kind of place Collum had never seen before, nor even knew existed.

A place of gentleness, where force was unknown. A horse's paradise, in fact, and in that sense a very Eden.

Gretchen described each horse as they walked over to his or her stall.

"I think we'll look at Butternut first."

Butternut was yellow, short, and almost fuzzy. She was a pony, Gretchen explained, and she loved to be scratched right behind the ears, like a dog.

The next horse, who snorted and stamped with delight when they approached, was Ajax, a piebald gelding.

"It's kind of an ironic name," Gretchen said, smiling. "He's really old and slow, but that's perfect. Slow and steady wins the race, eh boy?"

She flourished a handful of baby carrots with their greens still attached, a bouquet, and the horse mouthed Gretchen's palm and took them in delicately, first the small orange roots and then the flossy greens.

Collum was speechless.

This was a place, he further understood, where pain was healed, and riding was called "therapy." It was a place where there was no hitting or hurting, no contests, no winners and no losers.

Collum had never even known a place like this existed. For a while, as a boy, he had felt something like this, when his heart had been soft with love for his girl. But then it had been ripped away from him, and he had grown hard and calloused inside.

From stall to stall and stable to stable, the animals stood, quiet

and almost kindly. These horses, all of them, were almost preter-
naturally tame. They stood there, eyes shiny with love as their
flanks were brushed and their hooves lifted and cleaned of mud
and stones. They stood in the middle of the stables, tethered on
each side, as they were hosed down, curried, picked.

"Do you want to give Clemmy a sugar cube?"

"I don't have a sugar cube," Collum muttered, feeling put
down again.

Gretchen simply handed him a couple of hers. She was plump,
short-legged in her jeans, and cheerful. For a minute, Collum
stared at the crystalline squares that were transferred from her
hand to his. It was as though the young girl had offered him the
first sweetness he had known in decades. These were not props,
and there were no tricks—his hand held real cubes, composed
entirely of sugar. He almost felt like asking for one for himself.

Clemmy stood quietly. At the rattling of the sugar box, his
ears twitched. He turned his massive head, first to Gretchen, and
then to Collum.

"Here you go," said Collum, extending his hand.

"Let your palm really open up," suggested Gretchen.

Collum realized that he had been gripping his fingers. It was
a habit he had had all his life, this gripping and tightness, this
making of fists. His hand did not have to be a weapon, he realized. A grasping, hurting, grabbing thing that took and smacked.
He loosened his hand and put it in front of the horse's nose.
His heart expanded, and he felt the kindness of the sun and the
breeze's caress. Life could actually be good.

That thought held a sigh in it, a longing so deep in Collum
that he almost started weeping. If the world could be like this, he
thought, we'd need nothing and no one else.

Clemmy sniffed. His nose was warm and velvety. He took the
sugar cube from Collum's hand with flapping lips and a fondling

tongue. Collum enjoyed this like a boy enjoying his mother feeling his forehead when he is sick, each movement a caress as well as a question.

How are you, my darling?

Oh, Mummy. I feel so hot.

There, let's brush that hair off. You'll be better soon, right?

Yes. I'm better already.

Collum took off his hat. His eyes were now truly wet. If he were alone, he would have knelt and prayed here, as he once did as a child, when he'd prayed with all his heart to be delivered from his loneliness.

Each of the horses was as sweet as Clemmy. They smelled Gretchen's nostrils with their own, enormous nostrils. They said, very quietly, *huffff . . .*, as though to say, "I exhale with you because I can relax with you. I relax with you because I trust you. There is love in the warm air between us."

Yes, all that with a *huffff . . .*

Collum wanted that for himself. He wanted to feel a world in which warm air is exchanged between souls. He had always wanted that, more than anything or anyone. Even more than he wanted the girl he was looking for. After all, she had hurt him once, and could always do it again. Treachery was in her very bloodlines, the bloodlines of Judas himself, whose name was so similar to hers. And what was worse than Judas? A female Judas, that's what.

A Missing Ingredient

With all the ingenuity Heidi had—the ability to find the best sources for the best ingredients, clever whirring hands that could make things functional, tasty, or beautiful—something was indeed missing for this proud and capable woman. It was missing for everyone, almost without exception; it was the bane of existence for many on this hunger-panged planet. Heidi did not even know the name for it.

Perhaps, as the developmental psychologists had termed it, Heidi longed most for "object constancy." Babies needed to know that their mother was there even when she was not in sight, that she was there even when they closed their eyes or turned away. They needed to know that the loved one remained, even when she herself turned away, or was not there at all, for a time. Terror had to change to trust.

Unfortunately, there was little of this in adult life, where, instead, there was a preponderance of change, disloyalty, boredom, betrayal, and death—that ultimate evidence of inconstancy. Even the common midlife crisis, such as the one Heidi's husband was enjoying, could threaten the psyche of so staunch a soul as Heidi Dorcas Kunst.

Who was she? Who really knew her? Who really loved her? Who even cared if she lived or died? Heidi, like Jude, Collum, or any one of us, was lonely for a reliable friend in life, a companion who would, periodically, make the pain ebb away for one long minute. Make the bout stop. Like the trainers that led boxers to their corners, wiped them down, sprayed water into their mouths. One needed encouragement in life, between the rounds of pummeling. Heidi was longing for such sweet haven.

The catering business didn't fully help. Housewives envied her career, and career women envied the ease with which Heidi seemed to blend her work with her home life. She had updated her kitchen with a six-range stove, added a few freezers to the garage, and there she was. But she wasn't, really. All the food she cooked and all the clients she fed never nourished Heidi herself. The hole was always there, but most of the time she managed to ignore it. With her husband's instability—the name change, the piercings, the pewter-colored plait—the wound was tearing open again.

Heidi's unfillable void might have been caused by her past. Her parents had died in a catastrophic car crash when she was fifteen years old. That sudden horror, which made her life gape like the torn-up sedan the newspaper clipping had shown, seemed to be the key to her sorrow. But she had been in pain even before this blatant tragedy.

Heidi remembered how even when her father and mother were alive, she had longed for them constantly. They had never noticed Heidi more than in the perfunctory sense, and were always traveling somewhere else. She and her older brother, Mason, had been sent to boarding schools, and the family home was often empty, sheets on the furniture and dust on the kitchen range.

Once her parents were gone, Heidi couldn't remember a life that was different, closer, and warmer. They had evaded her with finality. Even the childhood home, with its gorgeous flower-filled vases and its carpeted walk-in closets, in which Heidi could smell her mother's scent of Bal à Versailles (clinging to the folds of her chiffon party dresses), was gone. Sold to a different family, one whose sense of the solidity of life had not been shredded and smashed.

Heidi and Mason had stumbled out of this mess together, left with the proceeds of the home sale and a sizable estate as well. They were given to the guardianship of the will's executor, a bachelor uncle who, while no villain, was no more caring than her parents had been. When Heidi graduated from Madeira School, her brother graduated from Wharton and started working in a local commercial bank. Mason offered to take care of his sister during her college breaks from the University of Michigan. Their uncle, relieved, had readily agreed to let her brother be her primary guardian.

But then Mason had ignored Heidi as well. When he was not working, he spent hours in an aspirational bar, proud to stand like a colossus in his suit and acquire knowledge of wine and women.

The University of Michigan was vast and loud, a horror after the niceties of Madeira, but in this place Heidi's heart laser-pointed on a junior called Daniel, whom she had met in business administration class. Business, because Heidi was determined to pin down the pinnable details of the world. She would be practical and careful, one foot in front of the other, numbers lining up into logical and predicable columns.

The class met from 10:30 to 11:45, and it was only natural that both of them would have lunch shortly afterward, meet on the sandwich line, and start talking. Daniel had noticed Heidi's dandelion of hair (the one thing she had trouble taming), and she liked the kind way he carried her tray for her, even though his own was heavy with a hearty, manly lunch. After the meal, he would take both trays and stack them in the right place. He seemed like a take-charge kind of guy.

Months later, after taking charge of her virginity, Daniel gallantly promised to take care of Heidi forever. His own hurry was perhaps prompted by his parents' divorce, which had occurred right after his leaving for college, and which had shaken him. Heidi and Dan agreed that life was full of awful surprises, and that a modest plan was the best way to live (it could then be embellished with optional, comforting fripperies). Dan would make the money, and Heidi would be his lover and wife, the mother of their future children. Both thought that they would have several, a passel of happiness, and that these children would have dogs and kittens and rabbits and a swing set.

As it was, they had barely produced Delaney—with a donor egg at that—who suffered from vertigo and hated all animals. Delaney actually seemed to hate everyone, her mother in particular. So even in the good days of early family-making, nothing had made Heidi whole. Because nothing out there could make you whole. Nothing on this tangible earth. Toys broke, books shredded, seasons passed, children grew, and passion ebbed and flowed. Husbands you met in business class might one day grow their hair beyond the collarbone, and change their names to Dante. Leaving you to have to expand your catering career so that life could go on resembling something normal and sufficient.

Drumming up business shifts sad thoughts away, so she dials her stalwart Jude.

"Hi, Heidi, how are you?" Jude says brightly. She's also been moping.

"Any orders for this week?"

"Hmm?"

"You usually call me by Tuesday, latest," Heidi explains. "It's Thursday morning! I wondered if you were OK."

"Oh, I'm fine! You?"

"Yeah, I'm great, been keeping busy. I've just finished my crewelwork. Orders slowed down for a bit, so I thought I'd make a little hanging for Delaney's locker at school."

"You're so lucky to have a daughter to make crewelwork for," Jude says, sighing as she thinks about her strapping boys, and forgetting Delaney's troubling stories for a moment.

"My boys are halfway out the door," she adds, "and they're only fourteen." Actually, only Joey was halfway out the door.

"Well, not my Delaney, I'm happy to say. Fifteen or not, she's not even going to that party the school is having next weekend. She's far too young for that sort of thing."

Delaney and Jude's son Davey were students at the same high school. They were invited to parties all the time, not only school-sponsored, but at people's houses, which was another order of party altogether.

From reading Delaney's stories, Jude knew not only that she wanted her mother dead, but that she had long gone to parties at the school and parties outside the school; that she had created a fake ID and loved to play beer pong and "hook up" whenever she could. Not, of course, that everything (or anything) she wrote had to be true.

"Won't this party be supervised or chaperoned or something?"

"Not to my satisfaction," says Heidi primly. "I mean, what's going to stop someone from cornering my Delaney somewhere, or spiking her drink with alcohol, or worse? Anything could happen when you add horny young boys into the equation."

"Mmm," agrees Jude, wondering if Heidi is referring to her sons, and if so, if she is being mean. Heidi always had a brilliant way with the hit-and-run.

"But back to the food order. You need some fruit soup? Or that mac-cheese the boys go for, the one with the Dijon-seeded Gruyère?"

"Yeah, sure, and Slam might—well, he's going out of town this weekend, so I don't know. Maybe just one of your artisanal hoagies? For tomorrow night?"

"Friday night? That's what you're giving him for his last supper?"

They both laugh at that phrase, Heidi thinking of death row, and Jude of the death of Jesus. Collum had been raised as a devout Catholic. He occupied her mind more and more lately, especially since he had stopped writing to her (her tempting note about her red kisses notwithstanding). Was he feeling guilty about writing to a married woman? Jude was glad she had not given him her address, but on the other hand her online profile and that little map with the arrow did say Putnam County . . .

Even more frightening, was Collum getting a divorce, as she'd seen in the tabloids? Could Catholics get divorced? If she brought it up, would he want to marry her now? The way things were going, would Slam perhaps not even mind losing her?

"Jude? I just asked you something."

"Wha—what? Organic, free-range beets!" Jude rattles automatically. That could have been the right answer, given the context, but it wasn't.

"What are you talking about? I've got you down for the Gruyère mac-cheese. Now, do you really want to give Slam a hoagie? I mean, not that my hoagies aren't extraordinary, but if he's going away . . ."

63

"No, don't worry; you know he loves the twelve-inch ones," says Jude, hurriedly catching up with the food agenda, "especially when you make him that side salad with the quinoa and the jicama."

For a moment, Jude feels that she herself is speaking in tongues. One often did when ordering from Heidi.

"And a tiny poblano on the side," she adds. "He loves that heat."

"He does?"

This time there is a long and miserable pause, perhaps brought on, on Jude's side, by that ambiguous word, "heat."

"What's wrong, Jude?" Heidi asks hopefully.

The only thing that reliably cheers her up is other people's woe. There seems to be some promise here, Heidi thinks. Jude always has problems of one sort or another, which is especially delightful. It would have been too obnoxious for her friend to have a handsome, athletic husband and naturally conceived twin boys, and not have any problems.

"Nothing's wrong."

"You know you can tell me."

In the past, Jude has confided in Heidi about parenting matters. Not the serious ones, which mothers had to be cautious about (Joey's mild ADHD, Davey's increasing withdrawal). To the limited extent needed, Heidi has given her good advice. For example, when Jude's sons had had alarming acne, Heidi knew just the right concoction to get rid of it. True, it was time-consuming to mix vats of red wine vinegar over the stove, and then add to it real oil of wintergreen and a dollop of Vicks Vapo-Rub, liquefied slowly in a confectioner's double boiler, but the results had been impressive.

"Let me help you," says Heidi eagerly. "I can be over there in half an hour. I'll bring my own chai latte, slow-brewed in a crock

I made. You'll taste the difference, especially if I add a drizzle of agave."

"What?" says Jude, finding the last series of words to be utterly defeating to her sense of the meaning of life.

"I'm coming over."

Oh, crud, Jude thinks. She'd have to get out of her yoga pants and tie-dyed T-shirt. She does have that much pride—the amount needed to dress up for Heidi Dorcas Kunst.

Looking into her closet, Jude finds a pair of khaki Capri shorts, which would look passable with sandals. The weather is warm; sandals would be fine. But nothing made of rubber or other nubby, vulcanized substances. No, the situation would call for delicate footwear that would be difficult to walk in, ideally with thin heels and tenuous straps. Digging into the back of her closet, she dredges up a pair of sandals from a few summers ago, when she had attended a wedding. The straps are woven of gold, silver, and bronze. She puts them on, then notices that her toenails are not painted. And she'll still need a "lovely blouse," to match the Capris and the sandals.

Now I see why I rarely have people over, she thinks, searching through her jumbled closet. I really need to get it together and socialize; less pressure on poor Slam.

Deep within, Jude finds a serviceable white shirt, part of that basic outfit that all women must have, as advised by helpful magazines. Now she would have to decide whether to tuck in or not, and if so, whether she needed a belt, and if so, whether brown, gold, or black.

The ringing doorbell ends her torment.

"Heidi?"

"Yeah, I took the shortcut," she says, stepping out of a champagne-beige ragtop convertible and closing the door behind her.

Jude drives a maroon van (the color had been optimistically

termed "beaujolais" when they'd bought it five years ago). It is often full of wrappers from the various quick-dining establishments frequented by her sons. Still, she knows she looks pretty good right now. The shorts, the shirt, the sandals! Why didn't she dress in ensembles like this everyday? It gave the morale such a boost!

"You know, we should get mani-pedis together," says Heidi slowly, staring at Jude's plain dun toenails. She is a flaw-fixator, one of those people whose eyes love to lock on the one thing wrong in another person's exterior—the wrinkle, the old stain, the bald spot or eyeliner smudge.

"It's a lot of fun." Heidi continues. "They give you a nice hot cream massage with it."

"That sounds—that sounds so yummy," Jude admits, imagining her hands and feet being caressed and massaged with hot cream, whatever that was. It sounded sensuous and just right, the antidote to all that ailed her. Again she thinks, Why don't I do these little things?

"You look troubled, sweetie," says Heidi, encouragingly.

"Me? Oh, no, I'm fine, really."

"Slam going away again, you say?"

"Oh, yeah, he's leaving on Saturday night."

"Saturday night? Why not Sunday?"

"He gets terrible jetlag. He needs an extra day before he can function at meetings. I mean, at the power level he wants to."

"Mm hmm," said Heidi, reaching into her bag to pull out a thermos of her special chai. "Do you have some nice mugs?"

"Well, I have lots of mugs—"

"You really need earthenware to bring out the aromatics."

"Is that the same as 'aromas'?" Jude really wanted to learn.

"No," says Heidi, her hands busy in preparation. She rolls the thermos in her hands, clockwise and then counterclockwise.

"Oh."

"I've added not only cinnamon and clove but also cumin. And a touch of black pepper, to tease out the sweetness of the agave."

"I have these gorgeous Wedgwood cups from England—"

"This is not Earl Grey, sweetie," Heidi admonishes, giving the thermos a final roll and a sharp shake, up and down.

"Let's go inside now; I'll look around your cupboards."

"No!" shrieks Jude. The house had not been cleaned for several days. The housekeeper had called in sick yesterday. If only Jude had known that Heidi would come over to comfort her!

"Don't be silly," says Heidi, striding inward. When she reaches the kitchen, she stands there pensively, hands on hips like a general surveying a recent rout, dead troops aground for miles in each direction.

"OK. I'm staying here today and helping you out. You sit, I'll find something to put the tea in, we'll talk, and then you'll watch me clean. I love it! You'll be doing me a favor."

"Fine," says Jude, surrendering. "But Hattie is coming in tomorrow. It's no big deal." Hattie used to come in every day in the better days. Now, she was always coming in "tomorrow."

"Is this the last view you want Slam to have of his lovely home? Off he'll go to a nice hotel in Italy. The kind with polished wood and ancient carpets. Huge beds you can bounce a coin off. Do you want him to look back and think about dirty dishes and sticky cabinets?"

"No, I don't," murmurs Jude, hanging her head.

Heidi picks up a sponge, sniffs it, wrinkles her nose, then squirts some of Jude's cleanser on it.

"Not the right cleanser, not the right sponge, but it's a start," she says, wiping victoriously. Then she pours Jude a half cup of chai and commands her to taste it.

"Good, right?"

"Mm, yes," says Jude, exhaling and even relaxing. Everyone should have a Heidi, she thinks. She had never had a sister, but this was probably what it would be like. They brought you tea, wiped Skippy off the cupboard, and asked you why you were sad. So you told them.

Jude Spills Some Beans

ctually, it *is* Slam that I'm a—a little bit, you know, sad about," says Jude, forgetting for a moment Delaney's assertion that her mother was a witch, and not to be trusted. The little smile on Heidi's face doesn't help.

"Slam, your husband, you mean?"

"Yeah. I'm sort of worried that—"

"That what?"

"That, you know—that he's having an affair."

Did you ever think of getting a life? thinks the busy, industrious Heidi. Then you wouldn't worry so much all the time. True, her own husband, Daniel, didn't work anymore, which admittedly was a problem to be solved ASAP. He had been a high-achieving assistant principal at an English-style boarding school nearby that featured cold showers in the morning and punishing hours of rugby.

One day, Daniel Kunst had kindly and innocuously answered the text of a depressed boy in the eleventh grade. Someone had misinterpreted the exchange, and his career had toppled. Now he spent most of his time at the local golf course, pretending that he had retired and was living the good life. Growing his hair and piercing his ears (and then one eyebrow) had not dimmed the pain and the shame, even as these acts seemed to annoy his imperious wife. Perhaps he had even written that text in the same spirit—the spirit of breaking all rules and boundaries.

Heidi was beginning to wonder if Daniel's bag of clubs was merely a getaway excuse to avoid her. Did *he* have a lover? Probably not, she concluded, her good sense returning. She knew that he still wanted her. They had sex three times a week, like it or not. And they both enjoyed the closeness of being a happily married couple. But it was hard to be with a man with lost ambition.

"Heidi? Do you think he is?" Now it was Heidi who was not paying attention. Jude was usually the one guilty of those lapses. Maybe it was the summer heat.

"What? Do I think who is what?"

"Do you think Slam is having an affair? He's always traveling, and you know how men are."

"No, I actually don't know how men are."

Heidi was not a student of literature the way Jude was; still less did she read the tabloids, which were so full of love's drama.

"Well, they have their needs," Jude patiently explains. "And of course so do women, it goes without saying."

"Needs? You mean sexual needs?"

"Yes, and Slam and I don't really—I mean we rarely—"

"Really? Rarely?" Heidi's face displays the consternation of a chef asked to cook the tuna all the way through, mixed with a touch of wild glee.

"Well, now and then, naturally. But he's really tired, the hours, the jetlag and everything."

"Hmm. I'll give you one tip. Men like the smell of licorice and pumpkin. Not together, of course. I'll make you some fenugreek/

aniseed cookies and pumpkin tartlets. Feed them to him, one a night, just before bed."

"Well, I can try it, I guess."

"It's like a love potion. He'll be on you like an animal."

"Is that what you do with Dante?"

"Is *what* what I do with whom?"

"Daniel. You know, make him the special foods, maybe toss in an aphrodisiac ingredient, I don't know, oysters?"

"Dear Jude, it's all I can do to keep my man's hands off me! Phew!"

Jude stares at Heidi, shamefaced. She has revealed a private secret, and Heidi's simply boasted. She'll have to balance this conversation. With a great act of will, she straightens her shoulders and asks, "And how is Dant—Daniel's job search going?"

"Oh, it's fine. He's in great demand," Heidi retorts, keeping her lower lip from drooping downward into a sad face.

A week later, on Slam's return from Italy, Jude tries the aphrodisiac cookies. Dressed in black baby-doll pajamas and wearing hot-pink mules with marabou puffs, she watches as her husband eats them all.

"Wow!" Slam says. "These are absolutely decadent!"

"You like them?"

"I'll say!"

Standing in front of the fridge, he flushes them down with cold milk straight from the container. He looks macho doing that, hoisting his libation, chugging victoriously.

Together, silently, they walk into their bedroom.

Jude goes into the bathroom for one last mirror check. She perfumes her hair and fluffs it. She puts a little body cream on her shins so they shine, and a dab of cellulite lotion on the backs of her thighs. Turning off the light, she swings the door open dramatically.

Even with the bedside lamps on, Slam has fallen into a deep and restful sleep, shoes and all. Worse, he has fallen on the diagonal, so that there is no room for her.

Sitting on the corner of the bed, Jude watches her husband for hours. At about two in the morning, his pelvis starts to rock in a familiar way, and he moans as though in pain. Suddenly, he shouts loudly, in Italian, *"Ahime! Ahime!"*

Twice.

Then he is still.

After a moment to absorb the scene, Jude wakes her husband, shaking him roughly, practically screaming in his stuporous ear:

"Is there any room for me in this bed? Move!"

With a kindly smile, still mostly asleep, Slam hauls himself over to the designated side.

"Night, *carina*," he murmurs, lips smacking as though he tasted something, or someone, delicious.

More Beans Spilled

D id you try them?"

"What?"

"My special aphrodisiacs? The cookies with the fenugreek and the tartlets with the—"

The two women sit outside in Heidi's garden. The automatic sprinklers hiss and whip efficiently. Under the shade of a Japanese maple, Heidi has arranged a lovely tea service for herself and Jude. An abundant white peony sprawls in a vase, sitting on a French bistro table with mosaic inlay.

"Yes. Slam loved them! He loved them!" says Jude, too brightly.

"They really worked?" Heidi has not actually tried these treats on anyone. She experiences mixed feelings again. She wants to believe in the power of her concoctions—and the volume of sales she might have—but she never wants Jude Ewington to be any happier than she herself can be. Which is not very happy at all.

"Worked like a charm. Seemed to make him really horny. I mean, he couldn't get enough. Phew!"

"Good girl!" says Heidi, adjusting the slant of her cherry Adirondack chair.

"No, Slam gets all the credit," says Jude, her mouth trying to hold a neutral expression. "Every bit of it!"

"I'm working on something else now. Care to try?"

Jude imagines Heidi's intimidating kitchen. Typically, pots bubbled on all six burners, and both convection ovens were going at full blast.

"Sure—what is it?"

"I've set out a couple trays to cool. Give it about fifteen minutes, and we'll go in. It'll sell out in a day, I can feel it."

"OK, sure. What's the market?" she repeats.

"It's untapped, and it's bottomless. Guess."

"Ummm—children with disabilities?"

Jude can't believe she said that. After telling Heidi too much about her private life with Slam, she was surely not going to talk about Davey again. Her son was getting odder by the day. It was summer, and yet the boy stayed in his room whenever Joey was not there, which increasingly was most of the time.

Joey was going back to boarding school in September. Was his twin the only friend Davey had? There had been other friends over the years (Jude remembered a Chinese chess-playing boy who'd since moved away, and in fourth grade a pudgy girl with a lisp), but none had lasted, and in the rough sociological divisions of high school, Jude worried that her son would not fit in anywhere. For better or worse, there was no kid like Davey.

"Disabilities, yes, I know what you mean," Heidi was saying, the word delicious in her mouth, as though she was saying "delicacies." With a keen and cruel swiftness, she had thought of Jude's peculiar son.

"Are you suggesting that I might find a culinary remedy for shyness?" she continues. "Awkwardness? Anti-social personality? Future Unibombers?"

"What did you say?"

"You know I'm just kidding, Jude."

"But maybe you've got something there," says Jude, beginning to seethe on behalf of her son. "You might make something for kids who resent their moms, and who secretly, I don't know, get fake IDs and use them to get wasted at clubs. Would that be profitable, too?"

Jude surprised herself. How had she managed to say all that to Heidi? She had tried to aim her response into one that would wound her friend (as her friend had just wounded her), but not so blatantly that she could be clearly accused of it. What was happening to her?

Writing to her long-lost love had opened some sluice gates, that was for sure. She loved whom she loved, and she hated whom she hated, and she was becoming impatient with all the hypocrisies one thought one had to endure.

"Hmm—that's an idea, actually," says Heidi, with what seems like real admiration. "Something to make them less rebellious during the pubescent stage? I'll give it some thought.

"But you know, Jude, even though everything I make is micro-calibrated in terms of nutrients, I'm not into health, as such. I'm into making something fun and yummy-yummy."

"That is exactly what you do, and so well," says Jude, relieved to get off the unspoken topic of their children. "Everybody knows that!"

"Yeah, the people do know it, and I've just about saturated that market, so I was actually thinking beyond the human market."

"Beyond?" Is Heidi talking about warlocks and wizards? Would she come out at last and admit she was a sorceress?

"Did you ever notice how many animals there are around here, Jude? Not just pets, cats, dogs, birds, but horses, for example?

"I just stopped by this place right near here. You know, Angel-

Fire? For kids to get riding therapy? Take a look at this brochure," says Heidi, dropping it into Jude's hands as though she were a process server.

"Look!" she repeats.

"Yes, yes, I'm looking," says Jude, resentfully unfolding the brochure. Yes, she is starting to hate Heidi. She can't stop herself. The perfection of all her surfaces, the industriousness, the sniping about marriages and children.

"Horses eat, too, right? I mean, there is even an expression, 'to eat like a horse.' But what do they eat? Their diet is dull. Hay and oats, you know? Why not make something they'd love, to use as treats for this training thing?"

"That's so interesting," says Jude, still wishing failure on her friend. She was one step shy of showing her all of Delaney's stories. That would shut her up.

"Yeah, it *is* interesting. That's why I have this brochure. I've got dozens of others, from other farms and suppliers. But this one, actually—I'm showing this to you for a reason."

Jude can't imagine what in the world Heidi thinks she knows about pets, particularly horses. She herself has never trusted animals, having grown up with cautious parents who felt that dogs were for biting, cats for scratching, and horses for throwing you to the ground and hurting your back beyond repair.

"I—I come from a different background from you. I know nothing about sailing, skiing, riding, Heidi." She tended to lump these all together as pastimes for people like Heidi, each requiring a special outfit and parents who ideally were WASPs.

"Yes, I figured as much," her friend retorts. "I'm not talking about you exactly. Look carefully at the wording here. It's a place for developmental therapy. That means it's for children. Children in need."

"But what—"

"OK, I'll spell it out. I've actually been noticing this for years, but I've been trying not to—"

Heidi stops herself. She does not want to ruin their bond. Jude is her closest friend, and she hers, even if they don't like each other. Even now, Jude was drinking her peppermint tea, and Heidi knew she was savoring each sip. The glazed celadon cup was hand-thrown, a gift from a Zen-loving client. Jude was reliable in her way. She was not only a neighbor—she was an appreciator. Heidi knew that Jude loved the peppermint tea and the glazed celadon cup that contained it. Heidi knew that life itself was made out of such containers—such tea and such cups.

"You've been noticing what?" Jude blurts angrily, interrupting Heidi's benevolent musing about the sanctity of well-served beverages. Jude is scared that Heidi was about to cross a line, and that she, Jude, will have to cross one, too. She does not want to see Davey as others see him. Up to now she has deflected those others and seen her son only through her own eyes, the loyal, loving, and generous eyes of a mother. Why would Heidi want to change that?

"This is hard, Jude. This is not easy for one good friend to tell another."

"What is?" says Jude, her voice flat.

"It's your son, David."

So there it was, Jude thinks, out in the open. "Oh, I know, he should get out more," she says quickly. "But I don't think he'd like *this* kind of thing, if that's what you mean. This horse thing."

"Jude, we've known each other for a while, right? I know your boy. He's always been quiet." Heidi's voice is soft and conciliatory. "That's all right," she continues. "Not everyone can be a man's man. Not everyone can be good at sports and all that stuff."

"Right," says Jude, tentatively.

"But now that he's entering his teenage years, and with Joseph away from home, you have to look out so that he doesn't turn into a real—a real weirdo."

For a moment, Jude can't speak.

"What do you mean by such a horrible, reductive word?"

"Well, my daughter, Delaney, you know?"

Yes, the daughter whose main writings consist of joyous plots to poison you, Jude thinks. To zap you like a roach.

"Yes," she says, powerful in her unshared knowledge. "Your daughter, Delaney. What are *her* insights into this matter?"

"Well, she's been watching David with great interest. They were in the same Spanish class. She talks about him all the time, in fact."

"David's very advanced in Spanish. He happens to be nearly fluent." That's why, Jude thinks triumphantly, he's a rising sophmore, and Delaney's a junior, and yet they've tested in the same level.

"Oh, nothing wrong with his language skills, I'm sure. But Delaney's watched him, not only in class, but in the cafeteria . . ."

Jude knew full well that Davey ate in a peculiar way. If you gave him a hamburger with French fries and peas (restaurants did not do this, add the peas, but mothers sometimes did), he would first eat all the peas, one at a time, each sphere pierced on a fork tine. Then he would eat his French fries from smallest to largest, dipping the tips into the circle of ketchup. Only then would he eat his hamburger, slowly and methodically. Each bit had to have the same amount of ketchup, lettuce, and tomato.

After he was done, and only then, Davey would drink his glass of water. He drank it all the way down, down to the last drops. He'd tip the glass for these, then say, "Ahhhh." That was how he ended each meal. In the cafeteria, Jude suddenly realized, Davey probably finished each meal way after all the others were done. Had Delaney really stayed on to watch him finish? And if she had, wasn't she the real "weirdo"?

"OK look," Jude says, her eyes damp and flashing. "I don't want to hear anymore about you, your daughter, or my son. Davey's the best—the best boy in the world, and one day you'll all see what a mensch—what a good and genuine human being he is. How would you like it if someone really judged you when you were a vulnerable teenager—if your whole life was judged by what you did or didn't do when you were—"

Without even consciously thinking about it, Jude knows she made mistakes when she was about her son's age, perhaps even unforgivable, irrevocable ones that had nearly ruined her life (and someone else's).

Jude lets her last thought hang unfinished in the air. She marches into the house and slams her teacup down on the kitchen counter. Heidi, right behind her, picks it up and calmly puts it in the sink. The cup leaves a little Zen circle on the granite, so Heidi wipes it with a moistened, waffle-weave, unbleached organic cloth.

"Later!" Jude barks over her shoulder, racing to her van as though she meant never to see Heidi again. Maybe she really wouldn't. Her anger gave her enough courage to contemplate cooking her own food from now on. Simple things: omelets, spaghetti. Meat loaf with normal beef and bread crumbs from a tin. Soup from a can, the old-fashioned kind, with sodium and heaps of MSG. All of it, she thought rebelliously. Iceberg lettuce in a glass bowl, with Russian dressing, *not* on the side. Glopped on top.

"Don't you want the brochure? Just in case?"

Heidi had taken a shortcut to the driveway and was ahead of Jude.

"Oh, fine!" Jude growls, swiping the horse-farm glossy from Heidi's outstretched hand. If it'll shut you up! That last part—she doesn't really say it out loud.

Disorders

Over the past year or so, Davey did seem to be developing an anxiety disorder, along with his obsessive style of eating. He hardly spoke to anyone but his own family anymore. Teachers had reported this, but Jude had not listened. She thought the way he ate was just a peculiar habit, charming even, and that Davey might one day become a great scientist or scholar. "The absent-minded professor," her parents had called people like Davey. There was no shame in that. Einstein had been peculiar as a child, and there was no one in the world her parents loved more than that genius with the wild, white hair. It was more than likely that Einstein had eaten his peas in an idiosyncratic way (perhaps likening them to planets).

But it was not the best way for a teenager to be.

While Joey, his twin, was easygoing and popular, Davey tended to spend time alone, listening to music. He didn't even like the Internet. If he had gone on Facebook, he would have no friends. Most teenagers had hundreds. Joey had nearly a thousand. Even his mother had one (not that Davey knew that).

He had had an enormous growth spurt over the past months,

and his limbs seemed lanky, out of his full control. Davey had always been clumsy, though, and had never gone in for team sports. In Little League, other players had been unfailingly sore at him; they had shouted at him to try harder, to quit dropping the ball or missing the ball, or whatever poor boys were supposed to do with that damnable ball, day in and day out, for all their growing years.

Now his lack of athletic prowess was even more regrettable. Davey could have made friends on teams, hearty mates to whom he would not have to open up, but simply pass a ball. The exercise might have helped his brooding. Staying inside all the time had also given him a pallor. His face was whiter than it had ever been, thought Jude, and the acne was returning.

Davey sat in his room wearing large headphones that blotted out all ambient sound. He liked torchy love songs, such as those sung by Barbra Streisand or Celine Dion. These he played over and over, sometimes hundreds of times. They made his heart swell with a sense of potential. His yearnings were not for adventures on the high seas; they were for the kind of soaring love that went all the way and withstood all obstacles. David Ewington was quiet and he was shy, but Jude knew he had something pure and true inside of him. The music spoke to that side, gave it hope and kept it alive.

It was suppertime, and mother and son were alone in the house together. Jude wanted to eat dinner with him tonight, just the two of them. Joey had gone out on a group date to the movies. The film would be a summer blockbuster, full of buildings toppling, cars crashing, and impossible heroics. Ten people were going, a pack of popularity, among them Joey's new summer girlfriend, whom he'd met at the mall the other day while his mother and brother were shopping together for shirts.

Popular, girlfriend, mall. Jude knew that none of these words would ever apply to the smaller, more awkward, power-ballad-loving twin, even with the new T-shirts she had bought him from a pseudo-cool store. But she was not sure she minded. Davey, she told herself again, would one day be someone extraordinary—if not Einstein, then a surgeon, perhaps, or a hostage negotiator.

She knocks on his door, but he does not answer, so she opens it and goes in. Davey doesn't notice her. He is singing along to the lyrics, which are about how no matter what, no matter how, the singer will keep on driving until she finds *You*. His voice, floating around in a tuneless but loud a capella, seems a bit like the wail of a deaf-mute:

"Come get you . . . ahhhhhh . . . can we take the rooooroad . . . *no matter hoooowwwww . . . !*"

His mother taps Davey on the shoulder.

He looks up, and she motions: "Take the headphones off."

"What's up?" he says, sliding down the headphones only slightly, gripping them as though he cannot wait to put them back on and shut out the world.

"Are you hungry?"

"Hungry? What time is it?"

"It's almost seven, Davey."

"Wow. I've been sitting here for almost four hours."

"Come down and have dinner. I've made spaghetti from Daddy's special noodles. I've got parmesan. And grape soda."

"Wow! Grape soda!" says Davey, without a trace of sarcasm. Like most teenagers, he loves sugary and salty foods, the junkier the better.

"Yeah, Heidi concocted it out of real Burgundian grapes and a certain low-gas formula she's been working on. I've got a couple bottles left. Let's go finish them up."

"Heidi, huh. I'll drink it anyway." Davey and his mother have an inside joke about his disliking Heidi's ambitious foods. Jude loves the way he prefers her own more humble fare, and how she can call pasta "noodles" with him.

They sit at the table, perpendicular to each other, like a couple in a corner nook. After making sure that each spaghetti strand is exactly the same length and bears the same load of sauce and parmesan, Davey eats heartily and asks for seconds. Jude feels the pride of feeding her fast-growing boy. For dessert, she has baked him an apple.

"Mom, I love it when Joey and Dad aren't here. They're so loud and so pushy, you know?"

"Well—yeah . . ."

"You know?"

"Well, yes. I do know. But I didn't know you felt that way about Joey."

"Well, I love him and he's my brother and everything, but come on! He's kind of a player. He's like Dad. Dad is always a success at everything he does, and that is admirable—but does he ever *think* about anything he does? And Joey, Joey is a born leader, as they say—but where is he leading everyone? Where are they all going? Does he even know?"

"You're very interesting and thoughtful," says his mother.

"Thanks. You are, too," he adds generously. "I wish it could always be like this. Nice and warm and cozy. Why is the world so full of angles and noise? And mean people elbowing, you know?"

"I do. Well, they're not always mean. They're just elbowish. They want to be first. Even in the pettiest ways."

"It's not a race, is it, Mom?"

"It shouldn't be. Unless you're talking about Darwin, and I hope we don't treat human life as 'survival of the fittest.'"

"It shouldn't be like that, but it is. Anyway, what am I 'fittest' for?"

"You have the rarest gift, a deep and intricate soul," she

answers. "And you'll enjoy that one day," she adds, although part of her doubts the truth of that statement. Yes, her Davey will be a success in the worldly sense, she is sure. But people with deep and intricate souls often suffer more than the elbowers. Though, of course, all of them suffer eventually.

Jude stands up to clear the dishes. From the kitchen, she calls out, "How's the baked apple?"

"Perfect. It's a perfect, perfect apple."

From her other son, this sentence might have stung of sarcasm, but not from Davey. The apple is indeed perfect: red, round, and sweet, the inedible core removed, and the hole filled with nuts and honey. She knows that Davey will eat the nuts first, then thoughtfully and thoroughly lick up the honey, and finally go for the apple. But that is all right.

"You know, sweetie?" says his mother, returning to the table with a small, folded brochure. "I've been thinking about something."

"No," says Davey. "No thinking. No plans. No agendas, please."

If there's one thing I'd change about you, thinks his mother, it's that you say "no" first. It wears me down, and it's not good for you, either.

"It's not an 'agenda'," she continues. "It's just an idea. I think about you because you spend so much time alone, indoors. And here we are, in the lovely countryside."

"Suburbs, really."

"Fine. Suburbs. We're not in the city. We have fresh air, land, a pool in the backyard. And did you even know how close we live to Angel-Fire Farm?"

"What's that—another wee farm in Putnam County? What do they raise, alpacas or organic aubergines?"

Davey is so clever. There is, indeed, a proliferation of "cute" rustic businesses in the area. Many of them sell dried-flower wreaths, enamel jewelry (usually depicting cats or ladybugs), and stone geese with tartan ribbons around their necks.

"No, it's a new horse farm, actually. You remember how you always liked to ride when you were little?"

"I actually remember *not* wanting to ride. It seemed like a good way to fall down and really break something."

"Oh you're right," she continues, chuckling affectionately, "you *were* afraid at those birthday parties with ponies. But not if the man held the rope, right? Then, after you got down, you'd give the pony a carrot, and slowly relax. Once, you asked if we could get you a pony like that, a nice tame one that you could get to know."

"What was I, seven years old? What are you getting at here?"

"Well, this place, Angel-Fire, is actually not so much about the riding and jumping part of things. It's more about getting to know and trust the horses, grooming them, communicating—"

"Mom, you sound a little flakey. Like you want me to use crystals or something. Do you think I'm really that strange?"

They stare at each other, and then Davey looks away. It is hard for him to maintain eye contact, but why should she force that? Why, indeed, is she picking on Davey? Jude hears her own words: "communicating," "horses." She thinks of *Mister Ed*, one of the television fixtures of her childhood. Why do all her efforts seem ridiculous lately?

But she is not talking about that kind of communication— the kind achieved with a trained horse that was given peanut butter, making his mouth move in patterns vaguely resembling human speech, which would then be dubbed. She is talking about the real thing—one being making clear expression to another— which animals do so well.

"No, of course I don't think you're strange at all!" she answers, with full conviction. But some people (like Heidi) do, or might start to, thinks Jude, and that is not good for Davey.

She can see a bit of wear and tear in her young son already.

"Your shyness really bothers *you* sometimes, right?" she continues.

"It depends if I'm alone or not."

"Is that a joke? You're not meant to be alone!"

"Really? Who said? Everyone seems alone, if you ask me. You and Dad. Joey with that constant stream of girls he can't tell apart. And then there's this girl, Delaney—"

"Heidi's daughter Delaney?"

"Yeah, that one. She was in my Spanish class. She ate with the weirdos at school and watched me all the time."

"Is she really a weirdo?" Jude asks eagerly, remembering that Heidi had quoted her daughter using that very word about her son. She excitedly imagines Delaney's crowd—chipped black polish, pierced tongues, pentagram tattoos. With wild maternal schadenfreude, she wishes a group like this on perfect Heidi's daughter. How long can her rebellious streak be hidden?

"You know? We shouldn't use those categories," Davey says, beginning to carefully remove the peel from the baked apple. "I mean, sometimes, the weirdos are the most interesting kids in the school. At least they think for themselves, and that is the beginning of wisdom, right?"

Davey is such a good and interesting person. It is poignant to have a unique child with whom you long to openly agree, someone you want to have a glass of wine with, to trade wise maxims with—but not be able to. Because he is your child, and you are his mother, and you have to raise him into someone who can have a go at the cold, cruel world the way you and everyone else had had to do.

"Here," says Jude, her voice strong and positive. "Look at the brochure; you'll see it's something that might really help you."

Obligingly, Davey picks up the brochure and reads it aloud. It says:

Nature. Man and beast. How often do we live with connection?
Is your child shy, awkward, socially withdrawn?

"Your '*child*'? I'm fourteen years old! Very nearly fifteen!"
"It's a figure of speech. Read it—they take kids up to eighteen."

Does he or she have trouble sitting still, making friends, control-
ling his or her impulses? Do you find them sitting in their rooms and
brooding?
Are you worried about your child's future as an active, positive
participant in the joy of life?
ANGEL-FIRE FARMS is the solution.

"Are they serious?"
"I hope so."

On our 15-acre facility, horses and their people develop a trusting
bond, one that brings them closer to the source of confidence!
Social scientists and developmental experts agree:
Therapeutic Riding is the best and most lasting solution to many
problems of adapting to the demands of school and society.
Your child, ages 7–18, will become confident! Hardy! Flexible and
strong!
Call for a complimentary lesson: 845-555-6987.

"Mom," says David, laughing as he puts the brochure down on
the table. "No offense? This sounds like a total waste of time . . ."
"Will you at least think about it?"

At the Angel-Fire House Farm

Even though he is a teenager, Davey half wishes his mother had accompanied him during his first Angel-Fire Farms visit. Perhaps this wish is part of his paradoxical problem—he likes to be alone, but not when meeting new people (or horses). Then he needs the comfort of friends and familiars.

It is Sunday, and Jude has promised Joey that she will drive him to a paintball party an hour away. Davey has not been invited, and in any case, would not have gone. So Jude drops one son off at the gate of the therapeutic farm, and keeps on going with the other, toward the imaginary world where guns mark enemies with brightly colored stains that stand in for blood. There is no therapy needed for that bloodlust; indeed, Joey is meeting friends there—alpha boys who, like Joey (whom they called "Joe"), are in the "popular" group at school. Boys she resents for not liking her gentler son, or speaking to him, even when they visit. Of course, Davey would hide and not even try to get to know them.

"I'll come back later," she promises him. "I'll peek in and see how you're getting along."

"No, God, don't," he says, opening the door of the van and

nearly slipping on the gravel path. "You'll only embarrass me. Just come at the end and pick me up at the gate."

"I'll see you at the end, then." Jude drives slowly away, her wheels crushing pebbles and then tarmac. She watches him in her mirror, getting smaller. He watches her, too.

When his mother is gone, Davey walks pensively along the long path, alongside a line of cars. The path winds upward, flanked by large grassy meadows where horses graze. When he gets to the top of the road, he sees clusters of parents hovering around their children, a large riding ring, and several stables.

Despite the presence of so many new people, there is something about the place that comforts him.

"Come," says Gretchen, the young farmhand, stepping up to Davey and taking him by the arm. "We've been expecting you. The younger kids are going to curry the ponies. I thought I'd show *you* the main riding ring, and then we'll see if we can find you a helmet that fits."

"I—I haven't ridden much before," says Davey, appalled that his voice cracks on the word "ridden."

"We don't expect any of you to know anything. We'll just get you comfortable with the horses, and see how it goes from there."

"Are you—are you one of the teachers here?" Davey hopes so. He likes her kind, round face, fringed by straight yellow hair.

"Oh, we all do a little of everything. Administration's actually where I spend most of my time. But everyone here is really, really nice. Horses especially," she says, smiling.

A broad-chested man walks into the ring, leading a large chestnut mare with a white star on her forehead and glossy black tail.

"Hey, cowboy!" Gretchen says to the man, who wears an oversize cowboy hat, chaps, and a bolo tie.

"Hey, Gretch! See you've got a new victim!" he replies, his grin revealing perfect white teeth. When it relaxes again, his mouth becomes invisible, lost under an old-fashioned handlebar moustache that ends in waxed tips.

"Come on over, Shy!" says Gretchen.

Shy? Why is she talking about his shyness? Davey wonders if his mother has said anything to the staff here about the specifics of his supposed problem. Social anxiety disorder is one catchphrase, he knows. Obsessive compulsive. Agoraphobia. Mom must have mentioned it; that was why he is here, while people his age (like his brother) are free to play paintball. He fumes with embarrassment, wishing he could turn and run away, or at least hide somewhere.

But Gretchen isn't talking to him when she uses the word "Shy." She is stepping over to the man in the moustache and ten-gallon hat, who is stepping over to her. His mare begins balking, and the man stops patiently. Looking over at both Gretchen and Davey, he confides in a whispery growl:

"Last class was hard for old Lula here. The kid couldn't help pulling her mane. Had palsy, poor thing. Little fingers gripped like vises. We tried to stop 'im, but he kept on doing it. Brave girl just stood for it, didn't you, girlie?"

"Awww," says Gretchen, reaching for a sugar cube in the pocket of her waist-high jeans. "Who's a good girl?"

"Don't give her one. I've given her several. Plus an apple core. She's right spoiled now, this li'l lady."

"May I pet her?" says Davey, as Lula comes up to him, nuzzling his jacket pockets.

"Sure. That's jest what she's here for. 'Slong as you don't pull her mane none."

"You from Texas?" asks Davey. He thinks he can recognize the accent, inconsistent as it is, and the exotic word choices.

"Yep, you got yerself a Lone Star guy right here."

"Which part?" Not that Davey knows any part of Texas, really. But he is drawn to Shy and finds it easy to ask him questions.

"All and any, pardner, all and any."

"And what brought you here?" Davey isn't usually so forward, but Shy has something in his own eyes that is vulnerable, as though he, like Davey, is not always comfortable in his own skin.

"What brought me here? You might say, the travellin' road."

"I understand," says Davey, sagely. He understands the need to flee, although his life has made it convenient for him to do so in his own room.

"You're a fine young lad," says Shy, forgetting that "lad" is a word more Australian than Texan.

"Probably the oldest one here, though," Davey responds rue-fully. Out of the corner of his eye, he keeps seeing little children, like five- to eight-year-olds, and it is embarrassing.

"How old'er you?"

"Fourteen."

"You're not old a'tall. There's a couple of cute teenage fillies that hang out together, probably older than you, I reckon."

"Older than fourteen?"

"Like I said, teen-age—got a 'teen in it—and they're right cute. I think they might be kleptomaniacs, though," he adds with a wink. "They got here a week ago, and I've been counting up the carrots. And it don't add up."

Davey nods, confused.

"Kiddin' ya about them carrots. It's good for 'em to be here, the lassies. No shopping malls, just nature. Horses, hay. It's paradise, mate, if you can handle the bloody saddles."

"How long have you been here?"

"'Bout a week or so. Oh, yeh, I was the newby then. I thought it was like a real ranch, you know? So when I first saw this place, I asked them—I asked them, right in their faces:

'You call this *dust?*'

'You call this a *corral?*'

'You call these *horses?*'

'You call this a *saddle?*'

'You call this *riding?*'"

Davey does not know how to respond to this somewhat the-atrical presentation, but nods in agreement. Shy continues:

"Yeh, I did, I asked 'em and no two ways about it," he pro-nounces, taking out a bag of shag tobacco and some rolling papers. "Mind if I smoke some out here in the wide open?"

"Feel free," says Davey, enjoying the turn of phrase. Feel free. He himself is feeling a bit freer already.

"But son, then I realized that this here place was another thing altogether. It's not about being a ranch with dust and ropes and ridin'. These horses are all old and most kindly. They been thrown away like rubbish. They did their service somewhere, and now they're here. The last stop."

"That's sad," says Davey, listening intently.

"No, it's not. This is where the story gets good, and it's true, which is more'n you can say for most stories."

Shy pauses to pile a pinch of tobacco on a rolling paper. Then he continues: "These fellas don't need to be broken no more, son!"

Shy says this intently, as though Davey were the one who had insisted that they all be "broken."

"No, I never—"

"—all they want is a scratch between the ears, a nibble of sugar, a nice curry brush along the flanks. I've learned to relax here, for the first time in my life," Shy concludes, flourishing a tightly rolled cigarette, and then lighting it.

"That's what I'd like to learn, I guess," says Davey. "To—to really relax. Sometimes I get so tense, and it's hard to breathe, and—"

"Don't I know it. I been there. What's your name, son?"

Shy exhales smoke to the side, swiveling his eyes to look at the boy. His face looks utterly familiar, the features resembling someone he once knew, someone who had made his heart soar and then yanked it back down to earth.

"Davey. I mean it's really David."

"David. The name of a King," says Shy. "A Jewish King, if I know my Bible, and indeed I do."

"I guess," says Davey, who doesn't really know his Bible. "It was my mother's grandpa's name."

"Is that so," says Shy, philosophically. "In the family tradition, you could say. That's real nice."

"What's *your* name?"

"Shy."

"That's what I thought I heard. '*Shy.*' I thought they—I thought they were talking about me!"

"Huh! That's funny. You're shy?"

"You mean you can't tell?"

"Not a'tall!"

"Oh my God, I wish you could say that to my mother!"

"Mebbe one day I will. Say that to your mother. Could happen," he says, with a handsome wink. Davey winks back, surprising himself, and they both laugh.

"So Shy—that's really your actual name? Is it short for something?"

Shy ponders the query, smoking.

"Cheyenne, I reckon."

"Are you part Indian?" Davey marvels. He is already starting to loosen the shackles of the old world and enter the new. Shy could be his guide.

"Some say one-eighth, and I don't say no."

"It's a place in Wyoming, too, right?"

"What is?"

"Cheyenne?"

"Sure it is, sure it is," Shy stutters, trying to keep up. He had not done too well in school geography. "See, son, I been all over. Been to Texas, Wyoming, the Blue Mountain Ozarks, you know, all of this great land of ours."

"Well, it's something I've been called all my life."

"Pardon?"

"Shy. I've been called that a lot. Especially lately. It's driving my mother crazy, and it's why I'm here."

"You don't seem that way to me, pardner. You'll do just fine. Know what? I guess you could give Lula jest one li'l sugar cube. But hold your hand flat, very flat. The secret's in the open palm, just give."

Treats

A week or so later, a truck rolls up to the farm. If a truck could be elegant, this one is, pale green with a magenta script logo on the side: "The Art of Food" (big letters) "by Heidi Dorcas Kunst" (smaller letters in darker magenta). Heidi jumps out, looking crisp in a double-breasted baker's jacket and pants. Three men follow her, carrying boxes up the stairs of the main building. They wear pale-green jackets, with the magenta script logo on the back.

Inside the boxes are treats Heidi has created for the horses of the Angel-Fire Farm. Why should animals eat no better than humans? Especially these animals, who do so much good for the children. Heidi herself knows several of these children, not only Jude's unfortunate David, who suffers from social retardation (Heidi personally feels it is Asperger's, with a touch of antisocial personality thrown in), but also many younger boys and girls who have everything from epilepsy to Down's syndrome.

Heidi knows them from knowing their mothers, who, along with their regular orders of food, also talk openly to her about their personal woes. As is the case with Jude, Heidi is only too happy to assist them, if only from the culinary standpoint.

Does she have anything that is good for hyperactivity?

Of course she does. Asparagus soup. It turns the urine green, which might unsettle younger children. The mother can then attribute this change to the child's being as wild as an ogre. Stop acting crazy, she can say, and you won't pee green anymore.

Suzy Shelton's ten-year-old daughter has violent tantrums.

For her, there are chamomile cookies, to which Heidi sometimes secretly adds a touch of valerian. Only one a day, she prescribes—but they are large.

For the mothers themselves she makes frothy shakes, which contain more than a soupçon of tequila. A touch of blue food coloring makes the drinks fanciful, if not exotic. "Blue Ladies," she calls them, and the uses of this frozen tonic are legend, even beyond the pale of parenthood. The secret ingredient is actually not the tequila but heaps of plain white table sugar, which the women have long forbidden themselves to enjoy in any recognizable form.

The new horse treats come on lollipop-like sticks, so there is no risk of anyone accidentally being bitten. Heidi has been testing them for weeks, and now they are the perfect size, shape, and flavor for the avid equine mouth.

These creations are actually Heidi's chef d'oeuvre, and she eats them herself. When the feeling that her life is not perfect overwhelms her, when she sees her husband's queue or hears her daughter slam her door so hard it shudders, she takes a nibble of "Ponipop" and is becalmed. There are secrets in the kitchen, ingredients and combinations that make life better, and Heidi is grateful she knows so many, and can always discover or invent more.

Shy loves Ponipops, too. Since their first appearance at the farm, he's secretly grabbed handfuls and stashed them here and there, eating them when needed to quell the voices in his head. He has lived long enough to suffer a series of bad scenes that can always be provoked in the present moment. The Pops put a stop to that.

There is a spicy taste in them like cannabis, he thinks, or resinous black hash. Shy, being of the land, knows a lot about the things of nature, its herbs and its seeds and the sap of its trees. He also senses not only the tender seed of the pine, but Omega-3 from walnuts, grown from soil that is moist and fertile with duck dung. There is also, Shy suspects, a calming heap of treacle in the Pops, what folks around here might call molasses.

Daily, he offers some of his private stash of Pops to David, his young protégé. They alter him in a most pleasing way, adding to the therapeutic powers of the horses and the people who work with them. The poor boy is no longer nervous at all, ever.

Indeed, after one nibble of the magical confection, Davey feels as though he can open his very soul up to the world as an offering. After finishing off two each, he and Shy gently giggle together at all their perceived troubles, which have now vanished like bubbles. At the end of the day, they wander the ranch, talking to the ponies and horses who rest and graze in their paddocks.

Oftentimes, the two men—boy and cowboy—sprawl out in the field with the grazing animals. They graze, too, munching peaceably on their good spheres of sticky, dark grain. Shy loves this ranch and these treats so much. He loves each and every horse he has met, not only Butternut, Ajax, and Clemmie, but Donut, Stewball, Tommy, and Hank. He even loves Darla, the old dappled gray who no longer likes to be ridden by anyone who weighs more than a hundred pounds. He is tired, too; he knows how Darla feels. Enough is enough.

Shy loves the people here, too. David, especially, is a wonderful person, one of the best souls he's ever met in his life. Maybe there is no need to be so angry all the time. Maybe people whose minds are forever at war with invisible foes are wrong. Maybe people can be forgiven for things they have done. Maybe he himself can be forgiven for all the things he has done wrong, whether knowingly or unknowingly, and all the things he has yet to do wrong, things he can't help. He has hurt his father, hurt Gingerean, hurt his own kids. Now he is hurting poor old Sydney in the wallet, and he will probably hurt many more people before he is done with this life.

But now he and this boy lie on their backs in the fields, looking at the clear, blue sky and talking quietly.

"What's your daddy like, son?"

"My dad? He's OK, I guess. He travels a lot, he's athletic. Kind of your standard alpha male. Why?"

"Oh, just asking."

"How about yours?"

Davey is really progressing. Before the ranch, he would never have opened up beyond the short answer ("He's OK"). Now, he is curious about Shy's life—and brave enough to ask him about it. It doesn't even feel brave. Bonding is as natural as breathing. In and also out. For me and also for you. His world is slowly expanding beyond his tightly gripped solitude.

He feels the grass around him, long and lush. He tears a clump out and lets it fall over him, sifting through his open fingers. He inhales the scent of the animals, the grass juice released by the tearing, the dark soil that sticks to the loosened blades. He smells his biscuit and tastes one bite fully. Grain by grain dissolving in his mouth. Even his skin feels good, the acne no problem as the accepting warmth of the sun caresses and offers healing to it.

"You really want to know about my dad?" says Shy, with a tiny touch of menace as he says the word.

"Of course I do. Anyway, I just told you about mine."

"You didn't tell me much. I don't even know his last name, or yours, for that matter."

Davey is slightly taken aback. "You could have looked me up on a list anytime. There's a list."

"I tried, actually. You're not *on* the regular list. You signed up a good week after all the others. Anyway, I'm not allowed into administration."

Davey wonders why Shy seems so agitated suddenly. But he himself gets that way, too. At least, he used to get that way,

"OK, well, my last name is Ewington," he answers simply.

"Hmmm. Very posh."

"Really? Never thought about it."

"That your dad's name?"

"Yeah, what else would it be?"

"I mean, is it your mom's, too?"

"Yeah."

"She didn't keep her own name, huh?"

"Well, not everyone does, I mean some women do—"

"No, I can see she can't think for herself, does what she's told, I mean she took his name and that's what was expected, I can see that clear as day. Very, very convenient, too. Women can just hide behind new names every day, like they disappeared off the earth or something, like they're not accountable for their words and deeds of the past. Like their come-ons don't mean squat."

"Is something wrong, Shy?"

"Nothing's wrong. Is your dad English?"

"No, why?"

"The name sounds English. I hate them, they're snobs. I'm glad you're not a Pommy bastard."

"What kind of expression is that? I never heard it before."

"Um—it's kind of a ranch expression," says Shy, recovering from his burst of curiosity. He takes control of himself. "Don't you go using it, now—you're too young to cuss." He winks, as he often does, but this time Davey does not return the gesture.

"Well, anyway," says the boy after moment, "my dad's just a regular old American. Nothing fancy."

"WASP?"

"Huh?"

"White. Anglo. Saxon. Protestant?"

"Not really. He's not anything that specific. Actually, his mom was from a Jewish family, but Dad is your typical all-American guy. Kind of a can-do guy. You might even call him a little bit macho."

"A dad like that can't be easy for a boy like you."

"How did you know that?"

"I had my own alpha male for a dad. He, too, was 'kind of macho.' Does yours ever beat you?"

"What? No!"

Silence.

"What? Yours does?"

"Did," says Shy. "Oh, he surely, surely did. But I'm past all that now. In fact, I never really bother to think about it."

Then why did you bring it up, thinks Davey, troubled.

"You mean like, a tap on the hand?" he persists.

"No, not a tap on the hand."

"A smack on the butt?"

"I said a beating, boy, and I meant a beating. Full force, fists and blood. I'd drop to the floor but he'd keep right on going."

"Wow. What about your mother?"

"She didn't do that. She cooked and cleaned and raised us up just the way her hubby wanted her to."

"So—she just, like, let him get away with it?"

"Oh, yes. Seems like she didn't want to get in trouble. The funny thing was, I trusted her. I really did. I used to think she *couldn't* do anything about it. But she could have. She could have tried just that little bit harder. Stood between him and me. Taken a few."

"That's sad."

"No, it's not." Shy has come to the end of his Ponipop, leaving only the long, white stick. He snaps the stick with a crack, then snaps it again and flings out the pieces.

"Because as I've lived and grown, son, I've come to the rather ugly conclusion that most women are cunning bitches. Not all, mind you. Most of 'em, though. Trust me on that one."

This doesn't seem right, but Davey doesn't know what to say.

"Now tell me about *your* mother," Shy says, continuing. "She must be such a lovely lady to have you for a son. She's of the Jewish persuasion, you mentioned?"

"You don't really sound like a cowboy anymore," says Davey. He is thinking about the delicacy of Shy's earlier phrase, "rather ugly conclusion," and the elegant word "cunning." And what is this interest in whether someone was "of the Jewish persuasion"? He has only mentioned that his father had a Jewish mother. And that is only because Shy had asked if he was Protestant.

"Oh, I've been around all types in my day," Shy is saying.

"Haven't you mostly lived in Cheyenne?"

"Where? Yeah, of course I have, mostly. I mean, there's plenty of good land there, I can tell you. No need to go far to find the wide open spaces."

"Then why did you come here?"

Long silence. A bumblebee hangs low in the clover.

"To be honest, and I want to be as honest as I can, I've come back to claim my lady love."

"Back? You've been here before?"

"I mean 'back East,' as the saying goes."

"A lady love? But you just said they—you know, women, were all—you know—kind of untrustworthy—"

101

"Yeah, most of them are sly little vixens that'll turn on you like that. There's no good in them, David. They'll break your heart. But I need this particular one. I wanna see her again. Dreamed about her for years and years, and then fate brought me here in my wanderings."

"Why do you need to see this person so much?"

"Give her one last chance, you know? We all have the right to repent, am I right? Confession, last judgment, extreme unction?"

"I don't know those words."

"You don't know the word 'confession'? The word 'judgment'?"

"Yeah, those particular ones I do, but—"

"I want her to confess—do you get it now? A wrong was done to me, but forgiveness is always possible, you see?"

"Yeah, I see. Uh-huh."

Davey is starting to feel uncomfortable, particularly as one corner of Shy's wax-tipped moustache is beginning to slip down-ward, toward the earth. He can see a trace of his upper lip, and how it wiggles and flaps as he forms his strange words. And then Davey can no longer hear the words. It is just wiggle and flap and paste and wax.

He is frightened of Shy, and stands up.

What time is it? Almost 5:30? He has lost track. His mom will be at the gate, parked in the van and waiting for him. She will be worried about not finding him.

Davey wipes the grass off his pants and runs, dropping what remains of his Ponipop. He is relieved when he sees his mother, comfortably familiar in her T-shirt and yoga pants, hair tied back with a plastic barrette. She has stepped out of the car and is searching for him.

When she sees her son, Jude's face opens wide with a smile that is as warm as sunlight and as pretty as the first birds of spring. Anyone can see that, even Shy, who stands not far away, seeing but unseen.

Judy and Collum, Age Fourteen

Now that a year had passed since her bat mitzvah, Judy Pincus was starting to keep secrets from her father. It was impossible not to. It was impossible to grow up and into someone new without keeping secrets from those who insisted that you stay the same as before. The same as they were. Who wanted you to remain exactly as they had taught you to be. Especially from a father who thought so much and so hard and so definitely, and who never stopped teaching and preaching.

The home: first and primary source of all brainwashing and literal domestication. Love me, be like me, think like me. In the end, living wood is turned into petrified stone. But this would not happen to Judy, who kept parts of her brain to herself and for herself, culs-de-sac of delicious, liquid emotional privacy. Feelings of love were one such area, a separate and distinct religion that Judy held too sacred to share with agnostics like her father. Yes, agnostics—though he professed to be "religious," and was of course loyally wedded to Judy's mother, his wife, he seemed to know nothing about surrender without reason. If he had ever done so, he'd forgotten it. (And forgetting was death and betrayal.)

For Judy, the words "always" and "forever" still meant something. And love was a pilgrim's voyage, full of risk. You couldn't find the answers to its questions without melting, without risking the very borders that kept you safe at home. It was as voluptuous and secret as her own budding body and the feelings it gave her. She longed, in some way, to be possessed, consumed. So how could she share those longings with anyone, much less her mother (who aggressively stirred Judy a glass of pink Instant Breakfast each morning) or her father, who chose to confront all feelings with tenets and calipers? Could she put a mental grid on the dreams, night and day, that often took her, piercing her through and spilling her, like the blade-point of a jousting knight? Like all girls, like all true, unjaded lovers, she wanted to tumble backward, come what may.

That was not on her father's agenda. No tumbling backward allowed, but rather a moving forward, productively, to maintain and restore what was good. Self-preservation—the Darwinian ideal, and certainly understandable in the logical sense. Who but a lover, a teen, or a nut would want to melt away? Even poets left their marks with black on white.

Normal people married their kind, distributed their values, and kept chaos at bay. For Jews, given their history, this was a greater challenge, and responsible parents took it on. Suicidality was not a great trait for tribal elders.

One of Mr. Pincus's main tenets—and a logical one—was that Jews were a vanishing species, as special as white tigers. A vital corollary was that they must marry only other Jews. That way, and only that way, more Jews would be born, and the people would not die out. They would survive forever, which was what God wanted. To marry "out" was to be a traitor, if not a genocidal murderer, one of many who would always be defeated in the end.

An unfortunate consequence of her father's marriage rule was that his child should not even consider dating non-Jewish boys. Most of the time, Judy found herself understanding, and even agreeing, with her father's logic. He was saying that even her earliest dates should be cognizant of marriage. When one falls in love for the first time, one often does feel that it will last forever, and in rare cases, it does. That is how many people get to have sixtieth anniversaries. Judy could, indeed, imagine getting married to the first boy to whom she gave her heart, and never envisioned the years ahead as a series of broken hearts and promises, as they more frequently turned out to be. She had a premonition that her first love would be her last.

But where would she find this Semitic suitor? Try as she might, Judy couldn't find any appropriate candidates. There were only nine Jewish boys in her entire freshman grade, and there was actually something wrong (for her) with every one of them. More precisely, there was nothing right with any of them. Five were too short and still had baby bodies, two had very bad skin, one seemed oblivious to his dandruff condition, and the one who was tall and smooth-skinned and flake-free was very immature. He snapped girls' bra straps, for example.

Although Judy could be, and was, friends with most of these boys (though not the dummy who used lingerie like a slingshot), that was as far as it could ever go. Her heart did not flutter when they came into the room, nor did it pine when they left it. The idea of kissing them made her gag, and if you couldn't even kiss someone, what was the point at all?

There was only one boy *on earth* that Judy could ever end up loving. Her fate was sealed on the day she first saw him. That boy was no Jew. If anything, he was the very opposite. His name was Collum Whitsun. He was Irish-American; he was a son of the streets; he was riffraff. Pure trouble.

Even his name was strange and different. And while all the

Jewish kids seemed destined for at least a B average and a life as (at worst) an optometrist, Collum had been left back! Judy, though a well-bred Jewish maiden, wanted him just the same. Perhaps even more. She could even imagine dirt under his fingernails, the soil of hard labor and the oil of machinery. This was a boy who would wax his car and look good doing it. She could see him chopping wood with an axe, as in a fairy tale of woodsmen. And she would be his girl, the one who made him speak his halting words. For whom he'd drop the axe, wipe his hands, and tumble.

Oh yes, the boy had to tumble, too. And the harder he fell, the more the earth would shake. A giant would fall for a princess, she thought.

Judy Shana Pincus was surprised that she was the only girl in school who seemed to think like this, who saw this perfect boy step in front of her like a miracle. Why wasn't everyone in love with Collum? Was he so magical that only she could see him? But all the other girls seemed to find him beneath them, and simply passed him by. They thought him rough and clueless. They thought him weird and even a little disgusting. And he gave off a "vibe" of nastiness. A chip on his shoulder that spoke of smallness and irritation.

Who needed that, besides Judy? Who saw the prince in that frog from the bog?

True, Collum had a distinct body odor (perhaps he bathed less than the norm, especially now that the hormones were running in some precociously masculine individuals), but Judy actually liked the way he smelled. It was a musky smell, like the warmth of a bed after you left it. She liked his dirty blond locks, which were not as fluffy as clean hair, but heavier, like a pelt, and swirly. Like hair of a boy that had swum in a lake, and emerged, shaking it out like a dog. Like a mutt. Big hands and feet. Shaggy.

Most of all, she adored his blue eyes. There was no word in the dictionary, nor, in *Roget's Thesaurus* (Judy checked) to fairly describe how beautiful Collum's eyes were, and how much she loved looking not at them, but into them.

One way of approaching their hue was to say that it contained more than one color. They weren't just blue, but orange-flecked and gray-rimmed. And not just blue and orange and gray, but sometimes red with provocative moodiness. Collum's eyes spoke. They demanded, they pleaded, they entered you and caught you up in an ancient drama your body recognized before your brain did.

And he was a boy who returned stares. When Judy looked into his eyes, he looked into hers. And the more his eyes met Judy's, the more her heart (and legs) melted. It was the way he looked out of them, and pierced you. Collum needed only to lift his eyes to laser-beam right into your soul. In doing so, he'd leave a hole that only he could fill.

Judy was a stare-returner. Maybe it was as simple as that. She wanted to know and be known. Collum reached deep into her, even to the private culs-de-sac she kept from her parents. They mated with their eyes, like true animals. Like actual white tigers, that rare breed. These lovers were rarer than Jews, even. They saw each other, and knew what lay ahead. Capture—and no release. A bite and a spill, and it's over. Collum had nothing to lose, and Judy (who had more to lose) wanted to lose it all. She really wanted to.

No hope for Judy. She was a goner from the age of fourteen, lost to a feral boy who would want her as much as she wanted him. And who wouldn't let go.

At first Collum did not realize what was in store for him, Judy-wise. He had his own problems that predated any story with this particular girl. His pains preoccupied him, although he'd noticed her already, in passing. She seemed to be a goody-goody. She already needed glasses, and sometimes wore them. She was pretty, but he hated the glasses, and bookish people made him sick. They had no use for him, anyway. He hated school; it was only a bit better than being at home, which was hell.

Collum would come to school guarded, enveloped in what seemed to be a private anguish. That pelt of hair, clearly uncared for. The posture of defense. And the face always hidden, chin down. To Judy, the first person who ever tried to see him, his malaise seemed like poetry, like depth.

Their first conversation occurred outside school, as Collum ran up the steps, thumbs locked under his backpack straps, head tucked downward:

"Your shoelace is untied," she said, voice higher than usual.

He slowed down only slightly, and swiveled his head in her direction.

"So what."

Amazing. A challenge. Jewish boys (most any sane boy) would at least have taken a quick, cautious look downward. Most would have then taken a moment to kneel and tie their laces. They didn't want to fall and hurt themselves. What is more embarrassing, after all? To bend and tie your laces—or to sprawl helplessly on the asphalt and maybe tear your pants, not to mention your knees?

Collum's entire being implied that to fall and hurt himself would not really matter, not really register at all. As though he could endure worse, and had, and could endure more, and had.

He ran ahead of her and into his homeroom, disappearing.

Judy of course caught him. It wasn't all that hard. Collum was lonely, and no one had ever seemed to have paid any attention to him. His grades were less than mediocre; he didn't play team sports or a blaring band instrument. What he could do really well was look interesting. Part of this was what God had given him, an uncanny physical beauty which was just beginning to emerge. And part was what God had cursed him with, a pain (born of a brute of a father) that roiled inside the heart of the boy.

"Can't you hear me?" said Judy.

"Huh?"

She was standing right in front of him, blocking his way up the staircase.

"I said HI. I'm JUDY. OK???"

He seemed to be listening. Judy took a breath and continued:

"Some days, your shoes are untied. Sometimes they're not. In case you're deaf, I've been talking about your shoes *every day*. Today, though, they actually happen to be fine."

"Yeah, so?" he tossed his hair with an attempt at defiance.

"So I'm trying to get your attention."

"Look, I'm going to be late for class."

"Yeah, so?" she said, echoing him.

"My—my dad—my father gets mad at me when I bring home too many notes from school."

"But you're never late."

"How would you know?"

"I've been watching you."

There was a pause before he spoke. A slight stoppage of time.

"You're wrong," he then retorted. "I was late a lot for a few months. Now I'm on time, and I better get going—" he pushed past her. Their shoulders brushed. He wasn't that tall, not yet. But his shoulders were broader than hers, and stronger.

"OK," said Judy, stepping aside, tingling merely from the touch of his shabby jeans jacket. "I'll let you go."

I'll let you go? Who was saying these words? Judy had never spoken in this way to anyone before, much less a boy. And she herself had never been late. Why did she suddenly sound like a thug? Because love is a bully, and it makes bullies of many of us, especially the too-passionate ones.

"I'll let you go," she repeated, "but I want to see you after school."

Collum stared hatefully at her for a second, seeing before him another persecutor. Get off my back, he thought. But at the sight of her eyes, his anger slid away. Right there, he saw a kindness, a patient attentiveness, which seemed almost holy to him. For just a second, he wanted to weep. And in the next second, he wanted to be with her, and this felt to him like joy.

This was Judy's first look at those eyes, full-on. There was malice there, and there was also hope. A certain vulnerability that caught her and kept her from breathing normally. She was actually panting, she noticed, and he noticed, too. Was there a trace of a smile there? A molecule.

"OK," he said, his gaze softening. "I'll see you after school."

Then he ran, head down, and disappeared into the safety of the cool school corridors.

After school, Judy waited, but Collum did not appear.

Oh, so that's how you want to play it, she said to herself.

Her calming friend Nessa, who wore thick braids that ended in covered rubber bands, came over. She and Nessa had bonded in the earlier grades, and while many of Judy's other friends had frozen into one dismissive clique or another, Nessa had remained who she'd always been—a loyal go-along.

"Wanna—"

"No I don't!" said Judy, too fiercely. She could see Collum running out of a side door, his shoulders hunched low. It was astounding to think that he was trying to avoid her, even more horrible to imagine that he had forgotten that she was waiting for him.

She watched him dart this way and that. She let him go.

"What did you say, Ness?" she then asked her friend.

"Wanna—"

"Sure! Let's!" said Judy. Whatever Nessa wanted to do—whatever anyone in high school wanted to do—fine. Gossip, eat pizza, shun the uncool, agonize over hair frizz or the perfect scented lip gloss. Study for the test. Root for the team. Whatever.

"I just thought we'd go to my house for a while. That essay, remember?" Nessa looked at her friend tentatively. Judy was really good at English, but lately, she seemed just a little off. Nessa, like most girls her age who kept the braid and wore white underpants, would grow up to avoid odd people on principle. But this was high school, and there was that essay to finish.

"I said yes, didn't I?"

"We can make real lemonade, too. My mom got a reamer. It takes all the lemon juice out really well."

Perfect, thought Judy. Let's spend the afternoon juicing lemons and writing our essays. She wasn't being sarcastic. It was easy to turn away from a passion she'd only begun. Maybe she'd also stop reading *Wuthering Heights*, which the librarian had told her she'd love. It was only making things worse and wasn't even on the curriculum.

For the next few days, Judy ignored Collum, but she did it in such a way that he noticed her doing so. He could wear his shoes with laces dragging; she would not say a word. He could be the first one into school, run here and there like a scared rat: So what? She was far too good for him. Millions of miles better, in fact. She was a nice Jewish girl, of the People of the Book. What was he? A savage. A guttersnipe. His grades were probably Cs—and he probably didn't even care.

Her father was right. Collum was a non-Jew, and not the classy kind that kept people like them out of country clubs. He was the kind that fixed things (like clogged sinks and carburetors), that made it possible for educated people to keep their nails clean. And he wasn't Heathcliff, either. He was just a bum without a novel to make him look better. Collum would surely not understand the niceties of her world, the refinement and study that had gone into her people since they stood at Sinai and received the Law. And the commentaries, later. He wouldn't even understand the Brontës, who made people like him look good!

And what was he doing now, on the ground, by the side door, slumped as though in a drug haze? Oh, well. That figured. He was just a sniveling, shaggy, BO-stinking boy, and he could drop dead, for all she really cared.

Judy stared at Collum as the school bell rang. He stayed where he was. Heroin, probably, she thought. Nodding off to his addictive drug, heroin, or horse, as the junkies called it. Or maybe just a big bottle of cheap booze.

"Hey!" she found herself shouting from the central staircase, as students ran up the stairs, passing her.

"You're going to be late!" she shouted again. Her voice seemed high and ineffectual. Not the kind of voice that was meaningful to addicts bent on self-destruction.

Collum's head was still down, and Judy now noticed that he held his hands over his face, blocking the world out. This is what happened in some homes, she thought, tutting with superiority. At the same time, there was nothing she wanted more than to be with him on his level, deep in those murky waters from which all trouble sprang.

The school bell was still ringing as she descended the stairs. Then it went silent, hovering in the air like a closed option, like the past that was now irretrievable. Silence and an open view of chaos ahead.

She walked over to Collum.

He seemed to sense her coming, letting his head rise a fraction, then settling it down again. He was beyond caring who saw him this way.

"What's wrong?"

"Get lost, OK?"

"What're you doing here? Go upstairs. Go to class."

"No."

"You'll be late for school!"

"So I'll be late. A lot of people are late. Now it's my turn."

"You'll get a mark. You'll spoil your record."

"Boo hoo. A mark and a record."

"You said your dad didn't like it when you were marked late."

Collum looked at her for a moment. He took his hands away from his face, lifted his eyes, and really looked at her.

Then Judy saw: a circle of dark purple around one blue eye. That eye was partly closed; the other stared out accusingly.

"What happened? You got into a fight?"

"Not exactly a fight. The outcome was pretty well known from the beginning."

His diction was more educated than she expected. And the words—"the outcome was ..." He was smart, just like her. He was sharp; he was deep. Her heart ached for him, a smart boy beaten by a brute.

"What do you mean?"

"*I* didn't fight. If I ever fought back, he'd—"

"Then who—"

"Who do you think?"

Smart as she was, Judy still couldn't figure it out. Her experiences had, up to now, been utterly limited and bourgeois. Everything bad she'd ever heard about had happened elsewhere. Nothing to do with her current path. It wasn't in the curriculum; it wasn't in the homework. Collum was beaten, and there—right in front of her.

"A—a bully?" There were older kids in the school, notorious morons (and not college material) who would not be past giving someone a black eye. Usually, they left girls alone, and this was one of the many reasons that Judy rejoiced in not being male. All that rough anger, all the fists and bruises! Of course, the Jewish boys were not like that. But most regular boys had a secret knowledge of it—sought it out, almost.

Yes, she was learning a secret about life now. She knelt, as though in prayer. Now, their faces were close. She was panting, unsure, and exhilarated.

"Collum—didn't you try to run away?"

"You're really not getting it!"

"What?"

"I've heard about you. You're richer than most of the kids in the school, different outfit all the time. What's your last name? Pinker? Pinkstein or something?"

Judy felt herself assaulted in a new and unusual way. Her father had hinted about things like this. Jews being singled out, ridiculed for their names and how they looked. Worse than ridiculed.

"It's Pincus. I'm not rich at all. Normal, middle-class, I guess, but not—"

"You don't know what my life is like, or how 'normal' it is, so don't go there, Pinkstein."

"Pincus."

"OK, whatever, Pincus."

"No, I don't know what your life is like. How would I?"

"Maybe I oughtta tell you. Do you want me to?"

"Yes," said Judy, falling even more in love. Was that even the word? In a way, this entry into another person's life—into a goyish boy's life—wasn't even a part of her. Judy left herself behind and stepped fatefully into a labyrinth.

As Collum spoke, she followed him into the heart of his painful, short life.

"My father is a drunk, OK? *A stinking, drinking drunk.* He works with his hands all day—that's why his arms are nice and strong. He's a housepainter, not the fancy kind of painter *you* might prefer, a *house*painter—and all day long he's at the bottle."

"Does he know about Alcoholics Anonymous—" Judy might have been in a labyrinth, but she didn't forget everything she knew. And she wanted to be helpful, after all.

"*Yes*, he knows about AA, you idiot! Oh my God!!"

"OK, I'm sorry. I just wanted to—no, go on with your story."

"No," he echoed, but his "no" was much more fearsome than hers could ever be. It was a wall that he could put up, and often did.

"This is too much for me right now," he said, beginning to shut down. Beginning to get up and start walking again. Who cared where? Away.

"It's not a *story*, OK? It's not an essay for the school paper. OK?"

"No, I know it's not a story! I'm so sorry. Please, please don't stop."

Collum wasn't good with pleading. He could retreat into a pitiless place. He lived there most of the time. But he relented.

"Let me just put it into simple terms that even you might understand: my father beats the holy living shit out of me whenever he feels like it."

"So your *father* gave you that black eye?"

"Oh, my God, you're a genius! So it's true!"

"What is true?"

"Jews are smarter than we are! Hallelujah!"

"How do you even know I'm Jewish?" said Judy, leery. Was this to be one of the "anti-Semitic incidents" her father always cautioned her about?

"That star you wear around your neck is a little bit of a give-away."

"My—my star of David? Oh, I got it for my bat mitzvah! You noticed? Yeah, it's actually eighteen karat, so the color—"

"Look, I don't notice shit like that, and I don't care, but you're standing over me, really close, so I'm actually getting a pretty good look at your chain and that Jewish star, your little bauble. I mean, it's in my face, for God's sake!"

While Judy was caught up with Collum's clever verbiage ("*bauble*?"—she really had assumed he was not as bright as she), Collum noticed that she smelled clean, like golden Breck shampoo, and that she had a beautiful long neck that fell away into the hint of female breasts. He trembled, just a bit, and Judy felt it.

She touched the boy's face with the tip of her finger. She followed its contours, forehead, wounded eye, piercing other eye, nose, mouth, chin. She was tender with him, and felt her own tenderness with a kind of reverence, not unlike religion.

A tear slid out of Collum's hurt eye, and Judy wiped it. He looked at her, his lashes long and wet, as dewy as a spider's web at dawn.

And then he got up, shook himself (and her) off, and raced into the school.

"What're you gonna tell them?" she said, panting after him.

"About what? Oh, this? Fell on my loose shoelaces."

"Well, they *are* usually loose."

"Not that they notice. You're the only one who's noticed."

"That's because I love you so much," she whispered to herself. Did her lips move? Did she actually say the words? It seemed so, because Collum's face, turning back, told her that he'd heard her.

The House of Whitsun

Collum's love was everything Judy had ever dreamed about. He showed it like a hero, in front of everyone.

They'd stood on the lunch line one day. Judy's friends—her peer group, that is, were getting used to the fact that she was eating with this boy, this scruffy kid. All of them were good students, and planned not only to go to college, but to Princeton or Penn. There they sat, holding their skim milk containers up, sipping through a straw and then stopping the sips to gossip animatedly about her. They were leaning over, to and fro, as though whispering intently. Staring and sipping, sipping and staring. Then one of them came up to the line, sidled near her, and said, "This will not end well."

She had actually said that, as though Judy and Collum were characters in some after-school special.

"Yes, it will," said Judy, without turning her face.

"I just got up because my milk container happens to be leaking, but as a friend I have to tell you that you're putting yourself in a bad situation," said the friend. Her name was Nina, and although she was an A student, there were rumors that her parents did her homework for her. She showed no discernible intelligence during school hours.

"Oh, shut up, Nina," said Judy, finally. "Get your moo-juice and mind your business."

"Judy! That's rude!" Nina froze. Her fears were confirmed; Judy was already going bad. She ran to her table as though running from danger, hand on her mouth, telegraphing shock.

Her friends gathered her in, resumed their whispering, staring at Judy and Collum as though they were Bonnie and Clyde.

"Where is the damned pie?" Judy bristled. The only reason she was *on* the line for this long was that the pie—her favorite dessert—had run out. Now she was forced to wait for a new batch to be laid out on the cracked ice.

"You go sit; I'll get it," said Collum.

"They won't give you an extra piece for me," Judy admonished.

"I'll give you mine."

He saw that she was trembling. The conflict had upset her.

"Let's just go. I'm not hungry anymore."

"We'll just sit far away from them, OK, Judy?"

"Where? They see all. They know all. It's unbearable!"

Collum had no idea that peer groups could hurt you like this. At this point in his life, his only friends were his older brothers. He spoke to no one in school except Judy. But he knew what to do.

The pies came out at that moment.

"I want you to dine on this in the presence of your enemies!" he said, swiping a slice off the ice and putting it on his tray. Judy loved these occasional moments of eloquence. Words, when they came to Collum, came to express emotion, loyalty, love.

When he spoke like this, she (the A student) was rendered speechless.

Collum took his tray and walked over to the whisperers. Judy followed.

They saw him approach: the mussy hair, the battered jacket, the shoelaces of his high-tops insecurely tied. The tray holding pie, and a gleam in his eye:

He spoke, with all the dignity he could summon:

"Any of you, any of you, makes a comment to my girl about me and her—about *us*—you'll—I'll—"

"You'll what?" said a girl called Maddy (captain of the debating team). "Beat us up?"

"Just shows what a lowlife you are," said her friend, Tiffney (who, despite her name, was a math whiz).

"Yeah, a thug. Just proves the point," said Susanna, whose father was a local judge.

"No—I won't hit you or anything. But you'll eat your words. You'll see that what you laughed at was true love."

The girls fell silent for a moment. They were, after all, fourteen years old. That word had not been anticipated. "Love" was not a word that was commonly spoken in the lunchroom. Yes, people dated, they went out. And maybe they loved in their way, or said they did. But to throw it out like that, like a dare?

As the girls looked at Collum, he met their eyes, and each and every one of those girls fell in love with that blue-eyed, hard-staring, soft-staring boy.

And there was more.

"I LOVE her," he said. He turned around, sure that Judy was behind him. And she was, tray in hand. Tray in his own hand, Collum swiveled his body and kissed her on the lips, a kiss so long and deep that she almost dropped her food. But nothing dropped but a bunch of jaws at the sharp girls' table.

Collum let Judy go, and started walking. He claimed a table for the two of them. Judy ate the pie he'd gotten her. It was full of peaches. Hard to tell if they were fresh or not, but she didn't care—they were sweet and moist.

That was their first kiss. It tasted like courage, love, patience, and good, juicy peaches.

If only Judy could have shown her father the actions of that day! Like a Maccabee warrior her Collum was, brave in the face of the enemy hordes. Holding his own against ridicule.

But of course, she could not bring Collum home, because her father would have asked many questions.

"Whitsun? What kind of a name is 'Whitsun'?"

She would have had to say, "Jewish, of course."

"Doesn't sound so Jewish to me, and I do know a Jew or two."

"No, it's changed. His grandpa changed it from 'Weinstein,' on account of all the anti-Semites."

The unreachable parts of her brain had made her wily.

"Into 'Whitsun'? Such a Christian sound to it."

"That's how he fooled them when he came from Poland to this country."

Now she had him. Her father would have liked to hear about this name crisis, about how a poor immigrant was forced to hide an identity because of fear of further suffering, but it was not in Judy's nature to continue to betray someone she loved with ever-greater bold-faced lies.

Collum was braver. Judy met his entire family—father, mother, and two older brothers, Ryan and Rob.

Going to Collum's home was like visiting another country. Judy's home had books and magazines that one could find in normal bookstores and on magazine stands. Collum's had "literature" in the form of crude pamphlets, black-and-white and stapled, strewn around in great piles that threatened to topple.

"My father is very certain in his beliefs," Collum explained. "He likes others to share that certainty, so he does these mailings," he added darkly, as they entered the ramshackle Whitsun homestead. It was a rainy afternoon, just after school. The exterior of the house was painted the darkest brown possible; inside, there were few lights lit, and the windows were heavily curtained. The effect was spooky and depressing.

The first time Judy visited, Collum had assured her that his father would be away for several more hours. His mother, Betty, who worked part-time as a substitute at a nursery school, usually came home at about this hour. Nursery school teachers were always catching something from the little ones, who were like petri dishes of viral infections, but Betty O'Dell Whitsun never caught anything.

"She's a rock," her husband would often say, but it wasn't clear if he meant it as a compliment, because his tone of voice always carried a sneer of hatred in it. He might well have meant that she was the cornerstone of his life; it came out, however, as though she were as dull and insufficient as a gray piece of granite.

Betty had learned to deal with her husband, it seemed. When Judy imagined the sort of woman who had three teenage boys, at least one of whom was regularly beaten, and a husband who struck his children, she imagined a sort of victim type, head bowed in submission. Betty, instead, seemed sanguine. She sang as she walked about her house (before she knew they were there), and when she did not sing, she whistled.

From where Judy and Collum stood, at the threshold of the dark house, they could hear water running in the kitchen, and Betty trilling a song in which she provided both the call and the response:

Oh, ya can't get to heaven,
Oh, ya can't get to heaven
On Patrick's nose

On Patrick's nose
Cause Patrick's nose
It grows and grows!!

"Hey, Ma!" yelled Collum. "I've brought a guest home for tea!"

"Hold on, now—what did you say? Is it my own Collum there?"

"It is, Ma, and I've brought someone home, so comb your hair and take off your apron!"

"Oh, she doesn't have to—" Judy attempted.

"But I *do* have to, when it's such a pretty girl he's brought home with him," said Betty, running out into the foyer to greet them. As she ran, she untied the strings of a soft-cotton floral apron, then used it to wipe her dewy brow.

"Oooh, don't have boys, I tell you! You'll always be washing and cleaning something!"

"This is Judy, Ma. I told you about her, didn't I?"

"You did. Judy: the girl who is perfect as a new-bloomed rose."

Collum and his mother were close. He was her youngest, after all, her baby boy. He felt good in her presence, and she in his. They had always been kind to each other, and no harsh surprises had ever ruined their expectation of mutual love and trust. All this Judy took in as she saw the way Collum and his mother looked at each other. She was glad he had someone like this in his life, and wanted his mother to like her, too.

"Do you want a nibble of something? I could make you both a nice cup of cocoa, or—"

"I thought we'd have tea together, Ma," said Collum. "A proper tea, with cakes and thick bread and butter and jam."

"But I haven't got cakes on the spur here, Collum. Would biscuits do? I've got those nice gingersnaps; they're always the last to be eaten. Don't you find that so, Judy, dear?"

"Don't I—?"

"Don't you find that if you lay out an assortment, say, of biscuits—chocolate, jam-center, graham, ginger—that the ginger will always be the last to go? It's like people are afraid of it, I tell you!"

Judy, whose parents favored rugalach, chose to agree.

"There, you see?" said Betty, leading her into the kitchen. "I knew I'd like you! And you'll eat a few of them, won't you?"

Judy nodded. She felt better now that she was in this room, which caught the sun, and whose curtains were white and airy. Betty's kind voice soothed her.

"Now let me see about the bread—I could toast up some of this loaf—we don't go for sliced bread in this house—and there is a bit of blackberry jam, I think—"

"Can I help you with anything?" said Judy, trying to be good. In her house, her mother did everything that the cleaning lady didn't do, which wasn't that much, and she, Judy, did even less. She liked the homespun quality of Collum's life, the "loaf" and the ginger snaps, which his mother kept in a round tin with candy canes on it. She liked Betty's flower-patterned cotton apron, and she liked the braid that Betty wore down her back like a young girl of olden days.

"No, I've got it. You two sit down, I'll just put on the kettle."

"Thanks, Ma."

"Thanks, Mrs. Whitsun."

"Now, dear, just call me Betty."

They sat down at a small round table in the center of the kitchen, around which five ladder-back chairs were arrayed.

"Would you prefer coffee? I do have some instant, and it's fresh from the grocery."

"No, I'd love tea," said Judy. Normally, she drank tea only when she had a bad cold, but suddenly the humble drink seemed far, far nobler than the aggressive jolt of coffee that her parents preferred.

"That's fine, then," said Betty, putting on the kettle.

In the silence that ensued, Judy listened to the sound of the wall clock ticktocking. It was an old clock, made of wood, and its subtle rhythms filled her with a sense of tradition. This clock may have ticked and tocked over in the old country, she thought. Suddenly, the thought of all those years and years made her tired. She wanted to be in the world now, where she was, and not be carried back. She could have done with a blast of radio, announcing the latest pop tune.

As though reading her thoughts, Betty said, "Yeh, it's seen the years, it has. That was my own mother's clock. We brought it over, one of the only real memories of the house of my girlhood. County Mayo, long ago. Ah, well. Time and tide."

"Is that from your old house, too?" asked Jude, noticing an enormous crucifix on the opposite wall. It was placed between two high cupboards.

"No, no, that's from my husband's woodshop downstairs," said Betty, as the water shrieked at its boiling point. She turned the flame off. The shriek retreated down the scale, and then was silent.

"It's—it's really impressive," said Judy, staring now at the large amounts of painted blood that poured out of the body of Jesus. There was blood on his head, rivulets from every thorn in his crown, blood from the deep, enormous gash in his chest, and blood from the centers of his hands and feet. The color of the blood was less red than maroon—a dark, clotted, and shiny color that made the drips look three-dimensional, congealed and impasto-thick.

"My husband, I'm proud to say, is a great artist. During the day, he is a house painter, and none is better for getting the job done, fast and neat, but then at nights and weekends, he—well, you can see the sort of work he does."

"I can," Judy agreed.

Mr. Whitsun Also Composed

Clearing the teacups and cake-plates, Betty Whitsun became pensive. "My husband also has the gift of music," she said. She held a cup in one hand and a spoon in the other, as though she were about to ring the cup and make an announcement. Her hands were in the air, and her face looked as though she were waiting for a cue.

"No, Ma," pleaded Collum, his face twisted like a martyr's.

"Oh, all right," said Betty, returning to her chores.

"Not today, thanks."

"Well, his compositions *are* very lovely," his mother insisted, now scraping the crumbs off the plates. "And Judy here seems to be interested in his artistic expressions, am I right, Judy, dear?"

"Oh, yes, of course I am."

Collum shot her a look.

"I am!"

"It's so easy for you young ones to forget that we parents are also people," said Betty, sighing. "Human beings, with hopes and dreams and passions."

"That's true," Judy conceded. For instance, she actually

thought that her love for Collum, and his for her, was deeper and more serious and abiding than anything her parents had ever felt. It was good to remember that they had possibly once felt as she and Collum did. Or—even more remarkably—that they still felt anything at all, at their age.

"Oh, yes," said Betty.

"Please, no," said her son.

"I think she'll love it, Collum, darling. It's quite lovely." She caught his miserable glare, and added, "and it won't be too loud."

"It's always loud enough to haunt anyone," said Collum miserably.

"Not as loud as the music you young folk listen to, at any rate, when Dad's not home."

She was referring to Collum's older brothers, who were teenagers, and liked banging music, rhythmic as the long march into Hades.

"I personally don't mind if it's loud," Judy offered, wondering from where the music would emerge. There didn't seem to be a record player in the room. In those days, music emerged from record players, often through speakers. There were lots of wires and knobs involved. The record would go round and round, centered by a small silver stick. A long arm would dance along the grooves of the record; at the end of the arm was a needle that followed them. Sometimes, a bit of dust, or a scratch on the vinyl, would cause a crackling sound, or a hiss, which only added to the drama of hearing notes emerge from a spinning plastic platter.

"Neil!" Betty shrieked into the kitchen air. "Can you come upstairs for a minute?"

"Your father's home?"

"Yeah," said Collum dully. "I did notice his boots in the corner of the foyer. Sometimes, he works odd hours. Emphasis on odd."

What Collum didn't explain was that sometimes Neil Whitsun was too drunk to work. On those days, he would lie in bed most of the day. Eventually, he would go down to his sanctum in the cellar and not be heard from until dark.

But music, Betty thought, could always cheer him. Let him come up from that gloomy basement he spent so much time in. Let him bring a note of gaiety into his life, the poor man. She never forgot the boy she had fallen in love with, the one with the sweet smile and the deep belief that life had a meaning, and that the meaning was good. She was touched that he still tried to express what he felt, what he knew.

"Ne-il?" she sang out more loudly. Then, with a broom, she banged on the floor, and cocked her ear expectantly.

"Neil! Neil! NEIL!!!!!!!!!!!!!!!!!!"

"YAAAAAAAAAAAHHH????"

Judy could hear a voice, sepulchral and goaty under the green-and-white checkered kitchen linoleum. The call and response of two lunatic beasts.

"CAN YOU COME UP, MY DARLING?"

"NAAAAA AAAHHH!!! 'FRAID I CAN'T!!!!"

"WE'VE GOT A GUEST, NEIL, DARLING! A SCHOOL FRIEND OF COLLUM'S! SHE WANTS TO HEAR YOUR MUSIC!!"

There was silence for a long moment, and then the menacing reply:

"*WHO* . . . WANTS . . . TO. HEAR . . . *WHAT*?"

He sounded like Oz, the great and powerful. Judy reflexively crossed her arms and legs against an onslaught. She, after all, was the "WHO" in question.

"A SCHOOL FRIEND OF COLLUM'S!!!!! SHE WANTS TO HEAR YOUR MUSICAL COMPOSITIONS!!!!!"

"*SHE* WANTS TO HEAR MY MUSICAL COMPOSI-TIONS??"

"YES!!!!!!!!"

"IT'S A GIRL, YOU SAY? A DAMSEL, FAIR?"

Betty turned to Judy.

"You tell him, love. Tell him that you want to hear his music."

"Oh, Christ almighty," Collum muttered, head in hands.

"You really want me to tell him?" She was still digesting the words "damsel fair." What was expected of her? On the other hand, the challenge was becoming fraught with romance, in a way. She was the damsel in this tale. Collum's maiden, with an ogre raging below.

"Yes, if you don't mind."

Judy attempted to shout. She felt stupid at the first attempt:

"I want to hear your music!"

"Louder, please," said Betty.

"I want to hear your music!!!!"

"With all you heart and soul, dear."

"I WANT TO HEAR YOUR MUSIC!!!!!" Judy bellowed, like a motherless calf. Oddly, the release of doing so almost brought tears to her eyes. She DID want to hear his music. This all seemed so extreme, so crazy, in a wonderful way. She wanted all of life to be like this, released and true. Full of hidden music, finally sounded out. Driven by a pulse of desperate passion, however pathetic the outcome. Very different from her father's nightly music hour, listening to the classical station on the radio.

Collum's father did not respond.

"Should I bang on the floor with the broom?" Judy asked Collum's mother, with a touch of eagerness.

"Wait," Betty responded. "I think I can hear him—yes—listen, he's coming up the stairway."

Judy listened with all her young body and soul.

By really concentrating, she could hear the first steps of Neil Whitsun, mounting upward from his basement. As he rose, the sound of his tread grew louder and louder. After a few more steps, he stood there before them.

The sight of him stopped the world in its tracks. The kitchen disappeared, time disappeared. The only thing Judy could compare this to was being at Radio City Music Hall, as the curtain rose and the sound of a kettledrum rattled your bones.

Collum's father was movie-star handsome. He had a thick head of hair, leonine, white. His face was long, the bones articulate, almost aristocratic. His eyes blazed like those of his son, and like Collum's, they were bright blue. His body, moreover, was tall and strong, with only a slight bend of defeat to the shoulders.

In contrast to his looks, Neil Whitsun wore a dirty white T-shirt and baggy khaki pants. On his feet were a pair of sagging black socks. He wore slippers, worn and humble.

Neil Whitsun took a long, almost rude stare at Judy. "So, you want me to sing to ye, do ye, girl?" he said.

Judy flushed under the intensity of his stare. She felt accused, as though this whole singing thing had been her idea, as though Betty had not mentioned it, not forced the situation. But under the circumstances, she had to play along. Even Betty was looking at her expectantly.

"Oh, yes, please. I hear your music is really nice."

"IT IS NOT NICE!!! IT IS FAR FROM NICE!!!" Neil thundered abruptly.

"It is—majestic," Betty offered, trying to guide Judy to the right level of reverence for her husband's gift.

"Well, I—I love majestic things," Judy stuttered.

"Yes, you may 'love' them—like a whore loves a shiny golden necklace with a most peculiar star—but do you REVERE and RESPECT them? That's the better question, now isn't it?"

"It—it certainly is," she agreed, her fingers fumbling to tuck her incriminating necklace into her blouse.

Collum kept his head down throughout this interchange. His fists were on the table, joints clutched so tight they shone white through his skin. All Judy could see, as she looked over to him, were these knucklebones, ready for self-defense, and his head held low, all blond curls and a touch of furrowed brow.

"I'll begin, then," said Neil Whitsun, with exaggerated politeness. "That is, if no one present has any objection."

The silence that responded showed collective assent.

He began:

LORDY. LORDY, SLAY ME NOW
KILL ME WITH YOUR BLOOD, SHED!
TAKE ME, BREAK ME, ANYHOW
TAKE MY HEART, EYES, GUT, HEAD!
MAKE ME MAKE ME MAKE ME DEAD
BUT NEVER SO ALIVE AND BRIGHT WITH
   REDDDDDD!!!! Blood.

Neil Whitsun paused to draw breath. There was white spittle at both sides of his mouth. His face was scarily flushed.

Judy quietly remarked, "That was good." She thought the "song" was over. Neil glared at her.

"I don't sing for your approval! And I'm not half done!"

And now, having rested, Neil's face became less red. Slowly, he began to dance, eyes closed, and to snap his hands in rhythm. His voice was now as tiny and high-pitched as it had been loud and deep:

Come to me come to me come to me come to me . . .
Take me take me take me take me
Rip my life out of its shell
Lift me from my living hell

Please . . . Oh Lord Oh Spirit!
Father, Father, don't you hear it?

Falling to the ground with the last near-inaudible word, Neil Whitsun seemed to have really finished his song this time. He lay face down, sobbing loudly and at length.

Judy actually liked this part. Particularly the rhyme of "spirit" and "hear it." But she said nothing, taking a cue from Betty and simply watching the man cry. Perhaps this was part of the performance.

When Neil Whitsun stood up again, his face was wet, and so was the front of his khaki pants.

"I have peed myself," he announced with dignity.

No one dared respond to this.

"You'll know you have sung well when you have peed yourself," he added proudly.

"That's a good pointer," said Judy, ever polite. In her insular life, she had never seen a man so drunk before. That's what he was, she reasoned. Not insane. Not anointed by God and/or his messengers. He was drunk. She had never seen any human being behave like this before, and the spectacle of this unhingement was slightly thrilling. My God, what people in the real world could get up to! The lengths to which they would go to express themselves!

"It'll never happen to *you*," he answered rudely, almost as though he had read, and dismissed, her thoughts. "I can tell just looking at you. Logician. Self-preserver, full of cunning sophistry."

For an inebriate, he spoke very clearly now, enunciating every syllable and slicing it clean from its neighbor.

"Cowardly cringer."

"Dad, Judy is a guest—" Collum began.

"Judy? That is who you brought into my house? A *Judy*? A cursed, stinkin' JEW-dy??"

Judy was not exactly sure what she was hearing, but the very scene was bright and thrilling in some way. It seemed important, in the way that her father's tenets seemed important.

"She's a very nice girl from school," said Betty, quickly. "We were just having tea and ginger snaps before you—"

"What's your full name, if you don't mind my asking?" continued Neil Whitsun.

Judy would have readily answered, when he cut in:

"It's Pincus, isn't it? Pink-ass, more like!"

Here we go again, she thought. Collum had called her "Pink-stein." Like son, like father. Judy became like her own father, and commenced lecturing:

"It's a biblical name. From Pinchas. These Hebrew names might sound funny, but they're regal. Like the tribes—Naftali, Gad, Menasseh—I guess they'd seem odd to you, too."

"Oh, don't list them for me. Don't I know only too much about your *tribes*. Know about you and your people, your tribal ways. Your father is a money-counter, eh?"

"He's—what did you call him? A money-counter? He's actually an accountant. You know, a CPA. Certified Public Accountant," she finished.

Neil Whitsun simply stared as her words stuttered to a halt.

"Exactly so," he said with satisfaction. "And he'll have some accounting to do 'later,' if you catch my meaning."

Judy didn't, but Collum and his mother did, and winced.

"Later, when it's far too late for payoffs and bribes, my girlie."

"But—but he also writes poetry," Judy weakly appended.

With this admission, Judy had hoped to appease Collum's creative father. For a moment, he did seem to retreat into thought,

132

but then he picked up a new head of steam and spoke rapidly, panting:

"Always prayed you would never meet my son, or any of my sons. But it's in the blood, isn't it? Take what you can, take over, rape, pillage, and plunder, right?" As he said "pillage" and "plunder," his mouth spat a little into the air.

"'In the blood'?" was all Judy could muster.

"You said it, not me," said Whitsun, with a smile.

"You mean that I'm—that I'm—"

"Of the Chosen Hebraic people?" offered Neil Whitsun helpfully.

"They really don't rape all that much," Betty noted.

"My father told me all about people like you," said Judy, summoning her courage. "I never believed him. I thought he was paranoid. And now here you are, with your dangerous prejudices."

"Yes! Here I am!" said Neil Whitsun. "And here I will stay. Vatican II did not stop Neil Whitsun, and neither shall the likes of you."

"Oh, now, darling, don't get yourself started!" said Betty.

What's he like when he's "started"? Judy wondered.

Vatican II had declared that there might be changes made in the Old Church doctrine. For example, that perhaps the Jews were not to be considered forever and solely guilty of causing the death of the Lord. That they were not evil and not to be punished eternally for their sins.

Neil Whitsun was not going to be lied to by the anti-Christs, Satanists in the garb of the Holy Roman Empire.

"In this house, there will be no changes made to the doctrines of Peter and Paul, and no forgiveness for the sins of the blood! Fancy calling me the prejudiced one, when it's you and yours who continue to deny, and to twist and to corrupt!"

"I'm not trying to offend you or stop you or do anything,

really, to you," Judy said, her voice wavering under his blue-laser glare. "I like your painting—and, and—your song was really kind of interesting—"

"Well, there's a start. You '*like*' this and you '*like*' that. What a great relief that will be to the Heavenly Hosts!!"

Well, I hope they're better hosts than you're turning out to be, thought Judy.

"Do you also like *him*?" he said, pointing to the bleeding crucifix hanging on the wall. "The Man behind the image? The Man behind it all?"

Judy sincerely hoped that this corpse-dummy, hanging in the madman's kitchen, carved and shellacked in garish crimson by Neil Whitsun, was *not* the actual man behind it all. She wasn't even sure she was comfortable with what "it all" implied. Her death? Her eternal banishment to hell?

"It's a very powerful portrayal," she hedged.

Of your insanity, she added to herself.

"What's that?"

Could he hear her very thoughts? She might have been whispering.

"A powerful portrayal of . . . humanity," she amended. If she really tried, she could see, in this form, the miserable deaths of so many victims of prejudice and hatred, the kind she was hearing right in that kitchen.

"Oh, He is powerful, He is. More than a portrayal, I must inform you, however. Can you feel it pulsing with the Holy Spirit?"

"Oh, yes!" In fact, Judy could see a vein pulsing in Neil Whitsun's forehead, under a lock of sweaty, gray hair.

"And you say you also liked my song?"

"Of course! You know I did!" Because, she thought, it showed me what my precious Collum has to deal with, and makes me love him more than ever.

"Well, now, maybe there's a chance for you, then," said Mr. Whitsun, seemingly relenting at last. He smiled broadly, as though he had decided to take the road of forgiveness. His tone, when he spoke again, was jovial.

"Betty! Go downstairs and get a few brochures. I've written most of them myself. You might want to have a look."

"Dad," said Collum, "Judy seems to have her own beliefs, as you've pointed out so well."

"But you see, son, *that* is the problem," said his father, still reasonable. "People with their own beliefs. And everyone thinking one is as good as the other."

His wife left the kitchen and headed to the staircase, which led to the basement. With a house as dark as the Whitsun's, Judy could not begin to imagine how desolate that basement might be.

"But as for you," said Neil, when his wife had gone. He wavered on his feet as he headed for Collum. "*As for you!*"

Uh oh, thought Judy. Here comes Mr. Crazy again.

Collum got up, kicking his kitchen chair behind him so hard that it fell over. He was much shorter than his father at the time, but he tried to look Neil Whitsun right in the eye. He had recently decided that if his father ever tried to lift a hand to him again, he would try to defend himself. He was ready now.

"What *about* me? I can pick whichever friend I want!"

"You can decide everything, huh?"

"Yes, that—that might actually be right."

"You're totally free, is that it?

"Free of you, someday, I hope," Collum said daringly.

Neil let that pass. The smile of forgiveness came back onto his face. It was such a warm and sincere smile that it was nothing if not frightening.

"And what did *you* think of my song, my Big Strong Man?"

"Do you really want to know?"

"It's why I asked you, isn't it?" Neil's smile wavered minutely, and his voice betrayed a molecule of worry.

"I hate your sick, crazy music, Dad, and I think your art is really grotesque."

Saying this, Collum winced and braced himself for blows, but his father simply closed his eyes slowly.

His wife had entered the room, arms laden with brochures.

"Help me to the bed, Betty," he said. "A little lie-down's what I need. I'm tired now."

"He doesn't mean it," said Betty to her husband. Laying down her papers, she took his arm and began to lead him out. Suddenly, Neil Whitsun stopped at the doorway.

"No! I promised her some of my pamphlets, and so some of my pamphlets she shall have!"

"Yes, I've brought the pamphlets!"

"Not all of them! Not the right ones! Not the newest ones! Only I know where they are!"

Dropping his wife's arm, he seemed to gain energy as he went to the staircase, descended into the depths of his private sanctuary, and returned with an armful of literature.

"Take these!" he commanded. "And now," said Neil Whitson to his wife. "You can escort me upstairs."

After a moment, Neil and Betty Whitsun were gone.

Judy looked at her boy. She loved him more than ever. She stuffed a mass of pamphlets into her shoulder bag, then took his hand in hers. As Collum's parents made their way up the stairs, Judy and Collum walked outside together, into the clear, fresh air of a spring afternoon. The sun seemed more shiny than it had ever been before.

Neil Whitsun had only drawn them closer.

Conspiracy Theory

ater that evening, however, Neil Whitsun made his son read his new pamphlet.

"It is my masterpiece," he said. "It says it all."

Secrets THEY Don't WANT YOU TO KNOW!!!!!!
Did YOU know?
THE HOLOCAUST HOAX WAS A PLOT TO MAKE MILLIONS AND THEN STEAL THE HOLY LAND!
WAKE UP!
JEWS are trying to take over the world!
They conceal themselves cleverly . . .
But smart people can tell because JEWS have a special smell!!
MAY THIS NEWS BRING JOY
To those PEACEFUL HEARTS
JOINED IN LOVE
IN OUR LORD JESUS CHRIST!!

Collum skimmed the pamphlet. Its words bore into him, hurting him, and he tried to return them to his father.

"No. Take it. It is yours to keep," said Neil, with a gesture of benevolence. His subscribers (there were about a hundred) had to pay fifteen cents a copy, to cover costs. His son was different. He was his blood and his life. But there would be conditions.

"I will be testing you on this material over the course of the year," he said. "Should you learn all my precepts, you will not be beaten. Should you fail, consider yourself the rebellious son who must be chastened. It is my duty as a father, and my right. I pray you'll understand that love and punishment go hand in hand."

Spilling Heidi's Beans

Although school is out for the summer, Delaney still keeps in touch with her teacher Ms. Ewington.

"I can't help but write to you," one of her emails says. "I just think you are the best teacher I ever had, and really I wanted you to know it. Because how would you know if I didn't tell you?"

That is sweet. Hardly anyone ever tells her she is great anymore.

"I think you're pretty great, too," Jude replies.

This is encouragement enough for Delaney. In her next email, she attaches a new story:

TO HELL WITH MAMA SPICEHANDLER

Mama Spicehandler always has a bag of spices. She carries them in a big stinking sack on her back. She is a hag and a crone, but no one knows that because she knows how to hide it.

Every day she puts on a mask so no one knows what a horrible and ugly bitch she is. But her daughter Deena knows everything.

This is what goes into Mama's foods:

MARIJUANA and MAGIC MUSHROOMS, depending on seasonal availability!!

She gives the food out to everyone, men, women, children, and especially horses! Mama Spicehandler should be given the death penalty, but she thinks she is too sneaky to be caught.

But her daughter Deena knows all about it.

She tells the police. They don't believe her.

She tells the contract killers. They ask for too much money.

She tells her favorite teacher.

The only person she can trust.

Maybe the teacher will do something! Anything!

Upon reading this story, Jude begins to worry about Davey. Surely there is no cannabis in the horse food, much less hallucinogenic fungi—and surely, Davey would not be ingesting that food, either way. Nevertheless, she finds herself calling Heidi. After all, Delaney has begged her teacher to "do something! Anything!" Jude feels mandated, which was something of a thrill in itself.

"I know this sounds wild, but are you using, uh, pot in the Pops, Heidi?"

"Excuse me? Jude, honey, what the heck are you talking about?"

"This is not a conversation for the phone, so I'd better come over," Jude replies, adding cryptically, "this time I might have to clean *your* kitchen, if you know what I mean."

"I really don't," says Heidi.

Driving over in her dusty maroon van, Jude thinks about what she'll say to Heidi. She is not going to tell her how persistently her daughter wants to kill her. That is obvious hyperbole. But Jude feels that Delaney's characterizations bear a grain of valuable truth. Heidi *is* a bit witchy, Davey *is* a little "weird" (but so are all the best people), and there is a good chance that those Ponipops are laced with something stronger than vanilla bean or nutmeg.

Whenever she picks Davey up from the ranch, he seems so loose and floppy. Equine therapy alone could not do that, could it? Work instant miracles? Shake out all the kinks? And sometimes, now that she thinks of it, his eyes do seem a bit red. Heidi's food simply changes your inner temperature; it dilates vessels and opens up pores. Jude herself has indulged in her pal's "tonics," and no amount of slushy ice can conceal that they are zombie-makers. Maybe the aphrodisiacs that she has given to Slam have been baked with absinthe, hence his sudden passing out (and vivid dreams). If Heidi is a dealer in potent herbals, she needs to know that her daughter is now aware of it.

"I honestly don't know what you're talking about," says Heidi, opening the door to her marble foyer. "As you can see, everything is perfectly pristine, as always."

"When I said I'd clean your kitchen, it was a metaphor," says Jude.

"Well, metaphor or not, the idea of your organizing my life— any part of it—is ridiculous. And your tone! You sounded so upset when you called; you sounded crazy. Are you having hubby troubles again?"

Jude ignores these comments. She races passed Heidi to the industrial kitchen, sniffing audibly.

"You may have gotten rid of the evidence for the moment," she says knowingly, "but I heard from a very good source that you doctor everything you make."

"A good source?" Heidi scoffs. "What good source? I've let you into my kitchen countless times! Would I have done that if I had anything to hide?"

"Well, yes!" says Jude, victoriously. "It's called 'hiding in plain sight.' Your daughter does it. You may think you have the perfect child, but—all right, I'll just tell you—Delaney's the one who ratted you out to me!"

Heidi finds this sentence to be so stuffed with input that at first, she can't reply. Then she screeches:

"Hiding? My daughter? 'Ratted me out'?"

"Mmm hmmm," says Jude, with joyous calm. "Sounds like you got the full picture, or should I say, the whole recipe."

"I 'got' nothing!" says Heidi, her voice still strident. "I 'got' that you're as strange as your son! Maybe *you're* the one who put stuff in my food!"

Jude withstands this insult. She replies: "So you're admitting there's 'stuff' in your food?"

"Nothing but the finest and freshest ingredients, grown from organic earth that has been lavished with duck dung, as you well know, and I am *not* going to dignify your accusations with any defense!"

"You just did," says Jude, trying to maintain her suaveness. Heidi's implacable perfection always rattles her. She is starting to wonder if Delaney's claims themselves are not a bit poisoned by adolescent bile.

"I'm sorry," she says, suddenly confused. "I just—Delaney wrote this story where she said you were lacing everything with hash and grass and whatnot—"

"And you believed her? Don't you know my child is a creative young lady? Isn't your class actually called 'creative writing'?"

"Yes it is, but—oh, my God," says Jude. "I'm so embarrassed."

"That's all right," says Heidi, benevolently. "What you need is a bit of my chamomile pudding. It's good for the nerves."

She serves out a super-sized portion in a Pyrex mixing bowl.

"Industrial, but it works."

"Thanks," Jude breathes, her head inside the bowl. "It's just what I need."

After that, Heidi has an alarm system installed in her kitchen. She also has a word with her daughter.

"Never, never, never again are you to go into my *sanctum sanctorum* without express permission."

"What's that supposed to mean?"

"Stay out of my workspace. My kitchen is my temple. You are not to touch my spices, or my roots, or my powders. Nothing."

"Do you think I ever did?"

"Yes, in fact I do think that. For one thing, food has been disappearing for years."

"Well, I do live here! I have to eat!"

"I'm not talking about your meals, sweet one. Every month a quarter pound of demerara sugar goes missing. And I can never fathom where all the kirsch goes. And some of the Ponipops did come out a little darker and chewier than the others, come to think of it."

"Maybe it's Daddy!" screams Delaney, flushing bright red. "He's here more than me! Maybe it's you! You can't prove anything! Just try!"

There is the admission. Heidi sighes.

"I don't have the patience. From now on, this kitchen is locked to you unless I open it. Alarmed."

"Fine!" says Delaney. "Who cares about your stupid little business venture! You're just a dabbler. You never do anything but make things look nice and fancy. You don't fool me. And your food stinks, anyway. Give me a burger any day. Seriously."

"I have just the remedy for your insolence. I'll get it from my root cellar. Don't you dare move, young lady."

Delaney disobediently moves; she goes from standing to sitting. She is not going to stay on her feet for five or more minutes while her mother scrabbles around downstairs.

When Heidi reappears, she holds before her a large horseradish root. These bitter herbs look phallic, thinks Delaney. She stands up from her chair and begins to run away.

"Stay put!" says her mother, grabbing her by the shoulder. "You need to learn that life is not all demerara sugar. You need to develop your palate. There is sweet, and there is sour, and there is salty. And there is bitter. It's an acquired taste, and all us grown-ups know it. *This* is bitter."

She puts the root in her daughter's face.

"Bite off a piece! Go on!"

Nibbling the tip, Delaney obeys.

"Now swallow it. That's just part one," says Heidi, as her daughter's nose and eyes begin to run, "of your learning experience."

More Learning Experiences

While Collum's father was no easy man, Judy's dad was no ant-free picnic either. Aaron Pincus, CPA, was a deep thinker who willingly—even eagerly—gave consideration to every aspect of every idea. If you asked him an ostensibly simple question, such as "What year did Columbus discover America?" you might get more philosophy than you wanted or needed.

Possible reactions to the question:

—What, really, is America? A concept? An ideal? The founding fathers had trouble with that, and oh, did they debate it. And yet at the time, they had slaves, and women did not vote. And don't even mention those unfortunate Indians, who were not from India, by the way.

—And do you mean the North America or the South America?

—Why do you choose the world "discovered"? The land mass wasn't there before? You couldn't see it? It's a question of perspective. When I meet a new person, I "discover" them? What ego! Like a two-year-old, who thinks that when he closes his eyes, the entire world disappears.

—Who was this Columbus? Was that even his real name? I don't know. Colombo? Colon? Cristoforo? Maybe I might suggest the Hebrew "Chaim"? (Aaron Pincus had heard that Columbus may have been a Marrano, or hidden Jew, hiding from the Spanish Inquisition. And what better way to hide than to travel afar to new lands that had no Judeo-Christian complexes?)

—And what is truly meant by "year"? Yes, the world turns around the sun in a year, but who says it all started 1492 years ago? Who says it is currently 1969? Who created this peculiar calendar, and which date did they date it from? (To Aaron Pincus, 1492 was not a real date. It was simply an artificial Roman construct, dating all time until and from the purported birth of Jesus Christ—and this was ironic, he'd add, given that the Romans were the very people who crucified people at the time. Lots of Jews, not just Jesus, that poor Jew—like so many others of his faith, before and since—were nailed to that cross.)

So when Judy needed help with her homework in school, she very rarely asked her father for it. It wasn't worth it. Each word released a testament. Still, there was no hiding from him. Although Mr. Pincus no longer practiced the Orthodox Judaism of his childhood, he brought these studies to bear on all of daily life. Nothing was simple, and without many "aspects." Everything in his world could be, and was, woven into his intense religious and sociocultural cords of understanding.

If Judy wore a violet-colored shirt to school, her father would say, "Beautiful! Purple was one of the colors in the Holy Temple. The dye was based on a plant source, purely natural. A gift from God."

That would really ruin the effect she was intending to have with her wardrobe choices. She thought violet was a hot and exciting color. Not an evocation of the Holy Temple and its divine plant source.

If Judy wore a blue shirt, similarly:

"Blue. Oh, blue was also one of the colors in the Holy Temple. The dye was based on a now extinct mollusk."

There was no need for Jude to associate one thing to another and another. She simply loved blue; it reminded her of the open skies above, unbounded by mazes of history and logic. It reminded her of Collum and her feelings for him, as deep as the deepest blue seas, continuous, billowing, flowing. Her father's mind had so many valences and charges, so many lines and borders!

Purple and blue were no mere colors to Aaron Pincus; they trailed a holy history. They brought him joy and inspiration that exceeded anything she was bringing to the picture. The lines and borders she shunned were written by God himself.

On the other hand, for Judy's father, yellow was the color of the stars the Jews had to wear under the Nazi regime. When she wore brown, her father was also disturbed.

"Brown is the color of excrement—the color of the Brownshirts."

"It's an earth tone," Judy insisted. "The color of the trees, or nature." Earth tones were "in" with her peers—orange, brown, yellow, burnt sienna.

"In this case, we are talking about the most *un*natural people on earth, worse than animals. May their names be erased from memory."

"May their names be erased from memory" was not a phrase reserved only for anti-Semites of the mid-twentieth century. It could include all persecutors of the Jewish people, from the Amalekites (for whom the phrase was coined, and possibly had worked, as no one but Jews now knew about them) to the Ku Klux Klan and beyond.

But how could names be erased from memory, Jude mused, if

her father kept bringing them up? Wasn't it better to just move on and say nothing?

The conversation would travel far past the question of Judy's brown shirt, which actually was a chocolate-colored polo shirt with a baby-blue collar and three horn buttons.

"They thought they were better than everyone," her father concluded (for the time being). "Well, I guess they were wrong."

And God forbid Judy should question the moral superiority of the Jews to the benighted peoples of the earth. From her earliest years, Jude heard her father say things like:

"See the headline? Anti-Semitism in the Soviet Union? What a shame! But it will end in the same way."

Which way? Judy would think, spreading marmalade and margarine on her rye toast. Her father, lost behind the large leaves of the newspaper, did not need coaxing. His monologue proceeded:

"In the end, the Jews will go free, another exodus. But the empire that oppresses them? The USSR? It will soon be destroyed."

At other times, Aaron Pincus might read aloud from his *Prevention* magazine, dedicated to the betterment of human health:

"Let's see, let's see," he'd say. "There it is! The new miracle drug. And who is part of this discovery? Of course: Goldberg and Friedman!"

Or Cohen, Levy, Bernstein, Finck.

As she matured and began thinking for herself, these fixations increasingly bothered Judy. Sometimes she dared to protest:

"*Jew-Jew-Jew!!* You're obsessed, Daddy!"

"I'm obsessed? *I'M* OBSESSED? The world is obsessed! Adolph Hitler—may his memory be blotted out—was obsessed! And why? Because he was jealous! Because we were better, smarter, one hundred percent more chosen, and that's what *he* always wanted to be!"

"You're taking a page from Hitler? You're obsessed because *he* was obsessed?"

"Look at him now. The worst villain in the world. A screaming loco with a little moustache. Crushed to powder, blown away. A failed painter, did you know that's who he really was?"

"No."

"Yes. He wanted to paint like a great artist, and of course in his daily life he happened to meet a Jew, an art dealer, who didn't think this punk was such a genius, and so little Ado got frustrated! He got mad! One particular Jew let him down, and then he got mad at all of the Jews? Isn't that crazy, Judy?"

For a brief moment, Judy thought uncomfortably about Neil Whitsun. Which Jew had let *him* down? Judas? Someone more recent? Was her friendship with Collum making things even worse? Was it, using another of her father's favorite phrases, "good for the Jews"? Would Neil Whitsun end up brandishing a burning torch and whipping their village into a frenzied mob? (And what if she let Collum down? Would he turn against her? Impossible.)

"Yes, the world has a lot of crazies," sighed her father, interrupting her brooding. Judy remembered that they were talking about Hitler, not Neil Whitsun. It was all a matter of proportion. But was her father right to be so vigilant? Did people like Whitsun, who started out as cranks, end up as Nazis? Not if they drank, she reassured herself. Collum's father was a harmless lush, she thought, almost fondly. He'd pass out before he could do a real genocide.

"Too bad he didn't buy his crappy paintings and hang them somewhere."

"Whose crappy paintings?" asked Judy, who was now thinking

of Whitsun's oeuvre, particularly the hanging Jesus with the shiny painted blood drips. Had she responded with enough awe to his work? Would his hatred eventually spread like mushroom spores? Would it carry into the future through his boys, Ryan and Rob, or even Collum?

"That Jewish art dealer. What a shame. A momentary decision, and a whole catastrophe follows. It's too bad it didn't go differently. But this dealer was a man of sophistication and taste, and who was this little Adolph? A *schmo* from *schmo*land! But then the talentless *schmo* begins to think, to brood on it: Who are these people to judge me? Where do they come from? And how do they manage to hold the keys and block the doors? Why do they own the galleries, and the stores, why do they ruin things for—"

"I know, I know, they used to say we ran the world."

"They still say it. They always say it! They come back to that! That's what Hitler said. Because he wanted what? To run the world. To have it his way! Like a spoiled brat, a bully! He had to have a tantrum! So get rid of the Jews, and you win the game?"

"I guess that was the idea . . ."

"Bravo! You run the world! Bravo! You're chosen! You're it!"

"Yes, if you want to murder people—"

"Which was no problem for him and all his helpers. Not even a little problem. But they couldn't win even when they killed off millions, and why, my dear little Judy?"

Long pause.

"Are you asking me?" said Judy. Sitting with her father and talking about psychopathy and genocide made her want to run away to the woods, where people could live pure and free, like Thoreau (a non-Jew), whom she had learned about in school, or like Robin Hood and Maid Marian. Maybe she and Collum could live pure and free one day. She'd read somewhere about communes, where people lived "off the land."

"All right, let's drop it for a moment," said her father, "just know that you have a destiny, and a good fortune ahead of you."

"Sounds more like endless persecution and torture," she muttered. "By a series of crazy loners—you know, people who keep pamphlets and spread crazy lies. And also those who can't stop thinking about the badness of people."

"What did you say?"

"Nothing." How could she have equated her father and Neil Whitsun?

"No. I'm curious. What did you say? I always like to learn from other points of view."

"Well, today we kids—my generation—are beginning to realize that people suffer from oppression all over the world. Since the beginning of time. Not just the Jews. Not just far away. Everywhere, all the time, someone is suffering. So to focus on just one people—I mean, it could seem selfish. Because, what about the other broken people?"

Judy was actually thinking less universally than she spoke. Specifically, she was thinking of her darling boy, Collum.

"So maybe it's time to smoke the peace pipe, Daddy."

"Who's not making peace? Who's not smoking the pipe? Ask me for peace and I'll give it," her father answered. His jaw was tightening. "I would welcome it, in fact."

"Please, Daddy, I didn't mean to make you more upset. I was just trying to explain how I—"

"UPSET?" he shouted. "WHO IS UPSET? ME? I'M PROUD! I'M PRIVILEGED! IT'S AN HONOR!!!"

Aaron Pincus's face looked distorted, swollen and red as a Concord grape. Was this always there, this panic beneath his bourgeois exterior? Judy, of course, did not share it.

"OK, OK, calm down," she said, feeling guilty for having hurt her father. She knew he had lost a large part of his family in the war and was somehow defending their lives. A lost cause. They were dead.

But those days were over. They happened long ago and far away.

"Everything is gonna be fine, Daddy," Judy said patiently. Why could he not see that the old hatreds were vanishing away, and that her generation would end them?

Her father's breath slowly returned to normal. He briskly wiped his face with a folded square handkerchief.

Judy wasn't sure if her father wanted everything to be fine. It seemed that he was at his glorious best in the outraged state: remembering temples built and destroyed, Hitler frustrated in his bunker, Jews rising like the phoenix from the ashes, trees growing from the desert (which were better than just plain trees any day). And yet, they lived in soft and harmless Brewster, New York. It seemed as though the worst thing that could happen here was that leaves collected in your rain gutter, or a bat got in the house.

Or your father got a heart attack. That would be bad, too, and not just for the Jews. Anyone could be toppled, any time.

Judy had overheard her mother nag her father to lay off the salt. She had heard her say that he had high blood pressure, and that "the pills" were not enough. That he was a pressure cooker that could actually pop.

"Should I get you a glass of water, Daddy?"

"Yes, thank you."

She was sorry she had upset him, but not sorry enough to let his words alter the hope she harbored for herself and Collum Whitsun. He was the son of a violent maniac, and maybe she was the daughter of another, more aggrieved one, but their love was stronger than vendettas, however lopsided or ancient.

Escape

Collum brought his father's new pamphlet to school. He had thought about it. Judy had to know what was going on in his home. She knew enough. Let her know it all.

As soon as classes were over, they ran for shelter under the football bleachers at the far end of the high school campus. It was raining heavily, and field sports had been cancelled. While most of the downpour fell with a heavy rattling sound on the metal benches, some dripped through the spaces between them. Collum took off his parka (what Betty, his mum, called an "anorak") and put it over himself and Judy, a little tent to keep them safe and dry.

"Comfy?" he said, wrapping his arm around her.

"Yeah," she answered, leaning her head on his shoulder. If only they could stay like this forever.

"I've got to show you Dad's latest writing," he said, rifling through his bookbag and handing her a wrinkled little pamphlet, mimeographed on cheap paper, the ink faded in spots. Neil Whitsun's "brochure" seemed so pathetic that way; even as Collum tried to straighten it, he felt doubly embarrassed by the feeble presentation of his father's thoughts.

"Give it to me," said Judy. "Let's get it over with."

Judy skimmed the paper, crumpled it, and threw it. It rolled a bit, then lay on the grass and the rain torrents beat it almost flat. Judy thought about the ink running, washed away into the mud. She nuzzled deeper under Collum's anorak.

"Your father's really crazy, huh," she said, loving the feel of his body's heat in the cool, wet air. "But my dad, he's got his own little fixations—"

"Yeah, but he's a talker, right? And your mom's always there, nice and smooth. My father thinks with his ham-sized fists, and his little lady shrinks away. A real mom would block him, you know that? She'd block him."

"If I were your mom, I'd take you away," said Judy.

Collum almost cried, but he contained himself.

"Yeah, where would you take me? She's an Irish lass, no skills. She's broken in. He's all she's got, and that kitchen, the boys. The family, sick as it is."

"I think—I think she even loves him, right?"

"He's got her brainwashed. Of *course* she loves him, which is even more insane than *being* him. She actually thinks love is greater than hate! Well, it's not, Judy, and you can watch that battle play itself out in my house every day."

Judy didn't know what to say. She was silent, sad. If love wasn't stronger than hate, then her father was right. She felt, just then, like kissing Collum. Stopping all this talk and just kissing.

"And I don't know how much more I can take of this. When he watches the news he gets madder and madder—and he takes it all out on me. As though every change in the world were my fault or something."

"It's 'cause we're friends, I guess," said Judy.

"We're more than friends. I love you. I *love* you," said Collum.

"He doesn't know how much. No one does. He'd go nuts if he knew. And he's all worked up about the war, and the draft—he talks about moving us all out, out of the country, even—"

"My darling, my darling," said Jude, feeling very grown up when she used such a word. "I see we are both in the same boat."

"Same boat?" said Collum, trying to understand. "My father will beat the shit out of me if he ever catches us together. My oldest brother's 1-A, and Dad will never allow him to spill his blood fighting for this Satan-ridden country. He's planning to pick us all up and ship us to Australia."

"Australia?"

"Yeah, he has some family there. What exact danger are *you* in?"

"Collum—understand this. Your father does not want you with me, the Jew. My father distrusts you, the Christian."

"I'm no Christian. I don't believe in anything," said Collum.

In the next moment, he shuddered as lightning began to flash, followed by the boom of a thunderclap.

"I believe in God," Judy acknowledged, as the sound faded. "I do, but in a universal way—not in all this kind of 'I hate you/ you hate me' stuff. That can't be right. I mean, it's like Montagues and Capulets. We must defy our fathers and forge a brand new path."

Their class was reading *Romeo and Juliet*. Judy had been impressed by how well Shakespeare understood her and Collum's world. What was in a name? In a clan? In a tribal grudge? When would it end?

"Let's run away. Soon, Collum, before everything closes down on us."

Collum insulted Judy by laughing in her face.

"Think I never thought of *that*? Even before you came into the picture? But you have to know what you're doing, Judy! Get real!"

Judy took his face in her hands and held it.

"I have money, Collum. Bat mitzvah money, which I never spent."

Both of them thought glancingly of how that sentence bore out some old Whitsunian fixations, but neither dignified such thoughts with any mention.

"How much?" was all Collum said.

"*A lot.* Enough to get away. I have a jewelry box, too. Three drawers, and they're almost full. Real pearls. A couple of opal rings. A gold bangle bracelet. And Collum, look at this."

She held out her golden Star of David, which hung on a fine chain around her neck.

"Yeah, I know, I know."

"No, listen. I told you. It's eighteen-carat gold, even the chain. That's really rare. It's special. It's worth a lot. My mother told me that when she bought it for me. Also eighteen is a lucky number in Hebrew. It stands for 'life.' Our life together."

Collum lost track of the plot when Judy described the necklace she was wearing. His eyes followed it down into her soft V-neck sweater. He grabbed at Judy, and with both hands took her breasts. He felt them, nuzzled his head between them.

Her body froze still; she was shocked.

"Stop it," she said, recovering. She'd felt woozy in an instant.

"When we get away, I'll give you everything. But stop it now. We really have to think!"

Judy wasn't sure what she had felt, but it had been frightening, and she needed time to process it.

"You'll really give me everything?"

"You mean my bat mitzvah money?"

"No, your—your body—you know . . ." he stumbled.

"What do you think? This is a game? I love you and I will do anything you want. But not now!"

"Whatever *I* want? Don't you want me, too?"

"Desperately," she said, not knowing fully what she meant. She did love him desperately, but her body was another matter. Parts of her still felt private and taboo. If he touched her any more she might scream out loud. That kind of touch felt outrageous, unthinkable.

Collum was far more experienced. Despite his youth, he knew all that a boy could know about sex. His brothers, with whom he shared a room, had secretly brought girls home for years, and the way they talked about these girls ("cunts," "twats") had made it easy for Collum to grow up. One of those girls had seduced him, only months before he had met Judy. She had done it on a dare from Ryan, the oldest.

In the middle of the night, while Collum was sleeping, this girl had woken him, grabbed his penis, and put it into her mouth as it hardened. He had never felt such pleasure. Then she had ridden him so hard and fast that he came in seconds.

"Now you're broken in," she said, laughing.

Now, when he masturbated, he thought of this woman, her mouth, the aggressive way she'd mounted him. He couldn't help it. He read his brother's magazines, studied the way women's bodies were made, and how to please them as they pleased you.

He had so much to teach his Judy.

"Don't you even want me?" he repeated, again reaching for her breasts.

"Of course I do," she said, her body rigid.

"You do what? You want to fuck me?" he said, audaciously.

"Yes. I will do that."

"Then say the words out loud."

"I will—I will—fuck you. OK?"

"If we run away, we'll do it every day, I promise you that. OK?"

"OK," she said, annoyed.

"Wanna start now? It's really fun!"

"*No!*" She was shouting because Collum was pulling her down to the ground with him.

"Don't you like this?" he was saying, touching her under her skirt.

"Could you please stop it?"

"No, I couldn't."

Silence for a few minutes. Worlds changed over. And Judy was a new person, one she didn't even recognize. Collum seemed new and different, too.

"I even have this cousin at NYU who doesn't really use his dorm. Maybe we can stay there at the beginning, I mean, when we run away . . ."

She was babbling, but her ideas were ignored and even her words distorted by Collum's mouth on hers and his fingers racing below. He had pinned her and found a promising spot to linger. Judy's eyes were beginning to close, and although she felt a tiny bit nauseated, she did not, or could not, move.

"Be quiet, now," Collum said.

"OK," she answered very softly.

Now he was the one who was talking.

"My brothers know some guys in the Bronx, I think," he murmured, still kissing her between words, still jamming his tongue in her mouth and stroking her down below. Her body was limp, as though he had murdered her. He put a leg between her own and pushed her apart, surprised by her lack of resistance.

Collum would have entered her, and she would have let him,

had the sky not cleared, and a group of high school players not happened by, whooping as they jogged in unison. Even so, he felt her shudder just as the coach blew his whistle, and was glad.

He had changed her forever, and from now on she was his.

A Heart Attack on a Plate

Janet Pincus made eggs and bacon for her husband every morning. She had convinced Aaron that most Jews, at least where *she* came from, did not share his obsessions. She came from what is called an assimilated background, where Jews shopped primarily on their Sabbath, and certainly did not "keep kosher." Susceptible to Janet's beauty when he met her, Aaron, like most doting lovers, abandoned a good portion of his old-fashioned principles. After all, what did they do but separate people? As Janet had pointed out, did he really want to be one of those sad individuals who eat tuna off paper plates while the rest of the world ate prime rib off porcelain?

Early in their dating life, Janet had begun by taking Aaron to a Chinese restaurant. "What could be more Jewish?" she had said, tenderly.

It was true; Chinese restaurants were raucous and clattery in a Jewish way, and what was a wonton but a *krepel*, the little meat dumpling one ate on Rosh Hashanah? The Chinese were so nice about staying open on Christmas and Easter. Jews would always have a table set for them amongst these welcoming hordes with their sizzling woks. They could even feel big and American here, if nowhere else.

Still, when Janet asked, "What could be more Jewish?" the obvious answers (wonton/krepel, Christmas welcome, etc.) did not come readily to Aaron's mind. Aaron had another upbringing, one with specific intellectual content, both historical and religious.

So if Aaron had answered Janet, he would have said, "The Torah, the Mishnah, the Talmud, the Holy Temple, the breastplate of the High Priest—all these are more Jewish than the Chinese restaurant!"

But love silenced him.

"Mmm mmmm," he said, sipping the tea that came as a courtesy, even before the food was served. It tasted different than his mother's Tetley, which, coming from Russia, she had always served in a glass, with a teaspoon of thick strawberry preserves plopped in for sweetness. To be honest, the tea was a little bitter, the small silver pot it came in institutional, and the cup without a handle either stupid or sadistic.

"What should we get?" Janet wondered, delightedly pondering the red and gold menu with its snappy cord and tassel.

"You choose, darling, you choose, and I will drink my tea and eat one of these interesting hard noodles here."

"Dip them into the duck sauce."

"From a duck, really?"

"It's like really sweet marmalade or apricot jam. Try it."

The waiter came over as Aaron tried to enjoy his Chinese noodles with duck sauce.

"We'll share," Janet announced. Aaron blushed. They had not even gone all the way (but would after the engagement), and here she was willing to share her food with him.

Janet ordered quickly, competently, dazzling Aaron, who had

rarely gone out to restaurants. The waiter jotted just as quickly, then spun away.

"In the meantime, I'll show you how to use the chopsticks," said Janet. This involved Janet taking Aaron's hands and helping him pinch up a noodle. After several tries, he could do it himself. He beamed.

Then a covered dish came, along with a large, silver tureen of rice.

Janet served Aaron a heaping portion of fluffy white rice. Then she uncovered the main course.

"NO! NO!" Aaron screamed, trying, as he did so, to throttle his own volume. Were shocks and disasters to assail him wherever he went? The sound came out strangled.

"What is it, Aaron, darling?"

"IT IS A VILLAGE!!" he said, pointing, horrified, to the hundreds of tiny shrimp that lay dead before him.

"IT IS A POGROM!!"

Since then, Aaron had come a long way. He still could not eat villages of tiny shrimp, nor could he abide the lobster with its awful eyestalks and antennae, but he would eat bacon. Geometric, salty, detached from its source, it reminded him of hard salami, the kind his father had hung from a string in the kitchen, and from which he would cut circles with his pocketknife.

Aaron also no longer refrained from mixing milk and meat, so he ate cheeseburgers. In fact, one of his favorite new jokes was:

"What's the most unkosher thing you could eat?"

"Pig's blood?" said Janet, for Aaron had told her that blood was unkosher, that it was considered the "soul" of an animal.

"No! A bacon cheeseburger on bread made with lard! On the first night of Passover! At the *Seder*!"

"Oh, when you're not supposed to eat bread?"

"Yes!" said Aaron, although his wife often did; you could not live on matzoh crackers for days if you wanted to avoid going crazy. Constipation was the least of it. Her flexible family had served both matzoh and fluffy dinner rolls at the Seder table.

"Oh, that's funny, on Passover!" said Janet appreciatively, when they were still dating. "Leavened!" she added, using the pertinent term.

But almost twenty years later, when Aaron was still telling this joke, Janet thought she would rather drink a tankard of boar's blood than hear it again. Really, it was childish—as though forbidden foods were a kind of adolescent pornography.

But bacon he liked, even though it was not really good for him. With his high blood pressure and cholesterol, bacon was truly a sinful dish for Aaron Pincus, for it is a sin to commit suicide. And the little twinge of guilt he felt every time he ate it didn't help his heart, either.

So from all this conflict, what else? Poetry.

Like many of those who toiled in the worlds of law and accountancy, science, engineering, or the actuarial field, Judy's father had aspects that often went unexpressed. Passionate aspects.

Janet did not really want to hear his innermost thoughts. They had been married so long that new information would have seemed outlandish. And Judy tended these days to roll her eyes when her parents took the foreground of her picture. So one day, Aaron bought himself a cardboard, spiral-bound notebook, college-ruled. Just for himself. Maybe, in time, others might have a look.

In college, he had actually had to major in accounting. His parents were immigrants and had begged him to be practical.

Now, he could attend the college of his own inclination. Aaron Pincus opened up the notebook to the first page and stared at the vast, blank expanse.

"A new land," he thought. "And I will be the explorer and the reporter. So, what do I see before me?"

After a few minutes, he wrote his first poem:

Born "a Jew"
Sounds like a sneeze
God bless you's
The answer, please.

It wasn't Shakespeare, but it was something. Thought and rhyme had come together, created where nothing had existed before. Aaron closed the book, then held it to his heart. Every man needs such a notebook. Though made of dead trees, such pages could someday outlive him.

Beyond Bitter Herbs

Heidi had promised her daughter more learning experiences. After being forced to eat the tip of a horseradish root, Delaney had felt only dread about what her next lesson might be.

A few days later, her mother wakes her before sunrise. She stands before her daughter's bed in a crisp yellow ensemble: sleeveless button-down blouse (striped alternatingly with goldenrod and pale cream), butter-colored bermudas, and bone-beige kitten heels accented with a yellow-white polka-dotted bow.

"Get up and get dressed," she says. "Today you're going to help me pack boxes and bags."

"OK, all right," says Delaney, still confused with sleep. She had been dreaming that her mother was a big whore, a madame in fact—one of those ladies who boss around all the other prostitutes, but was now too old for anybody to touch anymore.

In the dream, she, Delaney, had been one of those poor prostitutes, and her mother, the madame, had forced her to give a horrible old man a blow job. His thing had been all gray and twisted like a horseradish, and it tasted like poison would taste.

Delaney's mother had woken her before she could take revenge on all her persecutors. She would have bitten the man's thing off, and he would probably have died of blood loss. Then she would have run to the police and told them about the madame's illegal whorehouse, which employed underage children like herself, waking them too early . . .

"Can you hear me?"

"What?"

"I'm putting you to use."

Delaney, still half dreaming, feels the sting in this phrase. Another act of injustice. What else is new. Where do I bite.

"You'll be spending the rest of your summer doing routes. Lots of people order all their meals from me, especially in summer, when it's too hot to cook. And then there are the houseguests and their little requirements. Each week has special events.

"This week, there are two luncheons, as well as regular horse-snack delivery to the riding place nearby. We'll need to double up on Ponipops, since the staff eat them like candy. And don't you dare tamper with or taste a single one of them. Understood?"

"Mmmmph," says Delaney, turning her face away from the voice.

"Get dressed and come downstairs. No, on second thought, march down to the kitchen," says Heidi, imagining Delaney lolly-gagging in front of the mirror, wasting time staring at herself balefully without makeup, then hopefully as she started applying her lip gloss and eyeliner, and dabbing her zits with cover-up. Then she would have to decide which top made her boobs look good, and which shorts were short enough but not too short. And then there would be the shoe traumas—sneakers or sandals? And which sneakers—the hipster ones or the exercise-your-thighs ones?

As soon as her mother leaves, Delaney gets up and runs downstairs.

"I'm here in the kitchen, Mom!" she shouts, much quicker than expected. Heidi is almost impressed with her.

"Good. Come into the pantry."

This is an extra room that Heidi had made out of part of the four-car garage. Inside are two industrial refrigerators and an array of bags and boxes in various sizes.

"Hand over the bags which are clearly labeled."

"Can I just brush my teeth?"

"You're on a schedule now. We're packing today's delivery, and then you get fifteen minutes to wash up and get dressed. Work is good for people like you, with too much time on their hands and a fertile imagination."

"Ms. Ewington happens to like my imagination!"

"Well," says her mother, only slightly rattled, "that's fine for her. She's got the mind of a butterfly. Flit here, flit there, nothing solid anywhere. If all the world spent their time making up stories, nothing would get done, would it?"

"Well the *stories* would get done," Delaney can't help retorting.

Her mother stares at her coolly, then continues her instructions.

"You will take my car. Let me give you the address list and the suggested routes."

"Mom, it's only, like, six o'clock!"

"By the time you're ready, it'll be almost seven. You're already late. It takes half an hour to pack boxes, bags, and coolers. And then you'll wash up and get dressed. Do it quickly. If you don't get lost too often, you should be done by three-ish. And make sure to pick up the empty ware; people tend to swipe the coolers especially. Even the cheap old Styrofoam ones.

"When you're finished, you can take the rest of the day off."

Heidi suddenly feels a twinge of remorse for her only child, whose eyes are filling with tears even as she begins to kneel and put smaller bags into the larger bags and boxes. It is hard to figure it all out, and Delaney's bangs are in her face.

"Here, have a sip of my Morning Magic smoothie," says her mother. "I make it for my top executives—Mr. Ewington, your beloved teacher's husband, loves it before business trips. He says it turns him into a total road warrior."

"Is that a good thing?" To Delaney, such an appellation sounds like the exact kind of person she'd want to avoid.

"Of course it is! Want some?"

"Sure," says Delaney, with a touching subservience. Why have I not punished this child before? thinks Heidi. I had all this power to mold and to flavor, and I never used it!

Heidi selects ingredients from the coffee and coca plants, and pulverizes them with a pestle. To this she adds feral cow's milk (a legal rarity, obtainable only from India) and a new sweetener she has had a lab engineer, more viscous than corn syrup but less sweet than glucalose, the previous cloying sugar-free invention. She blends the ingredients with glacial ice (a fancy name for frozen Swiss water), topping it off with a sprinkle of diet powder, released from its gelcap. There is no reason for her daughter to look like a large filing cabinet.

"Drink this," she says, pouring the foamy liquid into a tall glass.

"Thanks, Mom," says Delaney, submissively lifting the glass to her mouth and downing it all. If she felt like a road warrior after drinking her Morning Magic, she would not let on. At least not to her mother, to whom a sincere personal compliment would have given more pleasure than any number of pulverized plants.

Despite her mother's shake, when Delaney finally arrives at Angel-Fire Farms, she is exhausted. It is almost four; she had been working steadily for nearly ten hours. After hauling three huge sacks of Ponipops up to the main office building, she is finally free for the day.

The air is fresher, and freedom more sweet, after working so hard. Delaney ambles around the farm. She pops her head into the barns and reads the horses' names (might be usable in her fiction, she comfortably muses). Sitting amongst the parents, she watches the younger children in the riding rings. Some seem completely normal. Some are limp-limbed and have to ride tethered to their ponies. Some seem too stiff, hands clenched so tightly that reins are held between their wrists. Some smile joyfully; others have expressionless faces. Delaney tries to link the parents to their respective children. Who is cheering for that joyless child—is it that woman with the perfectly straight black hair?

"Good for you, Evie!" the woman is saying out loud but softly, as though to herself. Her right hand punches the air without conviction. What would it be like, thinks Delaney, to have a child who does not respond to you, for whom your cheers and rallies are almost meaningless?

The class is almost over when Delaney sits to watch. After only a few minutes, the children are helped off their horses, and the parents wait for the teachers to escort them out.

Many of them cannot walk, she sees. The expressionless one does not smile when her mother scoops her up in her arms. She allows her mother to cover her with kisses, but does not kiss back. One of her little fists takes up a bunch of her mother's hair and holds it to her own cheek, and her blue eyes brighten. That is all.

Other children come out shrieking with delight.

"Momma, did you see? I let go of the reins and I balanced!"

As the staff lead the horses out, some of the children turn to say goodbye to them.

"See you tomorrow, Tommy!" says a boy in leg braces.

"I love you *so* much, Butternut," says a girl, slightly older. "Can I take off his saddle today?"

"If they say OK," says her mother, "and if you're not too tired."

When the girl takes her helmet off, Delaney sees that the back of her head has been shaved and has stitches.

It is a lot to take in. That girl probably had cancer, and had had an operation to take it out. Some of the children have mental disabilities, she knows, and others have physical problems she has never thought about before. Yet their parents are there for them, grateful to find a place they can get help. Everyone needs help, even if their problems don't show. For instance she, Delaney, has leaned on Ms. Ewington, but that might have to end, because Ms. Ewington has clearly told on her to her mother.

Isn't that kind of unethical? But who can she lean on if not her favorite teacher? And isn't that her favorite teacher's son right there, lying in the grass with somebody?

Delaney had wandered over to the paddocks where the horses are pastured at day's end. In the corner of the field, she is sure she sees someone familiar. It is the shirt she recognizes—a shirt David Ewington had worn almost every week during the school year, rugby-style, with red and white stripes, and a big white collar. These are not the colors of their school team (not that he would ever have been on it), and Delaney had wondered why David wore it so often. One day, she'd stood close to David on the lunch line, and noticed the unfamiliar school insignia.

"Why are you always wearing that?" she had asked, noticing him wince as the server put a ladle of peas too close to his mashed potatoes.

"Ah—please, keep them separate," David had said. She noticed how deep his voice was for someone his age, and how he already had the dark down of an incipient beard and moustache.

"I know," she'd said, "I hate it when the slop mixes together."

"Me, too," he'd said, smiling, then not smiling, looking at her, then not looking.

"So your shirt—?"

"What? This? Oh, it's from my brother's school," said David. "Babbington Academy, it's a boarding school in Massachusetts, not one of the really famous ones."

He had rarely said so much at once, but then no girl had ever asked about his clothes, and with so solicitous a face.

"You didn't want to go?" she asked, sympathetically.

"No, I actually did want to. I got in before my brother did, and in fact I went there for a little bit. But it wasn't right for me," he replied, arranging his cutlery just so and walking over to his usual table.

Afterward, when her clique had left, Delaney had watched David sit alone. She thought of going over and sitting with him as he ate his peas, tine by tine. But she had already been so forward, and he hadn't seemed to be that interested in her. She knew she wasn't pretty. Her mother was slim and starched, but Delaney knew that she'd come from a donor egg, and she knew she was a mess, with thick unruly hair, a square jaw, and wide hips that were not in fashion. The arty kids were slim and pale, and next to them she looked like a milkmaid, especially in the clothes that her mother made her wear, pastel blouses and dorky cotton bermuda shorts that zippered on the side.

Now she notices a familiar boy lying in the pasture, dressed in black jeans and the rugby shirt she'd seen so many times before. He is lying in the grass with a man who wears chaps and cowboy boots. That is all she can see until she quietly strolls closer.

The two of them are nibbling on Ponipops and talking about women. The older man seems to be saying something to the effect that females are bad, sly, evil. That you can't trust them. Well, she can agree with that—at least when it comes to her mother, that horseradish whoremonger.

But then she hears the man (who has a weird voice, alternating between Austin and Australia) go on to say:

"Ewington, eh?"

It *is* David Ewington! What is he doing here? Is this his summer job? She had no idea that he knew anything about horses. People who walked with their heads down and their hands jammed in their pockets were rarely sporty. The sporty guys walked tall and proud, legs apart and arms swinging. Their heads were big and prominent, held high so they could look down on their vast kingdom of fawning girls.

Delaney listens some more and draws herself closer. It is a good thing she wore her lightest sneakers (the laceless hipster ones she had managed to get past her mother). They do, in fact, allow one to be sneaky, especially in approaches on grass. Anyway, these two seem lost in their conversation, relaxed as two pond frogs.

She hears the guy with the cowboy boots say something about David's mother. Nosy! What business is she of his? Sometimes staff can get a little chummy at these places (Delaney remembered a tennis instructor at one of her camps, the one who had to stand behind you to demonstrate strokes, and feel your boobs). Yet David is answering him calmly, as though they are peers. Well, maybe they are, if they are working together, she reminds herself.

Delaney watches the cowboy sit up a bit, then rest back on his arms, looking up at the sky. She notices his weirdly uneven moustache that seems to have wax on the end. She hears him say something about "punishment," his voice getting louder on that word. This is getting good. Maybe this guy and *her* mother could get together, if they both like punishment so much!

All of a sudden, Delaney sees David Ewington stand up

abruptly and dart away, leaving the cowboy behind. It is as though they'd argued.

What has she missed?

Delaney stands where she is for a moment, then strolls away in what she hopes is a casual way. The cowboy never sees her as he follows David to the gates of the ranch.

The next day, Delaney awakens quickly. Early as it is, she is eager to do her rounds and see David again, maybe even talk to him this time. She alters her route so she'll arrive at the ranch mid-morning. There, she plans to repeat her pattern of the day before—first the stables, then the riding rings. Then she will go to the fields.

In the second ring, she sees him on a horse.

He is riding a tall roan mare with a beige mane and tail. Today, he is not wearing his red-and-white rugby shirt, but a too-small black T-shirt that looks good with his jeans, Delaney thinks. He sits tall on the horse, head leaning on her mane, as though he has found the perfect pillow. Delaney realizes that he is riding bareback. His legs hang free, but she can sense a light tension in his knees and thighs.

Davey feels alive on the horse, aloft and balanced high. His lips are moving, and if Delaney were closer, she could have heard him say, to his mount:

"Yes. You know me and I know you."

"Hi!" says Delaney.

The sound of the girl's voice breaks Davey's reverie, and he almost falls off his mount.

"Oh, hi," he answers, awkwardly but successfully regaining his balance. When he is sure he is safe, Davey waves one arm, like a rodeo star, for her benefit, then quickly puts it back at his side to maintain the necessary ballast.

"Would you please stay outside during the lesson?" asks Gretchen. "Or at least on the benches with the other families?"

"But I know—I know the instructor. David Ewington, right there? Anyway, his kid's not here yet, right? His student?"

"Davey, do you know this person?" Gretchen says.

Davey looks down at Delaney from the top of his horse. Gretchen sees that he is about to speak, and is silent. This will be good for him, chatting with someone from the top of a mount, balanced and strong.

"This is Delaney, a friend of mine from school," he says to Gretchen.

"Delaney?" Davey continues, "I am 'the kid,' and this is my lesson. OK? But what are *you* doing here?"

Davey is mortified but proud at the same time. Delaney seems to want to know things about him that he's always kept private. She is interested, for some reason, in figuring him out. He had noticed her attentions at school, of course—no one else spoke to him.

But has she actually followed him here?

"I'm—I'm—"

Davey feels sorry that she is now flushed and stuttering. Better than anyone, he knows how that feels.

"No," he says quickly, "it's totally *fine* that you're here, this is a great place. Are you looking for work here or something?"

"I already have work—my mom—I'm, I'm kinda just delivering my mom's foods and treats and stuff all over town, and this is just one of the stops, you know, that I have to make."

"Your *mom's* the one who makes the food we eat here?"

"And the Ponipops for the horses, yeah."

"Wow. Impressive." He is too polite to say that yesterday they had tasted very different, much drier.

All this time the horse, Maple, has not moved, but she is

growing restive, flapping her lips and tapping one hoof on the soft ground of the riding ring. Her tail flicks.

"OK," says Gretchen, "you two can catch up later. We have a lot of work to do, Davey."

"Sorry, sorry," he says, giving Maple a barely perceptible nudge to her flank. Immediately, she begins walking away, head high and eyes soft, happy to be summoned back to service.

"I'll wait outside for you, if that's all right," says Delaney.

"Uh, sure. Fine," says Davey, turning around to watch her as she walks away. He puts one hand on the horse's hindquarters as he turns, and keeps his balance beautifully.

A Visit from a Holy Man

One Friday afternoon, just after lunchtime, someone knocks on Jude's door. She's been polishing off some of Heidi's five-bean salad, prepared semi-raw and served tepid, and if no one had appeared, she might have found herself productively in the bathroom, as she often did not long after eating one of Heidi's fiber-rich repasts. She was always trying to lose weight, and Heidi always said that food with maximal roughage was the absolute key.

Such was life for the modern human being—semi-raw, tepid, avoirdupois, bowels. And that was for the lucky ones, with enough time and money to become solipsistic, internal and as self-protective as a threatened hedgehog (quills out, rolled into a ball). For them, life could be as slow as peristalsis, and not even as interesting.

The hand at the door is harsh. Perhaps it was even a banging fist, the kind covered by a studded leather glove.

Jude is not expecting anyone, much less anyone so avid, and finds her heart racing.

"Wh— who is it?" she squeaks, picking a fraction of pinto-bean-shell out of her incisor.

"It is Rebbe Malach," comes the voice behind the door. "Malach Gipstein, perhaps you have heard of me."

"No, I haven't heard of you," says Jude, racking her mind to think about all the charities she gave to, and which probably spread her name far and wide, all the way to the pious itinerant at her door.

"Rebbe Gipstein!" the man says, this time more loudly. "Learned fellow Jew from the town of Croton!"

It seems to Jude as though the man's accent and word choice are becoming, with each utterance, more and more Yiddish-sounding. Sometimes, on trips to the city, she'd been stopped by Chasidim asking her, "Are you Jewish? Are you Jewish?" They usually didn't want anything more than to give you a blessing, or a box of white Sabbath candles. But to find her out here? Did he know the boys' bar mitzvah tutor? Had he found a mailing list from the Temple they almost never went to?

"You heard from Croton?"

"Yes, I heard from it," she answers crossly, mimicking his immigrant locution.

"It's not so far," the rebbe continues. "You been there once or twice, to Croton which is on the Hudson?"

"No, not really."

"Oh, you should go, there is such a shul there, beautiful like the sunshine, such glass in colors like the rainbow! Red, blue, even green like a, like a—"

"Like a lawn, I know what green is like!"

"Not always," says the rebbe, stroking his black cotton-candy beard.

"*What?*" After a moment, her own voice pierces the silence, as though she wanted this bizarre conversation to continue.

"It's not always green, a lawn. Sometimes the rain doesn't fall, what can you do, and what you get is a brown, not a—"

"What do you want?" Jude interrupts. "I'm a very busy woman." She was. If the man had not come, she would now be watching a talk show about putting passion back into your life.

"What do you want from me?" she repeats, conscious that this question, itself, sounded a bit Jewish.

"Wat I want from you," answers the voice, with a touch of sadness, and no question mark. Just a declaration.

"Oy, vat I vant," he repeats, a poignant echo.

Jude is curious. She wants to open the door, but she remembers the heavy fist-knocking, and feels there might be some danger lurking in the arm that knocks, and the heart that wants. And yet, that voice is so plaintive. It reminds her of her own father, long gone. Her father would have smiled to see a rebbe at her threshold. Maybe it's an omen.

She opens the door.

It's a man, neither young nor old, neither fat nor slim. He's dressed in a long, black coat of a shiny-from-use material; matching trousers, pleated; a crisp white shirt (but no tie); white socks peeping out of the trouser bottoms; and black lace-up shoes that shine like patent leather. On his head the man sports a fedora of the kind that would be worn in a detective movie set in the 1940s and '50s, the kind used to obscure the face.

He does look like the pious men Jude sometimes sees in New York City, the ones who want to make a "mitzvah" with her. There were lots of these men, too, in pre-war photographs. These obvious Jews—dressed to be different—were targets. A holy people, a loyal people, her father once said, a people whose culture had nearly been destroyed in Europe.

Jude feels both repelled by and drawn to the man's banana-curled side locks and thick, scholarly glasses. There was variation in the beards of Chasidim, some were long and wild, others trimmed—and Rebbe Malach's beard was long and scraggly, the beard of a madman. You could find a chicken and a chick and the nest in that matted black beard. There was something, too, of the wizard about him.

For a moment, Jude even feels shamed by her own ignorance. How much he must have read, since boyhood, to wander the world so humbly, knocking on doors in the hope of doing good. How long must it have taken to grow those curly side locks and that sagacious beard.

Her own life is so bare of meaning. Yes, the boys had had bar mitzvahs, but these were social occasions. Jude defines herself as a "cultural Jew"—on occasion, she likes whitefish and smoked salmon, poppy seed bagels and blintzes. They remind her of her childhood. With her chicken soup, of course she sometimes takes also a matzoh ball. But these days, who didn't? Besides, on Heidi's regime, there were few of these heavy foods. Her culinary faith had long been diluted: gefilte fish became "quenelles," and seltzer, Pellegrino. Even the bar mitzvah food had been haute suburban.

The man is talking. To her. "So you open at last the door for a Yid." He says it like this: "*Yeed*."

"So I do," she challenges. She liked saying "so." So very Jewish.

"OK, so then I'll come in and make myself comfortable. And then I'll explain for you the purpose of my visit."

"So do you really have to come in? To the inside of my house?"

"Oh, yeh! That is what I really have to do!"

Jude stands at her doorway, still blocking it. Sentimental as the figure is, she doesn't want to be dragged into a long talk about charity.

"Look," she says. "In the end, are you going to just solicit some money, I mean, gelt, from me? Because my grandmother was a lifelong member of Hadassah, and I think that should count for something in this world."

"Meaning?"

"Meaning we gave already. In the Hadassah. I think she even had a gold pin that said 'Lifetime Member.'"

"You should never say 'I gave already,' because to live is to give and give. But Hadassah? Feh! I'm not from no Hadassah," says the man, leading the way past her, into the interior of the house. Jude follows, her smaller stride racing after his.

"And from you anyway I don't want any gelt," he continues, once he's located the large and tasteless black leather sofa that Jude's husband and boys love so much. The man then sits down with an affected "oof!," as though he has traveled far, on foot. A pilgrim, she thinks, on the road to the Holy Land.

But why is *my* house the Holy Land? Despite herself, Jude feels a tiny bit turned on. He's not so bad looking, if you can get past the weirdness. She remembers some lore about devout Jewish men not allowing themselves to be alone with women. This must mean that just being in her house is a taboo for the man. Another frisson runs through her.

"'Lifetime member,'" he chuckles, looking for the briefest second into her eyes. "Your beloved *bubbe*, may she rest in peace. And me, too. That's what I am. A 'Lifetime Member,' God willing, of the community of God. But your grandma, the Hadassah member—she had some manners? Or no?"

"What do you mean?"

"I wouldn't say no to a glass of tea."

"A glass—?"

"Yeh, I prefer glass, but a cup is good, a mug, you call it. Fine, all right, I'll drink from a mug!"

"And what kind of tea—I have cherry-mint, neroli infusion with rosemary, Lady Cordelia's Four-O'Clock Service—"

"Orange pekoe you don't have?"

"Oh, regular tea?"

"I like the Lipton, if you would be so kind. Orange pekoe."

"I'm sure I can find some regular tea, but it'll be in bags." Her father had enjoyed a nice cup of Lipton every Friday night, with lemon.

"What else should it be if not in bags? And with maybe a little sugar."

"White? Brown? Agave?"

"Nu, I should invent for you a wheel?" he says. "Sugar, thanks God, was already discovered, they make it very nice, a powder that dissolves like magic into your drink and makes it a little bit sweeter. That is what I want. A teaspoon, not more, regular sugar and some Lipton tea in a bag, this bag not dipped too long, and then I'll be—you know where I'll be? Already in heaven."

Jude walks into the kitchen, a little impressed. What a simple man he is, in the nicest sense of the word! What was the use of all this modern complexity? The man followed rules, dressed in a black-and-white uniform, and drank normal tea with plain old sugar. She remembered her parents doing the same, sometime before the prosperous 1980s, when cappuccino had come into popular parlance. Stealthily, it had ruined the essence of the ordinary world.

Lost Languages

A zoy gut!" says Rebbe Gipstein, when he finishes his tea.
"Excuse me?"

"So good, this drink! And now you want to know why I am here?"

"Kind of been curious. I mean, this kind of thing doesn't happen every day." Indeed, at this stage of her life, very little happened any day, and even less that was both new and pleasant.

On the one hand, of course Jude would love to know why a Chasidic pilgrim has come to her door and is now sitting on her husband and sons' favorite black leather couch. As though he owned it. On the other, she really doesn't care. She likes this man. He's like a copy of her father, without the angst. He could really be handsome, she thinks again (and again with the shock of eros), if he took off those glasses and shaved his beard.

"So maybe you'd like to know why a Yid is brought to the door of another Yid, yes?"

"Well, as I said, these things don't often happen to me."

"But my dear, they absolutely should!" he says, doffing his fedora with an odd flourish. Underneath, he wears a large woven skullcap, so his head is still covered, as in that old story Jude had read to her sons, "The Five Hundred Hats of Bartholomew Cubbins."

"Are we not all brothers and sisters? Do our hearts not belong to each other in love and loyalty? Is that not the true secret of our very survival?"

This was really the stuff of Aaron Pincus, her father. For the first time in a long time, Jude thinks of how he had been brought up, in the traditional way—to believe in a kinship of Israelites, a people united by history, no matter how far apart history had flung them. And now this holy man has somehow found her. Aaron Pincus has been dead for years, and yet his soul is calling to his daughter through this man.

"How did—how did you even know a Jewish person lived in here?" she asks the Chasid.

"How did I know?" Rebbe Gipstein closes his eyes and inhales luxuriously. His face is blissful, as though he breathed in the sweet savors of the Temple, frankincense and myrrh.

"You don't have a kosher mezuzah, this is true," says the rebbe, referring to the rectangular case that observant Jews put on their doorposts. "And this is very bad, very very unfortunate. You could even say 'a shande'" he adds, using the term for a horrible, blatant shame.

"I'm so sorry," says Jude, humbled to realize that in all her married life, she's never bothered to deal with her spiritual side. Jude had long felt certain that rituals separated people at best and drove them to battle at worst. She'd felt the pain of that as a Jewish girl in love with a Catholic boy.

"A mezuzah is an expression of faith unchanging, of loyalty unswerving. Not having a mezuzah can ruin an entire family," Gipstein continues. "It can mean that your children—you have children?"

"Two boys," says Jude timorously.

"Two? And they are both absolutely all right?"

"Yes, well, no—one of my boys has become more and more shy and withdrawn. To the point that—"

"One of the boys needs mental remediation? Say no more! Put up the mezuzah, and don't waste time! But make sure it is a kosher one, with the prayers intact."

Inside, he explains, there has to be a little parchment, with the prayerful verses inked by a scribe, on the parchment. These words say, in part:

"You should love your God with all your heart and all your soul. And you should teach this to your children, and talk to them of it when you are sitting in your home and when you are walking on the road . . ."

Judy Pincus remembers that her father had talked to her of all this. Talked? He had obsessed! And what had she done but not listen? Now, consequently, the door to her domicile is bare, and her precious son Davey, as precious to her as Isaac had been to Abraham, is wounded. If she does what she should, will God help him?

A beautiful melody rises in the air. It grips her.

"*Ve-debarta bam,*" chants Rebbe Gipstein, in the original Hebrew. "*Beshivtichah be-veisechah, uvlechtechah ba-derech . . .*"

"I have a son," Jude weeps, as Rebbe Gipstein revives the ancient melodies of Torah cantillation. "Even as we speak, he is getting treatment at a camp nearby."

"A camp nearby?" The rebbe stops chanting. "What camp? A Jewish camp that teaches him the Mishnah?"

"No," she admits, abashed. "A ranch, I mean, a farm with horses. With horses!" she shouts, as though realizing, for the first time, the desperateness of her situation.

"There is nothing so wrong with that, my dear lady. The Ba'al

Shem Tov, founder of the Chasidim, sat in the forest among the creatures of nature, and that is where he learned that God is truly all around us," says the rebbe. His voice is warm and kind and familiar.

"*Ut, ut*, my *sheina meideleh*," he murmurs, sweeping her into his arms.

One quick gesture, and she's enfolded by him!

Jude is shocked, but she is also delighted. After sitting with this man for some time, and hearing his timeless words, she would have expected his body to feel incorporeal, but his arms have the force of those hard knocks she'd heard on her door. Jude feels faint.

She falls into his lap, laying her head on this chest.

"*Zeit frei*," he says.

"What does that mean?"

"Be free," he replies, so indulgently that he seems to mean every sort of wonderful license. "Your life is in obvious bondage."

"It is," she sighs.

"So."

"So."

"So with your permission, I will come back and visit from time to time. A Jew is not in Egypt anymore."

"But *I* am," Jude pleads, her shoulders shaking as she now finds herself beginning to sob. Her longings are bottomless, inutterable. She misses her father. She misses her husband's real love. She misses the feel of life itself, which used to embrace her, but doesn't anymore. The holy man lets her wet his starched white shirt for as long as she wishes.

"*Zorg nisht*," he says, stroking her shoulders until they are still.

"Hmm?"

"Don't worry."

"Be happy?" she replies, trying to make a joke, alluding to a reggae song she once liked. But of course, the rebbe would not be listening to those vulgar songs on the radio. His answer is as literal, as serious, as one her father would have given.

"What 'happy'? All we can hope for is to be truly alive, and for that you have to live and no worries. So *zorg nisht, mein meidele*."

"Are you still speaking Yiddish?"

"Yes. The dying language of our eternal exile. But I feel that your exile is ending soon."

"Really?"

"You've longed for Zion, and Zion you shall have."

"I've messed up your shirt," Judy sniffles.

"*Dim trafferth.*"

She picks up her head and looks the rebbe hard in the face. He had rolled his "rrrrrs."

"That sounded like a different language!" Does he know them all? Is he less angel than demon? For a moment, she is frightened, not of a strange man, but of being tricked by hope.

"It is a different one. But it is dying, too. Rebbe Gipstein pinches her cheek affectionately. "Welsh—such a good and musical people. They are Hashem's children, too."

"Of course."

"I said, in the Welsh, 'no problem at all.' Now please get up. My legs are sleeping.

"But it is of course a problem," he sighs, as she stands. He stamps his legs to restore the circulation. "It's a tragic problem when a culture or a language dies, like our own poor *mamaloshen*. Gaelic, Welsh, Ladino. I learn them all.

"Because life is life," he concludes. "And we who are alive must guard it to the last spark."

"How?" says Jude, her voice pleading. She doesn't want him to leave. "How do we guard the last spark?"

"What's past is not past and what's dead is never dead," he

replies, replacing the hat on his head. "A little ash can blaze again. Do you understand?"

"Oh, I want to!"

"*Taiku,*" he says, now in Aramaic. He's walking to her foyer.

"Tell me what that means," she pleads, grabbing the Rebbe's arm to make him linger.

"It means that some questions will never be fully answered until the world to come," he answers, swinging her door open wide. "But that does not mean we give up trying to answer them."

He walks away, long strides of black trousers, gabardine coat swaying.

Delaney's Season

When Heidi asks her daughter how her delivery job is going, she is surprised at her reply. Delaney smiles and peals out: "I love it!" Is she finally learning to appreciate her mother's special genius? Heidi knows she herself is not a conventional artist, as so many yearn to be, but isn't her cuisine a form of creative expression? It is wonderful that Delaney can see that.

Her daughter has never before been so clear-minded and buoyant. She had always been a difficult, complicated girl, always with an angle and a grudge. In fact, when she'd heard about her daughter's story, Heidi had not been quite as shocked as Jude had thought she'd be. Of course she knew her daughter wrote. The girl had done so for years, and fancied herself to be talented. In fact, Heidi had read many of her daughter's works, as well as most things her daughter created on her computer. She'd just never paid attention to the "Mama Spicehandler" tale. From now on, she would be even more diligent.

With a child like that, you had to be on your guard. Frankly, it was exhausting running a business and knowing that it could be undermined (your very life could be undermined) by not only a midlife-stricken husband but also a subversive daughter who tries to hurt you not only in word but, increasingly, in deed. If she'd known motherhood was going to be like this, she'd never have struggled so hard to achieve it. It is she who needs to be taken care of, for a change.

But now, Delaney is strangely happy. This is good, of course. But on the other hand, it seems so unlikely—what teen likes to rise at dawn and drive all day in the heat, delivering food for other people (and animals) to eat? Heidi determines that she will keep an even closer eye on her daughter to see what, indeed, has brought her such joy. Could it be that she has met some boy on one of her stops? David Ewington, who is at Angel-Fire (thanks to her), is out of the question ("weirdo"), but could Delaney have met someone older? Someone with a pickup truck who will take her in the back of the cab?

Heidi had not had the benefit of parents when she was Delaney's age; her uncle and brother had not watched her properly, and there were times when people tried to take advantage of her. But she was no Delaney. She'd had a good, practical head on her shoulders, and knew how to navigate in this perilous world. Delaney is a baby. A cranky baby, perhaps, but a baby nonetheless.

What in heaven's name is making her so delighted?

Though Heidi thinks it impossible, David Ewington is, of course, the source of her daughter's new mood. Along with baskets and boxes and bags of her mother's foods, Delaney has brought a part of herself to the boy: her original words. In fact, she has written a tale just for him. In it, a young man and woman meet, fall immediately in love, and ride away on horseback, the man sweeping the woman up in front of him on a roan horse with a cream-colored mane.

Davey reads her words and smiles, head turned toward the text.

Then he lifts his head and looks at her.

She looks into his eyes all the time that he looks into hers. Like a blinking contest, but no competing. Sharing.

"Is this me and you?" he says, voice cracking as it sometimes does.

"You can see that it's us?"

"Uh-huh."

They continue to gaze at each other as though they are the first male and female on earth. They feel important, responsible for each other, true.

They do not kiss that day, but their eyes pledge everything they can feel at their age and stage.

Patriarchs

"Where have you been?" said Neil Whitsun to his son.

"At a friend's house. Why?"

"*Why?* Don't take that insolent tack with me, young man. I don't have to answer *your* questions! In fact, it is quite the reverse, as the Bible says."

"Oh, what exactly does the Bible say, Dad?"

"It says that a man must subdue a rebellious son! Come downstairs for a pamphlet and your beating!" he said, running to the basement.

"Oh, I'll come downstairs, but there will be no more beatings!"

Collum ran behind his father and tackled him on the last three stairs. They tumbled downward in a death grip, thudding on the landing. Neil fell on Collum as though possessed, not merely striking him, but wrestling him to the floor with all his body and his might, biting and scratching. The two of them grappled like bears, with loud and dangerous thumps and grunts.

Betty, at the top of the stairwell, said "Stop," but she said it so quietly that no one paid attention. In any case, she was not relevant. The men were at war, and this time it seemed a battle to the end. Somehow it would end.

Collum knew this. He had seen his father grow weaker every day, and he, stronger. He was nearly sixteen now. With a sudden jerk, he flipped himself over his father and held him down with his hands and knees.

"*You* will *stop hitting me—or else!!!*"

Old Whitsun, groaning, reared up as much as he could, and full-on spat in his son's face.

Collum leapt up from him and raced up the staircase. He ran out the door. Without looking back to see if his father got up (or could get up), he ran as long as it took to get to Judy's house.

He knocked on her door like a madman.

Judy opened it and whispered fiercely, "Are you crazy? My parents are home! We're having dinner! This is not the plan!"

"The plan?" he answered, trying to keep his voice sane. "My father and I are about to kill each other! This is it, Judy!"

"You want my parents to see you like this? They're not going to—"

"I DON'T CARE! WE HAVE TO RUN! NOW OR NEVER!!"

Aaron Pincus stood at the door.

"What is all this commotion here?"

"Oh, it's just a friend from school, Daddy. Math class. We, uh, we sit next to each other in class, right?"

Collum nodded, panting. He nodded too many times.

"And so—?" urged Aaron.

"He's having some trouble with his father—"

"What kind of trouble, young man? Come in, maybe we can help you. There's no need to shout. Here, we will talk like civilized people."

"OK, Collum?" said Judy, following her father into the house.

"*OK, what?*" he replied, looking around wildly for escape. Coming into Judy's house and sitting down with her parents was not the plan. She needed to just pack up and go. But having no choice, Collum followed her into the heart of her family home.

"Sit, please," said Aaron, stretching his arm out and pointing to an extra chair at the dining table. It was big and mahogany, and to it was attached a deep, tufted cushion for comfort.

"Janet?" said Aaron. "This is Judy's schoolfellow. He will be joining us for dinner. I'm sure you don't mind setting another place."

Janet Pincus was a bit taken aback, but went into the kitchen and brought out another plate and tumbler, along with some cutlery and a folded paper napkin with blue flowers on it.

"Mathematics class, yes?" Aaron continued amiably as his wife scurried.

"Yes," said Judy. Collum remained silent, trying to regain his normal breath. Her home made him nervous; its monumental stability made him feel small and bad.

"So let's do mathematics. We were three here and now we're four, am I right? And what is your name, if I may ask?" said Aaron, as his wife offered Collum a mushroom-smothered chicken breast from a serving dish.

"No thanks, I'm not hungry," Collum said to Mrs. Pincus, embarrassed to be sweating so much. Was that blood on his face? He took his paper napkin, wiped his face and neck, and heaved a great sigh. There *was* blood on the paper. He crumpled it and held it in his left fist.

"I asked you your name, if you don't mind answering."

"Oh, sorry, my name is Collum."

"An unusual name. From where does it derive?"

"Oh, uh, I think it's kind of an Irish name," he said, pouring water out from a pitcher and nervously gulping from his tumbler.

"You're very thirsty, I see. You're sweating, like you've run somewhere. So tell me, what is it you are running away from?"

"His father is always—" Judy began.

"Yes, my father—" Collum could not finish either.

"What is the problem? Your father—he is drinking to excess, maybe, leading to family violence?"

Collum stared at him coldly.

"You got it," he answered, annoyed at his father for fulfilling this man's sociological stereotype. Annoyed at Judy's father for thinking the Jews were so much better than anyone else. "He's drinking to excess," he repeated, "leading to family violence."

Collum had a good ear for languages. If you didn't know better, you'd have even thought he mimicked Aaron's voice, the voice of a pedant to a despised student.

"I feel sad for you, young man," said Aaron, sighing. "From such problem drinking come so many, many other troubles. A beating, maybe?"

"A beating, maybe?" Collum echoed, his inflection perfect.

"He has terrible problems with his father, Daddy," Judy intervened. "He hits him all the time, really hard. And his brothers, too."

"Oh, you know the whole *mishpocheh*?" asked Aaron. "Not just the son?"

"Not really," Judy backtracked. "But I've heard the details. Collum comes to school, and you—I can just tell."

"So," said Aaron, chewing a button mushroom thoughtfully. "Your math classes at school have led the two of you to a bit of closeness, it seems, outside of school. Should I suppose that the first person you call on when your father is drinking to excess is my daughter, Judith?"

"I never ask her to help me; she just kinda cares, and—"

"Such an expert she is, on drinking?" said Aaron. "This, I didn't know."

"Lots, you didn't know," said Collum.

"Aaron," said Janet, putting her hand softly over her husband's. She knew it was bad for him to lose his temper. He didn't do so very often, but he had called their daughter "Judith," and his face was getting red.

"Yes, my dear? You have some contribution to make to the current situation at our dinner table?"

"Aaron, darling, it's nothing. They're school friends. Nowadays, kids call each other and they talk about everything and it means nothing special. Boys and girls, Jews and non-Jews."

It was one thing for his wife to get him to eat all the forbidden foods, to serve the world's worst *treif* up to him on a plate. But he was not going to swallow this "nowadays" nonsense about matters of love, marriage, and family.

"Is that right, Colin," he said, "it is right that it means nothing special when you come here at night, sweating and shaking, and with marks on your face, to see my only daughter? Or is it something else?"

Collum hated having his name mispronounced. Even more, he hated the way Mr. Pincus was looking at him now, his mouth twisted with what seemed to be disgust. Collum felt like a crawling bug ruining an otherwise splendid meal.

"Yes, you're right," he answered, spitefully.

"I'm right?"

"Now that you put me on the spot, Judy does mean something very special to me."

"Collum—" Judy cautioned.

"No, Judy—your Dad *is* right. He knows it all, just how rotten a goy I am, the son of a drunk, beneath your contempt, stupid and thick! I don't deserve to be at your beautiful table, or even use your nice paper napkins," he said, balling up the one he had used to mop up his blood and his sweat, and throwing it down on the floor.

"You're a little bit like my father, Mr. Pincus, if you don't mind my saying so," he continued. "He's a drunk and he beats me, but you hit pretty hard with your words. They hurt, too. If you didn't hate each other, you'd really be good friends, or should I use your word, 'special' friends."

"Me? I don't hate him or anyone else," said Mr. Pincus. "If I'm upset, it's because I don't want you to be with my daughter in this way. There are very few Jews left in the world since the Holocaust. One third of the nation is dead. My whole family is lost to me, murdered in violence. This is my only child, and I want her to maintain our ties."

"Well, forgive me, but I personally don't care how *many* Jews there are. This one's the one I care about. Maybe I can help her with this impossible burden you've given her. Of keeping a community alive."

"A burden! My ignorant young man, this 'burden' has been an honor and a privilege, from generation to generation, for thousands of years!"

"Then does one little person really count?"

"Collum, please!" Judy implored.

"Yes, one person counts! Each one is a vital spark! Didn't Judith tell you that she's not allowed to date non-Jewish boys?"

"Actually, it never came up. As a matter of fact," Collum continued, "with all that you say separates us, why do *you* think we are as close as can be?"

"No, Collum!" Judy shouted.

"So—you're 'close,' you say? And how long has the 'closeness' been going on?"

"Daddy, no, listen, we're just friends," Judy pleaded. "Math class buddies!"

"*Stop lying!*" Collum said, between gritted teeth. "To him and to me and to everyone! Have you no shame?"

Judy was silent, ashamed on all fronts.

"I don't hate Jews," Collum continued. "Maybe my father does—he hates everyone, even a lot of Christians, hell, even a lot of Catholics—but I don't, that's for sure. I look up to the Jews! I love them. Anyway, I love one of them. Judy. And she doesn't love 'non-Jews.' She loves ME."

Judy wished she could disappear. Her father's hurt stare bore into her.

"A love affair. So beautiful. Maybe for this I should celebrate?" he said. "I should take out maybe the schnapps from my break-front?"

"I'm not asking you to celebrate. But leave us alone. Maybe I have potential. I can be your friend, too, not your worst nightmare. I mean, I've defended Judy to my father. I fought a battle royal for her."

"And for this you are proud? For defying your own father?"

"Yes, actually I am. Under the right circumstances—"

"Maybe you are right. Maybe you two are both from the same piece of cloth. I asked Judith not to date a gentile, and this she promised me. She made a vow! So to lie to your father, to fight him like an animal—good things, yes?"

Aaron's face was now purple and blotchy.

"Collum, could you please, please just go," Judy said quietly. She tried to meet his eyes, to find him in this chaos.

He would not share his eyes with her. He sat there puzzled. Go? Where was he to go now? She was a little girl trying to please her father, a good father unlike his own, but he was cornered. He had nothing in the world. No one.

Still, Collum stood up, and Judy stood up, too. They went to the door together, and stood there, alone for a moment.

"Go back home and wait for me," she said.

This time, he did look into her eyes.

"Really? Go home? I *can't* go home, Judy!" he said, beginning to crumble and cry. Judy's heart began to break for him. She saw it all and would remember it all. His sad blue eyes shone gorgeous in the night, sad for the love of her. She wanted to grab him, to cover and be covered with kisses. She wanted to lose herself in her boy and never look back. She knew they would be happy. But her parents were waiting for her, and she steeled herself.

"Yes, you can. Pretend to make up with your dad. I'll do the same. I need a little time to get ready. I can't just run when it's like this."

"*I* was willing to," said Collum, tears pouring freely as she shut the door behind her, leaving him alone and outside.

Matriarchs 1

"Well, *I* have got a *fabulous* dessert," said Janet ridiculously, after the visitor had gone.

She and Aaron had sat soundlessly, frozen until their daughter returned to the dinner table. But now that all three were together, as on every other night, perhaps normalcy would return. They could have peach crumble, couldn't they? Janet thought they could.

"Is this all a bad dream, Judy?" said Aaron. "I pictured you with a nice man one day, from a nice family. Maybe even a doctor, a lawyer. And now there is this wild boy and his violent, drunken father, an anti-Semite yet—"

"It's—let's try to have a new dream, Daddy. Something that you might not have thought about before. Collum is nothing like his father. He's special, he's alone, he's his own person. He's different."

"Yes, not so many Jewish boys are fighting their fathers."

"But his father beats him!

"Not a surprise, and not an excuse. He beat him back a real beating, not just self-defense, but as real offense. To end the matter."

"He defended me. Us."

"Today. But maybe tomorrow he'll beat you, too?"

"That day will never come."

"He'll get drunk. He'll call you Shylock. He may even want you dead and gone. You think his father's words go nowhere?"

"Collum is a good person. He'd never be like that! He's interested in Judaism, maybe he could study, you could teach him, he has no one—"

"From this boy, you will get misery. His family will not disappear. They will hate you and they will hurt you—they will even destroy you. Is that the life you want for yourself? For me and for your mother?"

"Well, that's possibly a little extreme," said Janet, trying to introduce a more pleasant tone to the proceedings.

"I mean, look at the Lindens," she continued, "you know the nice couple that we had over for cocktails a few years ago, when I was trying to get on the flower committee? He's Presbyterian, and she's Jewish, and they could not be happier or more lovely people."

Aaron considered this for a minute.

"The Lindens, you say? Like the tree?"

"Yes, I suppose their name is the same as the tree," said Janet, getting up and walking into the kitchen to fetch her peach crumble. She had also made real whipped cream.

In her absence, Aaron Pincus rose from the table and intoned:

"I'll give you *trees*—the lindens, the elms, the oaks, the pine trees of Bavaria that you could smell all the way to Dachau but it didn't stop the stink of death, and most of all—"

He clutched at his head, as though to stop it from thinking.

"THE POPLARS! THE POPLARS OF PONAR FOREST!!!"

Janet called out from the kitchen:

"What's that, dear?"

Judy cried, "Calm down, Daddy, your face is so dark!"

"THE POPLARS IN THE FOREST!" her father screamed, so hard that he felt his chest would burst, but didn't care. It was the loudest he had ever screamed in his life, and he screamed for the lives of all the lost and martyred:

"BY THE DITCH!
WHERE THEY SHOT THEM!
YOUNG MEN! BOYS!
MY COUSINS, UNCLES—IN LITHUANIA!!
AND NO ONE—NO ONE EVEN SAID A WORD!!!!"

With that, a strange expression became fixed on his twisted face, as though his eyes had seen the contours of that ditch.

Aaron Pincus dropped to the floor. Heavy and hard, like a shot person collapsing.

Janet Pincus, coming into the dining room, let go of the dessert tray. It clattered downward. Dishes, spoons, crumble, and cream. Reflexively, she bent down to pick up the pieces, to clean up the mess.

Judy stared at her father's prone position for a good thirty seconds before she could move. Shards of china clinked as her mother lifted them up from the floor. Finally, she heard her own voice shrieking:

"Call 911, Mommy!! He's dying!!"

Her mother dropped everything and ran to the kitchen phone.

Judy knelt down to look into her father's eyes. They stared at her, half unseeing and half pleading. He could not speak, and his face was contorted in deep disappointment. It twisted more, into hatred, and froze.

Judy was deeply horrified at herself. How could she have brought him to this point? She was terrified that he would never come back from this moment, that he would remain this way, forever frozen in accusation.

Only when the ambulance arrived did Janet address her daughter.

"You should stay put. Finish cleaning up the mess."

"But Mommy—"

"First of all, you're too young to see such things. Second, I want you to keep your mouth shut. All right, Judy? You've said enough for one night."

"I didn't mean to!"

"You knew your father was sensitive! You knew the effect this very conversation would have on him!"

"But I didn't plan for Collum to come over. I never wanted that—it was his idea, not mine."

"You should really start to think about the consequences of your actions. I don't blame *him*! That poor boy! But really, Judy, you're a smart girl. Where did you think a friendship like that would lead?"

When Aaron Pincus had oxygen on his face and was strapped securely on a gurney, the emergency technicians raced him out to the ambulance. Janet followed, leaving the front door open.

Judy stood in the doorway of their home, watching men load her father into the back of an ambulance. Her mother got in with the EMT people. She sat by her husband and stroked his face. Then the driver got in, the doors were slammed, front and back, and they were gone.

She continued to stand at the entry to her childhood home, neither inside nor out, but in between.

Matriarchs 2

For the next week, Judy stayed home from school, twisting in bed with a raging fever. Her mother, softened by her daughter's illness, took care of her, bringing her cold compresses and cups of weak tea.

On the seventh day, her mother asked Judy if she was well enough to let her go out for more than a few hours. Each day Janet had gone out to shop for groceries and to see her husband in the hospital. Now she had been invited to her friend Mimi's house to unwind and relax. All these days, Janet, too, had looked pale and wobbly, and Judy had worried about her.

"Sure, Mommy, have a good time."

"Should I bring up some toast and orange juice before I go?"

"I'd like that."

"And a fresh cold compress?"

Her fever was down, but Judy said, "Yes, thanks."

"OK," said her mother when she had brought all the creature comforts she could think of to her child. "You have the little TV set, your OJ, toast. Do you have something to read?"

"Yeah, I have my *Seventeen* magazine and some stuff for school."

The class was now finishing *Romeo and Juliet*, and Judy wanted to keep up. Her good friend Nessa had dropped off her notes.

"Good, all right. I'll be back in about three hours or so. Want me to call you from Mimi's and see if you need anything? A Baby Ruth or something?"

"No, I'll be fine," said Judy.

She hadn't expected her mother to leave for so extended a time. But now that the opportunity had arisen, Judy knew that she would try to reach out again to Collum. As soon as the sound of her mother's sturdy stride faded and the front door shut, she sat up and strategized.

Collum was at school; she couldn't go there. Maybe she could go to his house and leave him a note. All this time since her father had been taken away by ambulance, she hadn't been able to speak to her boyfriend. When she had called his home, his father had answered, and Judy had hung up immediately.

Only Betty would be home at this hour, she thought. It would be nice to say hello to Collum's mum, confide in her, even. She would write a note for Collum and give it to her for safekeeping. Betty had a soft heart. Neil Whitsun was a monster, but Betty was the heart of that family. Thank goodness Collum had her.

Judy took a piece of loose-leaf paper from her three-ring binder. She began writing, explaining that her father had fallen ill and was still lying in the hospital. He'd suffered a "cerebral infarction on the left side." He would have to go and get rehabilitated so he could recover and walk and talk the way he once did. He might even still die.

As she wrote these words, Judy started crying. Her tears splashed the page as she continued:

"So even though I want to be with you and give you everything—"

She blushed when she wrote that. It seemed so silly now, she almost crossed it out. But she left the words as they were and continued:

—even though I love you so much, we have to wait a while. We have to.

I can't leave my father now. What if I never saw him again? How could I live with that? On top of which my mother, who is very angry at me, is a nervous wreck.

I know you have to get away from your horrible mean disgusting bigot of a father. And I know you will. And I know that we will be together forever, no matter how long it takes. But this is not the right time, OK? We have eternity, Collum, so let me have a few more days, maybe a week or so.

I'm going to help my mother take care of my father. When the time is right, I will show you that love is stronger than anything else in the world.

Yours, forever, Judy

Running into her parents' bedroom, she took a long business envelope from her father's desk, folded the paper in, sealed it, and kissed it. Tucking her thoughts in and sealing them up made her feel hopeful. This letter was not just a letter. It was a document, a contract. It was her vow.

Now she jumped on her bike and cycled over to the Whitsun house as fast as she could. As she stood by the front door, Judy thought she could hear Betty singing, as she liked to do as she did her chores.

She listened. It was hard to hear the words, but something in Betty's voice unsettled her. She was singing in a guttural way, as though she'd been drinking. And the song sounded like the one she'd heard Mr. Whitsun sing that day she'd visited. A cruel chantey. Betty was chuckling, too.

Poor Collum, she thought, almost paralyzed with fear. The way he had to live. That bleeding statue. She could feel it all now, now that she stood there alone. That was how he must have felt all the time. And all she had for him was a promise, some words tucked into a business envelope. But time would show him that her love was true. A friend to the end she would be.

Judy took the letter out of her pocket. She'd folded it in half, and now it was wrinkled, too, and warm and soft from her body. She smoothed it out over and over. When it was straight and nearly whole, she kissed it again. Her eyes closed, as though she were kissing her own Collum. For a second, she felt a twinge inside of her, remembering his touch below the bleachers, and how she'd swooned with desire and surrender.

Judy slipped the note under the front door. It went to the other side and was swallowed into the Whitsun household. There was no more she could do. She cycled away, back to her own home, jumped back into bed, and waited to hear from her boy.

Collum's Vigil

The night of Aaron's stroke, Collum had come home. With nowhere else to go, he'd tiptoed into an eerily quiet household. Had everyone gone to bed? Was that possible after such a big fight?

"Is that you, son?" said Betty, calling out from the master bedroom. Wordlessly, Collum walked toward the sound of her voice.

His father lay atop the olive green chenille bedspread, hand gripped on his chest, eyes closed tightly, as though in pain. The top buttons of his shirt were open, and Collum could see the white hairs of his chest. Betty hovered over her husband, daubing his face with a damp washcloth. She looked up to see her son in the doorway.

"Welcome back, dear," she said, a bit flatly, as though concealing anger. "We were worried about you, darting off like that. It might be better if you went to your room now."

His father looked terrible. Had he had a heart attack? No, Neil was holding his hand over his right side. Collum knew the heart was on the left.

Relieved, he went in, pushing past his mother.

"I want to talk to my dad," he said, with an authoritative voice.

Betty backed away in seeming deference.

"It is a question of my ribs, son," said Neil Whitsun from his supine position. His voice was low and sepulchral.

"Do they hurt much? I was only trying to get you off of me, but—"

Neil Whitsun interrupted him:

"Adam lost a rib so he could have a woman to support him in life. In my case, it is a bit different, eh?" He glared at his wife.

Collum wondered how his mother could be implicated in this.

"HE is YOUR son now, and I am done with him. You have raised up a traitor in our midst, and I cannot have that."

"I'm sorry, I'll try harder," his wife said, simply. It was as though she had said this many times before. But she meant it. She would try harder. One always could. It was amazing how hard one could try.

She glared at her son in an unusual way:

"You must never, never again act like you did tonight. How could you hit your own father?" None of the other boys had ever lifted a hand to her husband. He was not a perfect man, it was true, but this boy was the worst possible son for a man like this. And now he was growing big and strong and defiant.

"In the old days," Neil said, chewing his words with slow delight, "such a son would have been stoned to death in public, and good men would have cheered. Such a son have I long endured and foreseen the evil of."

"You did foresee it, luvvy," said Collum's mother, soothingly.

Collum wondered at her essential loyalty. Did she really mean what she said, or was she just trying to survive?

He, too, was only trying to survive—and he would do so by assuaging his father for as long as he could, while he waited to hear from his girl.

"Father, forgive me," he said to Neil Whitsun. In his mind, he added silently, "'cause I'll never forgive *you*."

Dodging

N eil Whitsun had other battles to fight beside that primal one with his devil-son. The Church itself had betrayed him with all kinds of reforms; it had introduced the anti-Christ to the central halls of the Vatican. And now the country he lived in was slowly going mad.

But he had a family to take care of, three strapping sons and a wife who depended on him for guidance. Time was not stopping for him; it was moving inexorably on and challenging God's and his own authority. A war was being fought on the other side of the world, and sons were being drafted. Ryan's number was especially terrible, and if nothing was done, he would be sent to the other end of the world to help save some sly, slant-peepered heathens.

Worse, in his objection to the growing war, Neil had motley company. This was a time when teenagers all over the country were escaping the draft. Some went to Woodstock, others to San Francisco. Many fled to Canada or Sweden.

Woodstock? San Francisco? Canada? *Sweden*? Well, his family was not going to handle this like a bunch of indecent, dirty reprobates. Rob had tried to grow his hair; of course, he, Neil, had put a stop to that with a good razoring. In fact, what his boys needed was to get away before more changes occurred. Jews were dating and mating with Christians (why, there had been a Jewess in his house not long ago—batting her eyelashes at his young-est!). Negroes jigged with fair-haired girls. Women were trying to wrest power from their men, men were beginning to go soft and weedy. Rock and roll, unisex, revolution.

Neil Whitsun would have no part of this rotting, cursed Gomorrah. Thank Christ, he'd been given a way out. There was family in Australia. His father's people worked on a cattle station and said there was plenty of opportunity there for men who knew how to earn their wages. Yes, Collum would lose a month or so of school while they settled in, but what did that matter? His boys were not scholars, sitting in their ivory towers and ruining every-thing with their casuistry and false idols.

Anyway, Ryan and Rob would love the new land. They would share its values and adore the manly ways of it. Both were short, snub-nosed, and muscle-bound. Collum was different: rangy, handsome, and smart as Satan. Betty coddled him too much. He was her baby; she had spoiled him. Only Collum was soft enough to cry when he was hurt.

And only he had ever dared to strike his own father, thought Neil Whitsun. He vowed that such an outrage would never hap-pen again. He would work him hard, this boy, and break his spirit. Collum would get the toughest horses. Mankillers. Yes—the one who would be drafted would be not Rob or Ryan, but soft-eyed, temperamental Collum, drafted into a different life down under.

His father had been planning this escape for months. It had little to do with that girl of Collum's, but she would not see him again. The boy would be corralled by his family and flown to Aus-tralia. There, he would be teased and mocked for his accent and his softness. He would work in the baking sun until his looks and talent whisked him away and back into the world. And so they sold the house and flew away within a fortnight of Collum's desperate dash for refuge.

For decades Collum thought of Judy Pincus, not knowing why she'd never called or written after that night. She had loved him, maybe, but over the years he imagined her cramming for tests, getting her idiotic A's, posing in the cap and gown to please her mummy and daddy. He could see her continuing to wash her hair with Breck shampoo and drying it in her nice pink bathroom. He could see them all eating that chicken smothered in mushrooms, wiping their faces with napkins that had floral designs. He imagined them listening to classical music, reading books peaceably, with no hurt, bleeding boy to disturb them.

After all, she was the one with the nice, normal family. A typical Jew, he came gradually to think, acting sensibly, playing it safe, and waiting for the best possible deal.

Correspondence, or Social Intercourse

Jude S. Ewington takes a long, transformative shower. She stays under the steaming jets for what seems like forever. Her mind and body travel. After she dries herself, still naked, she writes to Collum:

Collum—there is a man in town who reminds me of you. Your father would be so upset if he knew that I said that, because he's not only Jewish. He's a Chasid. Do you know what they are? Super-religious.

Collum replies right away:

Well, I did have a crazy beard when I played that Neanderthal. Didn't you ever see Mancave? *It was the first one I directed, so I'm embarrassed by how many things I could have done better. But I made my point, I think, about the essence of man.*

Jude answers:

Yeah, I saw you ravishing away. And it made me feel really bad about so many things.

What things? Collum asks.

That you were so far away. That you looked so good, even with that straggly beard. Even carrying a caveman club, you had that elevated poignancy. It made me feel bad that we'd never had a chance to make love. I think it would have been amazing.

And Collum replies:
When I find you, will we "make love" then?
Let's use the right word now we're being honest, shall we?
Will we finally fuck—like you promised?

Jude does not answer, though oddly, she feels sure that it would be right to say "yes." Her attraction to the Chasid is opening her up in every way. Even the word Collum uses, "fuck," seems open and real and true. It's the right word for a powerful act. Archaic, Anglo-Saxon.

The boy she'd known was raw like that. Real love, at its source, was raw like that. Yes. She could say "yes" now.

The Seduction of Slam

Under Heidi's watchful eyes, David and Delaney are growing closer. She has begun sanctioning this relationship, thinking that the timid Ewington boy will have a tempering effect on her headstrong teen. Now, the two of them come over regularly after his therapy at the ranch. Slowly, they have made their way to Delaney's immaculate bedroom, where the curtains match the bedspread, and the curtain ties match both. At first, the door had been kept politely ajar, but after several visits, it is shut.

What Delaney does not know is that her mother's senses are first-rate. Not only are her taste buds evolved, but also her sense of hearing. Eschewing the full invasion of privacy that a hidden camera or tape recorder would entail, Heidi simply listens at the door whenever she can. To her great satisfaction, David and Delaney tend to do no more than talk; there are few ominous silences that Heidi has noticed. Most of all, she enjoys listening to them chat about their time on the farm, gossiping about the various workers there.

It is especially delicious when Jude's name comes up in connection with one of the farmhands. David and Delaney seem to think that someone with an odd name (sounds like "Shy") is all too interested in this married friend of hers. This worker has tried to find out what she is like, what her maiden name is, and—most ominously—exactly where she lives. Perhaps Jude has interacted with this man at pickup time. It would have all seemed very innocent, thinks Heidi, straining to hear more details about the stalker/paramour. The countryside is full of such gigolos. Here and there a foolish housewife had fallen for them, hoping for a way out of the humdrum. (Thank goodness she, Heidi, has business sense and a career, and no time or inclination for such foolishness.)

Heidi has met many a "bolter" in her day—a married woman who runs off with another man, often one with an outlandish profession. Several women in her mother's horsey set had done this, one with a golf instructor, another with a polo player. She has never seen Jude near anyone with a Titleist ball or riding crop, but you really never know. That woman is one of the quieter ones, come to think of it, with her wan little complaints about her husband and her refusal to dress well. But she does show a flare of temperament, here and there, as she'd done about Delaney. Such women can surprise you, like a frog with a fly. Now you see it, now you don't.

Frankly, Heidi does not think that Slam deserves this kind of treatment. Her own Daniel had chosen to "find himself," but Slam seems to be working his way back to the financial heights of his former consulting career. If he flies a lot between Italy and Putnam County, Heidi believes it is only for the pasta. She, of all people, can appreciate artisanal foods—even if the man's own wife does not. And if they are not sleeping together often enough, perhaps it is because Slam does not feel acknowledged. Instead, Jude probably whines about her own stunted life, and tries to hold him back. Misery loves company, she thinks, but it's not a very sexy kind of company. And now there is some sleazy hired hand in the picture, Jude's supposed admirer.

Heidi is Jude's friend, but this flirtation will have to be stopped at once. Slam will have to be informed; he is a man's man and will know what to do. Heidi lures him over with a request for a tasting of his newest *tubetti*. She promises that if she likes his product, she will tell everyone in her food chain about it; moreover, she will use it in her own catered foods.

He is strange when he gets there, though. Sitting in her kitchen, sipping a glass of her chilled Beaujolais, Slam cannot look more relaxed, even when she begins to explain what she knows about his wife.

"There is talk," Heidi begins ominously.

"Always is," he says, setting a large pot to boil and measuring out a sheaf of his product.

"About your wife, Jude."

"Uh-huh," Slam says amiably, adding a dash of sea salt.

"And a man."

"Oh? A man?"

"Yes! An employee at the place where your son is taking riding lessons. And I overheard Delaney saying that he was quite the 'cowboy'!"

Slam chuckles. "Well, that's good. Davey deserves the best instructor. Hope some testosterone rubs off on him."

Is that all he can say? What if the testosterone rubs off on Jude?

"No, no, you misunderstand," Heidi insists. "This cowboy fellow, he seems fixated, obsessed with your wife!"

"Oh boy. This is—yum. Good and crisp; I might pair it with Alfredo, whaddya think?"

He is talking about the wine!

Heidi embellishes more and more, but nothing changes Slam's calm demeanor. As the water begins boiling agitatedly, he coolly tosses in the pasta.

"'Bout thirteen minutes, then we're in heaven," he says, referring to the cooking time.

"You know, Slam, speaking of 'being in heaven,' a woman like your wife might get her head turned by some smooth-talker."

"Maybe a goat cheese salad? And *then* this pasta course? But then there is the element of appetite . . ."

"Yes, appetite," says Heidi, trying to sound suggestive. "It is rumored that the female's is stronger than the male's, at least in middle age."

"Well, everyone loves good food," he says placidly.

Slam is thinking only about selling pasta to Heidi, perhaps going into business with her. Whatever she is saying about anything else does not interest him in the least.

From this, Heidi deduces that he does not care about his wife—and that what Jude has told her about his apathy is true. A man so blasé about his woman being pursued by a handsome ranch hand is a man who is no longer remotely in love.

And yet, unlike her own husband, Slam is so sexual. What a waste!

His body is amazing, she notices, broad-shouldered and bubble-biceped. She watches his right arm stir the pasta as his left reaches for a drop of olive oil to prevent sticking. Yes, the oil will lubricate the situation, Heidi silently agrees, staring at Jude's evasive mate.

His hair is still so black and so thick, his nose big and Roman.

She's heard about his tennis prowess, too—the source of his nickname, or perhaps that was a hint of something else? Slam is, she realizes with a thrill, a real man, with real work, and a focused lust for that sensual blend of grain, eggs, and oil of which one never tires.

Pasta, pâté, paste, she muses. Wheat, stalk, seed, and harvest. His wares are ambrosial, essential, like Barolo wine and the rind of an old Camembert.

Yes, this man and his culinary calling—so complementary to her own—fascinate her, all the more so when the fire is put out at the peak of al dente.

"Ready for the taste of paradise?" says Slam, draining the water through a colander, his face rising out of steam as from a cloud.

"Put it on a fork and bring it to my mouth," she says, leaning over him and entering the water-vapored air.

"Say 'ahhhh.'"

Heidi's lips part and her tongue quivers lightly as the food enters her mouth. La bocca, she thinks, drunk on the little Italian she knows. La bocca, la pasta, la bocca, la pasta. She is crazy for him, swallowing the harvest he has reaped and is putting inside her.

She tries his pasta hot. She tries it cold.

She admires the firmness of the tubes, and the width of the space inside them. Each is a hollow walled by strength, softening and swooning each time it meets the boiling water. Over and over, they cook the pasta. Over and over she compares and contrasts, pondering all the many things that food can do. And not just food. But Slam does not take the hint in all of Heidi's well-wrought gustatory phrases. He is just not as appreciative of the metaphor as he might have been.

"I think I prefer it hot," she says. "*Boiling* hot."

And: "*Putana*. Something that your mouth won't soon forget."

And: "The texture? Sauce should be thick enough to give you the mouth-feel, but thin enough to run down your chin. I like a slippery sauce.

"You, too?" she prods.

Heidi gets nothing but the most literal of responses.

219

"Yes, I think that *would* be a nice dish," says Slam agreeably. "I don't think, though, that the texture should be too firm—some people make a kinda snobby fixation about that, but I want the food to be easy to eat, and then they eat more. That's economics 101. As for the spicy sauce," he continues, "that's your call.

"A lot of people don't like it that hot, certainly not *arrabiata*—scratch that off, if you want my advice—"

Heidi is, in fact, becoming *arrabiata* with Slam's willful (it seems) obtuseness to double entendres, but hope keeps her going.

"Anyway, 'hot' food," he is saying, "uh—I don't think it makes sense from the volume-sales standpoint. It's known to cause satiety, so from purely the business end—"

"*Look!*" she bursts out, "I'm sick of purely the *business* end!"

Slam does not understand her pique.

"People won't want as much of it," he explains patiently. "You sell less. Fewer profits."

"Slam! You talk about 'satiety.' I'll tell you about satiety. My husband Daniel hasn't made me happy for a long time . . . In fact, there are times that I think he must not like women very much at all!"

"Oh?" is all Slam can say. From what he has heard around the tennis and golf club, Dante does like women. In fact, he likes them so much that he is not a bit particular about them.

But maybe he neglects his own wife. She does seem pretty underserved.

It would, in fact, be all too easy for Slam to turn off the burners, take Heidi by the hand, and drive her off to the nearest motel. He could screw her all day long until she finally relaxes enough to act like a normal person.

It could be nice, actually. She would be so grateful, not at all like his wife, who is often annoyed with him, who expects him to make up for the fact that she is growing older, that he is, too, and that the kids are no longer babies but big, strapping teenagers.

How are men supposed to make up for all the losses women never fail to notice and obsess about? He could fuck someone else's wife easily enough—that would count for a lot in her ledger. But Heidi's own husband could never get off so easily. Just the same, Slam could never easily appease his own wife. What about tomorrow, they all worry. Or worse, what about yesterday! Why isn't today like yesterday, and why can't tomorrow be like today?

Pasta is simple. You plant, water, cut, separate, add some eggs and a pinch of salt to the mix, and boom! Happiness for both seller and buyer. Passion between people is another thing entirely.

Even if they each get what they want, however briefly, what is next? Slam could see the whole affair—the frantic sex, the tears of shock, relief, regret that Heidi would spill, and the endless fraught moments that would follow.

Not worth it. Slam is sympathetic and kind (he gives her an extra sack of pasta, gratis)—but refuses to take Heidi to bed.

As he walks away, he suddenly feels kind and warm toward all women, his own wife included. It is so hard to make them happy—not just his wife, apparently, but Dan's wife, too. Why is that? He pities them, and resolves to treat Jude more kindly in the future, time permitting.

The Holy Ghost

Rebbe Malach Gipstein continues to visit Jude Ewington. He is her secret, her holy of holies. His accent is a turnoff, a Jewish cliché, but his zeal fascinates her (she's even affixed a mezuzah to her door). His mission, he said, was to awaken her soul from its quotidian slumbers. And she wants him to; she feels lucky, and chosen by him. He had told her she was special; she believes him.

She had been so young when her father had had his stroke; now, she is eager to learn all she can about the ancient ways. Jude sometimes imagines herself as the Rebbe's wife, donning the *sheitl*, grinding the Friday-night fish. It seems too complicated. Maybe not his wife, actually. His lover, then? Is that even thinkable? Is she simply transferring her feelings from Collum to him?

When she asks the rebbe what his first name, Malach, means, he tells her: Angel. Now, sometimes, Jude can't concentrate when the man speaks of holiness to her. She knows what's really holy, deep down. She knows what's true, in the Eden-garden way, what can't be faked. She wants that holy union.

Jude is beginning to obsess about stripping Malach, layer by layer. She's seen the hat come off, but now she wants him to toss the skullcap, too. She wants to peel off that long black jacket, that crisp white shirt. She'd lift up his tzitzis—the fringed undergarment worn by pious Jews—and then finally . . .

What would she see?

She tries to discern his body under the clothes. She can't seem to forget the hug he'd given her, that first day, when she had cried. He had held her, and his arms had been strong, his chest hard as a rock. When she'd sat on his lap, there were thighs, hard as stone, and—something else. It was true. He'd said that his leg was asleep, but that part of him was anything but.

Truthfully, the Rebbe's body is awfully developed for a man who all day studied Torah, and sometimes the Talmud. And his face, hiding under the glasses and the beard—it, too, is quite rugged and tan. His smile lines are deep and his neck is muscular.

Yes, Jude is increasingly hot for Rebbe Gipstein. "*Heis*," as he would have put it in the Yiddish tongue, the dying language alive in his mouth. Thank God his holy quest has brought him to her door.

It happens in late September, what some call Indian summer. Jude is off from teaching, and Slam is off in Italy again. It is a Friday, the eve of the Sabbath, when her dream to know love comes to life.

It comes so true that Jude almost feels sick to her stomach at the shocking joy of it. It is as though Malach has read her mind and knows what she had been thinking of all summer long, even before she had ever met him.

"We seem to desire each other," he quietly announces.

"We—we do? You desire me?" This is the greatest of surprises.

"I do not believe in lying, so I will tell you. Very much. I desire you as much as Israel desires God. No more perfect union could be imagined."

"And I desire you as much as God desires Israel," she attempts. She will remain in this holy vein, if it is called for.

"You are my vineyard," he answers.

"And you are my—my vintage," she replies, faltering a bit. "Harvest," she amends. "My reward for being so good all my life."

"*Have* you been good?" says the angel, taking Jude's hair out of her barrette and loosening it. She throws her hair over her face, recklessly.

"Maybe too good."

"Let me look at you and see how good," he says, advancing toward Jude. He lifts her hair out of her eyes and holds it in his fist like a trophy. He stares at her naked face until she blushes crazily.

"Without my *shtreimel* and without my yarmulke, this you also need to see," he adds, whipping off his fancy hat and skullcap.

His uncovered hair is so blue-black shiny that Jude wants to laugh. It is a Superman color, a Hollywood dream of Apaches and strength.

"Wow. Look at you! I've been daydreaming about this for such a long time, I have to admit," she says. "I've imagined you and me together in my pool."

"Your pool would be our *mikveh*, where you and I would purify ourselves, body and soul together."

"Purify?" She hopes the pool has enough chlorine in it. Sometimes, the waters turns a faint green, and Slam has to "shock" it back to the right balance.

"Yes, and sanctify—as the marriage prayer says: 'Behold, you are sanctified to me.'"

"The marriage prayer?"

"God and Israel could be together, yes," he says.

"But Malach, you actually know that I'm already married—"

"According to the laws of Moses? According to the sacred laws of God and his chosen people, Israel?"

It is true, she concedes. She and Slam had had only a civil ceremony. Her father had died by then, and her mother had never cared much for religion. Slam's parents, from a mixed marriage themselves, preferred the classic wedding march and only the most basic of vows. No one wanted the drama of the broken glass, signifying the destruction of the Temple and millennia of exile.

In Malach's eyes, their paper bond is nothing. A sham and a *shanda.*

Jude looks up at him, shamefaced.

"I've never been properly married, have I?"

"Not as yet. May I consecrate you to me now? Shall we cleanse ourselves first, and make ourselves new again?"

Jude is happy to hear a catch in the Rebbe's voice. Poised as he is, wise as he is, love has humbled and awed him.

She takes his hand and leads him to the backyard.

"Here is my pool."

"It is not what I imagined when you said 'pool,' no, but still it is a body of water, and sufficient, I guess, for our needs."

"I think so, too," says Jude, happy that her husband had put a stockade around it for safety reasons. They would be hidden from the neighbors.

"Are you too modest to take off all your clothes?" asks the rebbe, beginning to unbutton his starched, white shirt.

"Yes, a little," Jude admits. She wonders if her body is good enough for a man like him. So handsome, underneath it all.

"So let us leave each one undergarment. I will leave my shorts underneath, and you will leave your underwears."

"My bra and underpants?"

"No, the bra top you should take off," he says sternly. "The breasts are not used for the procreation of the human being, only for the nourishment. Israel is the land of milk and honey—so in conclusion, there can be no shame in *shadayim!*" he says, using the biblical word.

Jude complies. She takes off her pants and her shirt, and then she takes off her bra. Malach cannot take his eyes off her.

"Even more beautiful as God made you than with raiments," he whispers.

"More beautiful, really?" She is heavier than she has ever been, and like most women her age, self-conscious about her arms, shoulders, breasts, legs, stomach, knees, ankles, bottom, waist, neck, and hands.

"Clothing. Just a shell for the body, obscuring the light."

"Yes, exactly, take off yours now," Jude retorts. "Come on, all the undershirts—"

"I'm doing that."

"Well, hurry. I'm standing here alone and you have everything on."

Even as she speaks, he tosses off garments.

"Now take off your pants."

He does so, so quickly that he falls to the ground, trousers entwining his legs. Twisting, he manages to kick off the heavy gabardine, but falls in the process. He lies on the earth, on his back, wearing only cotton boxer shorts.

He looks beautiful, she thinks, sprawling on the ground.

And she looks beautiful, standing above him, looking down with her hair flowing to her shoulders and her breasts naked and bare, as the scripture said.

"Rebbe?"

"Yes?"

"Why aren't you—"

Something has popped up and sprung out of the boxers; Jude stares at it.

"Why aren't you circumcised?"

"I'm *not?*"

The rebbe begins talking quickly. He tries to convince Jude that his foreskin had been much bigger before. And that this remnant of it was like the Shechinah that floated over the people of Israel . . . A tent in the desert, spiritually speaking . . . The Christians called it the Holy Ghost, but the Jews really knew it meant oasis . . .

Jude is staring, open-mouthed. His torso is ridiculously well-muscled. And while the hair on his head is that Hollywood hue, Jude follows a long trail of blond, leading from navel to groin. The hair on his arms is flaxen, too. It gleams like gold in the sun. This person is so handsome that she gasps.

He isn't who he said he is. He isn't a man sent from heaven to heal her soul, but the one who had broken her heart. Whose heart she had broken. They'd broken each other, long ago. Now here he is.

"Take off your glasses," she orders.

"And by the way, somehow we never discussed this matter, but your sons are not *entirely* legitimate."

"Oh, shut your mouth, 'Rebbe.' Really! Not one more god-damned word, even if it wins you the Oscar. Glasses off, *now.*"

Silently, as though with a sense of relief, he complies. Jude finds herself looking into a pair of sheepish, deep blue eyes.

"Oh, Reb Malach—you are *my* angel, and have always been," she says, knowing her own Collum Whitsun. She has not seen him for over thirty years.

The rebbe stares at her as he pulls at his beard. It comes off in one piece, and he tosses it aside. The side-locks are next. Left and right.

227

A long silence.

Collum rises from the ground and she meets him halfway. They grab and hold each other tightly for a good, long time. Without his paint, his disguises, his extensive research, method acting, and poignant linguistic tricks, Collum is her helpless boy again. He is tender, searching, and vulnerably simple. Jude can feel his pain and his desire, that powerful blend that never failed to move her. He's come back. And the feelings, too. Why had she been so afraid of them? She was glad he had found her. People were made to be found, discovered.

"Did you know it was me all the time, Judy?" he says, trembling so much she trembles, too.

"Yes," she lies. But it is true. In her soul, there is no difference between the boy, the rebbe, and this gorgeous man whose body is now hers. They are all about love, as impersonal and perfect as that. She would take them all; they all blended into a quivering white beam in which she sees and can be seen.

At last.

"And do you love me still?"

"Do I love you," she answers, exhaling as she nuzzles him with her mouth. They kiss each other again and again. With each moment, she rises. She has never kissed like this, even with Collum as a teen. There is knowledge there, and homecoming. There is pain there, and relief of heartache.

"This is good," he says. "This is right. Here is my heaven."

More Discoveries

Davey walks home from school, thinking of Delaney. He has decided to skip the last period, a review for a quiz in a subject he knows cold. In this new autumn term, he feels changed, more social now. He has even begun to help with the Angel-Fire kids on weekends, now that Shy is gone. He has never fully believed the stuff Delaney had said—theories about his mother, and how Shy was obsessed with her, and that he had left town because of some gossipmongers. Yes, the man had a crazy moustache that sometimes seemed glued on, but some of Delaney's friends had green or purple hair. Some even shaved their heads and had their scalps tattooed.

Now that he is with Delaney, Davey has learned a broader range of self-expression himself. He is proud to be her boyfriend, kiss her under the trees on the high school campus, wear a cologne that she says makes her crazy. In a good way.

Davey really likes that kind of crazy. He will be fifteen in a week, and she is sixteen—they are not kids anymore. They can express even more of themselves if they want to. He thinks, for example, that he will be a good lover. He has touched her breasts

229

many times, both over and under the shirt. Each time they felt bigger, as though they had grown under his hands. Delaney also tells him that each time, his hands are bigger. He has measured himself, and it is true—his body is growing, almost as though he is reaching out for adulthood as fast as he can. Delaney has put her hands on his body, too—and it feels so much better than anything he could ever do to himself. Her hands are soft and loving.

His brother Joey tends to talk about sex when he is home, but crassly—"anal" this and "blow-job" that. It is kind of disgusting, Davey thinks. Touching and being touched by Delaney has been special, and beautiful, and all the time they have looked into each other's eyes. Not when they kiss—he knows you close your eyes for that, but when they have lain in the grass beyond the view of the stables, where he and Shy had once talked as friends. They have lain on earth that is part sand and part scrub and part weeds, but still heavenly, his flannel shirt off and cradling her head as he rises above her, and then her arms reaching up to stroke the skin of his chest and slide along his arms. And then down his long waist, and under his belt and down the back of his jeans, cupping his ass and pushing his hips down on hers . . .

Davey walks quickly into his house, running upstairs to masturbate. And then he hears—he thinks he hears—odd, sickly sounds, alternating between high-pitched pants and deep primordial groans.

"Oh . . ."

"Ahhhhh."

"Ohhh . . . ohhh . . ."

Davey stands at the top stair of the staircase, frozen. He moves one foot to the landing, which creaks loudly.

"Honey?" says his mother. "Is that you? What time is it?"

"Mommy?"

Crazed, Jude and the rebbe rush around the room, frantic to

alter the scene. The rebbe manages to put on his tzitzis, his boxer shorts, and hat. Jude can manage only her bathrobe.

"Are you OK, Mommy?" says Davey, opening her door.

His face changes from concern to horror when he sees a man there.

"*Who the hell is that?*" he screams, frightened. Davey stares at the man's long bare legs, his arms emerging from a fringed and yellowing undershirt with strings hanging off it.

"This is my, my personal spiritual advisor," says his mother, rattled to hear her gentlemanly son curse. "Didn't I—didn't I—tell you about him?" she stutters.

"No, as a matter of fact, you didn't. I didn't know you had 'spiritual' problems," he says sternly.

"Well, honey, I do. I was very sad and had lost all my faith in things."

"Permit me to make an introduction, I am Gipstein, Rebbe Malach Gipstein," says the man, stepping over to Davey and taking his hand. He shakes it briskly, then pats the boy on the back in a fatherly way.

"So I'll be leaving at this time," he continues, as though he were making a community announcement.

"Oh, yes, yes of course," Jude responds, just as loudly and formally.

"Let me just get you your yarmulke . . ."

"Don't forget the pants, dude! Mom, really, who is this guy?" says Davey.

"I'm actually a rabbi, David, a student of the Tor—"

"What did you say?"

"To—? The Five Books of—"

'No, quit it. My name. How'd you know my name?"

"What other name should a nice Jewish boy have," says the rebbe, appearing only slightly rattled, "but the name of a king?"

231

"And you look so familiar," Davey continues, but the rebbe puts on his thick glasses, and even his eyes are obscured.

"If you have seen one Chasid, my friend, and I say this with all the love a Yid can have for all the Yiddin, you have seen them all. The beards, the glasses, the socks, and the coat. In fact"—he waxes loquacious—"this is not even a beard—I saw a beard once that came all the way to the waist. Once, a rebbe said to me, 'where is your beard?' and of course, naturally, I showed him my beard, *nu*, what else is growing *mit* hair from my chin," he babbles, his Yiddish getting stronger, "and he says, '*You call that a beard?*'"

"Hang on—were you—are you Shy?"

"Why I should be shy? I am not ashamed, for the Lord our God is with me at all times, including, I hope, even now."

That was close, thinks Jude, as she shuts the door behind the rebbe personified by the world-famous talent Colm Eriksen. It was a nice performance, and the actor paused to touch the mezuzah in the traditional way, kissing his fingertips, then bringing them to up the brass-covered scroll.

"It really wasn't what it looked like," says Jude, abashed, to her son that night at dinner. She isn't lying—it *looked* like she had been in bed with a Chasid; *actually,* she had been in bed with the love of her life, a beautiful boy who'd been whisked off at fourteen to Australia.

Separating his vegetables from his potatoes, Davey says, "I'm not gonna judge you. Bodies are beautiful, and you only live once, but I really wouldn't do stuff like that in the bed you and Dad share, you know what I mean?"

"I do know what you mean," his mother answers, shamefaced.

"By the way," her son continues, spearing a pea on a tine, "I'm thinking of getting a tattoo."

Jude doesn't have the strength to challenge him, but simply asks, "Of what?"

"Just one word on my heart: 'Delaney.'"

The mother could caution her son that tattoos are permanent, and young love is not, but given the circumstances, she isn't so sure of anything, and probably has no business giving advice.

Plaisir d'Amour

Collum and Jude need privacy, so they begin to patronize the Teeter-Totter Inn. It's a horrible motel, near Teeterboro Airport, but it will do. Slam stayed there once when his plane had been grounded due to the weather. It was the only place with vacancies that night, and he'd complained about the seediness of it. That's fine for Jude, who wants only to be anonymous with her long-lost boy.

Something in her wants Collum to know that nothing matters but their love. Collum doesn't care where they are, as long as he has her, and Jude doesn't care either. She's not a suburban wife; she's a lover. So she doesn't need fancy sheets and a huge soaking tub. The toilet paper does not have to be folded in a special way, and the shower doesn't have to thunder like a South American waterfall. Love, she now knows, is the final luxury—and more than equal to all the others.

In theory, then, nothing in the world matters to her but the absolute rightness of this moment with her man. In practice, Jude recoils a bit the first time they open the door to their chamber. But she hides it; she's doing penance—to show Collum how far she's come from the days of her bourgeois childhood. She'll starve for him, freeze for him. She'll sit in an ugly room with a blinking overhead light, where you can hear airplanes taking off nearby.

"Shall I carry you inside?" says Collum. "Like my long-lost bride?"

"OK," she says, with a touch of sadness. Looking at the dreary curtains, she knows that this is not her husband or her bridegroom. Life is cruel in exactly this way. The décor is a stern reminder of limits and losses. She is already married, to someone who no longer needs her. This is only the long-lost lover of her compromised life. She had lost him long ago, and is now trying to grasp a molecule of happiness, somehow. And this is the room for it: a soiled cubicle near a second-rate airport.

Nonetheless, they enter the room as one.

The bed is sunken. It's covered with a stained comforter, which Collum tosses away onto the linoleum floor. The sheets underneath are purple and shiny in a sickly kind of way, like rotted meat. There's a large, square plaque near the headboard; it has a coin slot in it. The sign says, "Magic Fingers."

"Shall we?" says Collum.

"Shall we what?"

"Make some magic?"

Jude thinks he must be kidding, talking like that in a place like this. She hardly knows him and his tastes; she isn't sure. Odd that you can kiss like that when you hardly know anything about someone. When all you know is how much he needs you and how much you need him.

But then she realizes that he's being ironic about the "Magic Fingers." That makes it fun. They'll need two quarters to make it go. Jude fishes in her purse, finds one. Collum gives her the other. Just like that—they're a couple.

Once the second coin drops, the bed vibrates. It's palsied, raucous, incompetent, arrhythmic. It's silly. They sit together on the hectic bed. Its shaking makes Collum's cheeks shake; it's ridiculous.

She laughs.

"What?" he says, laughing too. Even his voice shakes, "whaaaaaaa"—like a billy goat's. "At least the sheets are soft, right?"

He rubs them a bit too hard and an orange spark shoots out. "*Ouch!*"

She bursts out laughing again as he sucks his finger. Jude tries to get a shock, too, and she does it, and he roars. From then on, Collum and Jude feel the weight of the world vanish. They make magic sparks together 'til the bed lies still. It's a crater, and they fall into the center, limbs tumbling over limbs.

Collum drags the mattress off the bed and flings it on the floor. He lies down on it; he pulls her down to him. Nowhere to fall, and no more surprises.

"We're old," he says, kissing her. All joking, disguises, and shocks have stopped, and his kisses feel different than they did at the beginning. There's something besides desire in them, a bit of rue. Unless he's being playful, Collum defaults to sad, Jude sees. And when he's sad, there's something wary in it.

She remembers the boy he was, broken and hurt by a ferocious father. Broken and hurt, and she hadn't been able to help. But she can help now, and she kisses him with all her love, with pity even, making promises she can't expect to keep—promises no one could keep. Her kisses say, "I'll never leave you." And, "there's no one else." And, "nothing will ever change."

Most of all, they try to say, "You'll never feel pain again. You've had enough pain." When she puts that thought into her kisses, she feels that kindness itself is what hurts him most.

"I dye my hair now," he says, pulling away, as though to stop this love stream. He's a restless boy now, sharing in show-and-tell.

"Have a look!" He leans up on his elbows, chuckling ruefully. "I don't mean this tar paint. The blond's fake, too. The Nordic blond I'm loved for, the one you see in all the pictures. Either way, I'm gray as a granny. Go on, have a look at the old mop."

She grabs a hank of his hair and peers at the roots. Yes, she could see the white. There was no black and there was no blond. No color at all. Gone. She was sad to see it, touched that he let her.

It wasn't only that it was white; it was thinning, too. Here and there, she finds spray on his scalp. Painted pores. She doesn't want to know this.

"I dye mine, too, Collum," she says reassuringly. It's a voice she's used with her sons. "Who doesn't, at our age?"

"OK, not sure about you, but I happen to be an Aussie male, and it's creepy. But I have to. I also wear a girdle," he advances. "On camera at least. Got a little tummy now, see? A little jam roll?"

He unzips his pants, and she is relieved that he's not wearing any spandex below. She does see a bit of whitened stomach, a soft roll of flesh. Collum pinches his fat so hard it turns white.

"It's lipo for me in the end, I suppose."

"Oh, come on," she says again, with a mother's kind voice. "We all gain a few pounds over the years. Everyone I know wears Squeezys," she adds, mentioning a popular brand among her generation. "They're not really girdles, they're foundation garments."

"Oh yes, luv, they are girdles!"

"No, they're black and sexy—"

"I've come as I am," he admonishes, playful. "But if YOU are smuggling a girdle into this room under the guise of Squeezys I will know of it, young lady—" he grabs her skirt and lifts it.

Jude is, in fact, wearing a "foundation garment." What an

idiot she is—she'd thought she'd pull it off in the bathroom. She's forgotten the game.

Both laugh as Collum wrestles her girdle down, falling silent when he succeeds, leaving her naked from the waist down. Jude lies very still, fully clothed on top (a cashmere V-neck, a pretty bra below). Her skirt is up, and Collum can see everything she tends to hide away. Light streams in from the motel window. Her lover can see her stomach, loosened from childbirth. He can see her legs, where they meet at her . . .

"What do you call this?" she said, drawing her knees up, tightening her thighs.

"What do you mean?"

"You know," she says, wishing more than anything to let him at it.

"I call it a cunt, of course. Now put your legs down for me."

Now he can see her cunt. And down he goes, so tenderly, so brilliantly, nuzzling her so that she disappears into a loving, spiral glory. And that is just the beginning of a day that disappears and never ends.

Collum and Jude had found a sanctuary in time, like the evening when God rested from his toil. There was nothing between or outside them, no secrecy, no rushing and no shame. No one would burst in and ask them questions, such as "who the hell" this man was. Collum was hers and she was his, before Joey or Davey, Slam and Gingerean.

In those primordial moments—so rare—Jude found a deep, collected sense of life; it washed over and warmed her. She was more than safe. Life held no danger, no misunderstanding. She was loved as she had always needed to be loved, and held as she had never been held. Collum was with her, and he seemed happy. Now, finally, he gave his Jude everything he had, all that he had saved for all those years. And now she knew how much he had to give.

They began meeting every day from two to five o'clock.

It was amazing that sex could be so heavenly even after the sixth, seventh, twentieth, thirtieth time. They were hungry, making up for lost years. They were vengeful, greedy, lusty, rude. Twice, three times in a row, and nothing but the same thing, over and over, as much as was needed to calm them down.

They were finally calm. They weren't so lonely anymore. They'd had their fill, they knew it and were stilled. Slowly, workaday thoughts crept in again. Jude wondered what kind of things Collum liked to do—besides this. She loved books (after all, she taught writing to high schoolers). Did he like books? Despite the small paunch, he seemed to have spent a lot of time in the gym. But she hated gyms. Did he like to take walks? Should they drive somewhere and take one? Did they both like strolling in the city, or would a nature hike be better?

Collum slept beside Jude as she began to puzzle their differences. They'd moved up to a better hotel, and then a really good one. But something was getting lost, even as the packaging of the toiletries was more and more gorgeous and the bathrobes more fluffy.

Even when everything smelled like sandalwood and felt like the emperor's own silk, Jude was falling away. Between bouts of increasingly tiring lovemaking, he snored the way Slam did. Maybe even louder, with sudden snorts that seemed almost rude, almost flatulently abrupt.

The air outside their lovers' nests was cooling. Collum was not a boy anymore; he was a man, and she knew very little about him. He muttered when he dozed, but Jude could neither understand his words nor guess what he was talking about. If he was practicing yet another dead language, she couldn't have cared less. When he awoke and reached for her, he hugged her in place, so she could not sleep comfortably. Judy was aware of the bones in his arm, his hard chest not a pillow but a stone.

Paradise was always temporary. In the end, man and woman were going to be evicted. He had to earn his living by the sweat of his brow, and she would bear children in labor and pain.

She and her husband had played those roles. He had been her first actual lover, the one to whom she'd lost her virginity. She had never thought of their lives as roles, never realized their passion would end. Slam was not like Collum, not tender and enclosing, but self-absorbed, virile, and mechanical. He knew exactly what to do, and did it powerfully well. It was he who had turned her into an eager lover, female to his male. First, they had done it many times a day.

Then every day.

Then several times a week.

Then once a week.

Then once a month.

Then on special occasions.

Then almost never. That was when the corset and heels had come into play. The cheerleader outfit. Viagra and the role of *bonne francaise*.

Then never, no matter what. Not birthdays or anniversaries. Nor when Slam came home from Italy after a long time away, and she had tried every last trick and lure she had. They were done in that department.

"Do you think that will happen to us, Collum?" she'd been bold enough to ask only a week before. "Do you think you'll ever want me to wear the proverbial corset and black stockings?"

"Take longer to get to you? Nah!"

But just after Columbus Day, Collum awakened from a snoreful doze. He smacked his lips, rubbed his eyes and said:

"You know, luv, I've been thinking about that merry widow—"

"Merry what?"

She was brushing her hair in the bathroom. Restoring it to the look she had when they entered the motel. Tied back in the barrette. The mother of teens, respectable and tame. That person was Jude, too. She was real and true, and Jude knew her.

"Merry widow. You know, you mentioned the sexy gear, the corsets and that sort of thing."

"Mm hmm?"

"You know how you complained that, ah, your husband didn't care? Well, I would care, a lot, ah, if you don't mind putting it on for me . . . sometime. D'ya still have it, baby? And the stilleto heels, you know?"

"Stilletos?" said Jude glumly, also noting the generic word "baby."

"Won't say no to that, me Sheila!"

"Then I won't say no, either," she said, too brightly, dejected to be hauling out her kit again. These items were no longer "proverbial." They were sadly all too real.

So she hauled them out and heaved them up. She rummaged through her closet to find the discarded ensemble. Jude was very sad as she donned her costume, tucking each breast into its confining cup, and hitching her garters. Was this both the first and last man whose breath she'd take away? For how long could she morph into a courtesan or pinup? How many tricks must she play to get the desired result? And did she still desire it?

Here it was. She felt the blasphemy in the very question—had she tired of him, too?

Stilettoes in the air, Jude began to notice—to fixate on—the broken red veins around Collum's nose, from that sun in Australia. She might be a middle-aged woman trying to be sexy in that phony, pinup way, but he was a middle-aged man who decided if and when she was. And she resented him.

Who is he? Why does he want her to play this role? Why on earth are they humping like this, as though it matters?

She is suddenly tired not just of him, but of thinking about any of this "love stuff." It confines her so that she wants to scream.

A growth spurt. Her boys often have them. They tend to hurt.

Escape from Paradise

J ude isn't being entirely fair. Ever since Collum asked her to
tart up a bit, she's been bitchy about whether he really loves
her. Of *course* he loves her! What else is he doing, dropping
out of the world (no movies, an angry producer) begging her over
and over again to be with him?

Does she have any idea how many people in the world adore
him? How many would change places with her? But he doesn't
want any of them. She is the only woman for him; she always will
be. Life doesn't give people too many retakes—yet here she is,
balking as she'd always done.

She'd betrayed him before, excuses or not. And here she is, dil-
lydallying. A man can only take so much. Even a man in love.

All Collum wants is for Judy to leave Plum Grove and "start
over" with him. But he is starting to suspect that Judy is never
going to run away from the comfy life she has, any more than
the first time. Not even to Tahiti, where he keeps a large house
running with the help of ten servants. His wife, Gingerean, had
known nothing about it; it was always his private refuge, his
dreaming place.

243

Collum had bought it when he'd made his first killing in the movie business. And even back then, decades ago, he had bought it with Judy in mind. He wasn't a kid anymore. He could make this happen. She was being a mule, and this part of her drove him mad.

"Let me call for my plane," he says, dragging on a cigarette as they lie together, spent again. "We could make our first lap anytime. To LA, maybe, then overseas. Bit by bit we'll leave 'em all behind."

"But I—I want to. I will, but I'm not ready to leave—just yet."

"Not ready? Where have I heard that one before? We're middle-aged now! How much bloody longer can we wait, Judy?"

"I can't just cut off all ties, Collum!"

Jude is thinking of her sons. How on earth could she take care of them all the way from Tahiti? Not that she has to tend to them daily, but they aren't fully fledged, and she cannot simply abandon them. And she does love teaching her writing course.

"Well, *I've* cut all ties, as I did the last time, as you might recall."

"I do recall," she says, remembering how he'd run to her home from that battle with his father.

"You don't believe I'm serious?"

"Of course I do," she says, appeasingly.

"Don't you condescend, snotty! This is my bleedin' life I've cut off."

"Did you just call me 'snotty'?" Name-calling was new.

"I did, and I'll do it again," he says, thrusting his jaw like the pugnacious kid he is. She actually never liked that part of him, especially now that she is getting a taste of it. He could be crude, and not in a way that was titillating. Quite the opposite, in fact. Crude and reductive in a way that ruined any spell.

"Well," she answers coolly. "From what I read, you were having a nervous breakdown anyway."

"I was having a what?"

"Nervous breakdown. I mean, you were losing it, Collum. Call it a mid-life crisis, the price of fame, I don't know. But you were fine for a very long time without me. So you can't blame me for everything bad that happens in your life. And the things that go on in your head."

"What things?"

"Collum, I'm just saying that I can't fix everything! I can't make all your pain go away!"

"You said you would."

"Did I? I was about fifteen years old at the time."

Collum feels his temper rise and knows things will go bad. Over the years, he has turned more and more into his father. He knows he has, but there is nothing he can do about it. The beatings and abuse have come back in his mind, and like Neil himself, Collum now fights unconquerable demons. They madden him. They want everything that is good in him to die. He is fighting and fighting for that good, but where does that fight ever get him?

With a threateningly calm voice, Collum asks Judy to repeat what she has said. About his supposed "breakdown."

"About your going nutso?" she says lightly.

He decides to laugh it off.

"Yeah, all right, I do go bonkers now and again. And who wouldn't?"

"I'm not the poster girl for normal myself," says Jude, suddenly seeing herself as she is, naked with a near-stranger, discussing Tahiti with a guy she hasn't seen for more than thirty years. And counting the ways they're both crazy.

"Nah," he says, collecting himself. "No, right. I know I'm abnormal. So are you. Love you for it." He takes a deep breath: "But—but just to clarify—you don't believe I've cut things off for *your* sake?"

"In part, yes," says Jude, trying to be honest (they have been so honest up to now; it seems a virtuous sign of love). "But I also think you're like me. Tired, a little washed-up. The fun ran out. The work was drying up. Tell the truth, Collum. You came to me only as a last resort."

His face turns red. Again, he collects himself.

"No, my dear," he says, with an exaggerated patience. "YOU came to me. When your marriage dried up. When you got a bit bored. Fishing through Facebook, if I recall. Poking at anything that seemed remotely likely."

"OK," she concedes frankly, "That's true. I was dejected and felt past it. But you leapt at the idea. I was a way out. Just like before—you needed to run away. Love becomes like a lifeboat, you know? It doesn't have to, but that's what it is sometimes. You bailed on your life and there I was.

"Collum. Admit it. You're the one who took it to this level. Hunted me down. Tried to make it real."

Collum listens to what she says. He considers it carefully.

"*Tried* to make it real," he repeats. "Is that what you said?"

"Well, it's real—I mean, look at us—but it's not the answer to all of life's big quandaries, now, is it? And I'm starting to wonder, is *anything* the answer to all of life's big quandaries?"

"You have never taken me seriously," he responds, each word rising in volume, "NEVER thought I was good enough. NEVER believed how much I loved you. I've hated you for that. Did I not say that I bought you a house in Tahiti? Long ago? When things were flush?"

"Stop shouting. This whole afternoon you've been totally rude to me."

"Hoity-toity. You think you're better than me. You're a bitch."

"OK, now you're being really—"

"DID I NOT SAY THAT I BOUGHT YOU A HOUSE IN TAHITI??"

She nods, silent. Yes, you said it, you lunatic. Just go there and lock yourself in. Stop screaming and stop hurting everything you touch.

"Thank you. And did I not I fall down the stinkin' bog for love of you?"

"Collum, I can't be the reason—"

"I'M TALKING!!!" he roars. Jude has never seen Collum this way. Then again, she'd never seen his last fight with his father, that moment of fury and payback for a lifetime of hurt. He was out of his mind. A lost boy, kicked out, exiled out of his own very sanity.

For a moment she feels pity for him, and this makes her try again. She will apologize if it helps. If it gives him some relief. If it stops this scene and turns it around.

"Sorry, my darling. I'm so sorry. Shhhh . . ."

Jude puts her hand on his; he flings it off with a broad, harsh gesture.

"I have come here a broken man. Yes. I drank. Yes, I cursed and rowed. Yes. I said awful things about certain peoples of the world, the blacks and the kikes and the bitches and the benders. But who do you think started all that pain inside of me? Huh?"

"I always thought it was your father, Collum."

"IT WAS YOU, JUDY! YOU! YOU! YOU!!"

"But—"

"HE never deliberately lied! You did! Bloody snob like your dad! You all thought you were too good for me; you had second thoughts about the guttersnipe, didn't you! The riffraff! The little snot-nose!

"DAD never turned on me! You did! That man was true to his

247

heart and soul!! I gave you MY heart, not once, but twice now. Twice I sniveled and begged for your mercy. But it was never enough, not then and not now. *I* was never enough for the likes of you. I TOLD you I've cut off everyone and everything, and you don't—you don't—it means NOTHING to you!"

"No, I believe you, Collum," Jude stutters. "Of course I do. It means—"

"YOU, little Jappy Princess Kikerton, YOU couldn't possibly understand the PAIN I'm in and the lengths to which I'll go to stop it. I've cut myself off. I'm bleeding from loneliness. I'm a stump of whatever I was. But that's not enough for you, is it? But guess what? I'm as good as any one of your perfect rabbis, clean as that Rebbe Gipstein you were so fond of, clean as any Jew, your CHOSEN cocks, your KOSHER dills."

"You're being really weird."

"That's not weird. I'll show you weird."

She hopes he is joking.

"Please don't."

"I will. I'd be happy to cut something else off, if you know what I mean!"

She doesn't.

"Hey, Collum—I love you and you're—you're overreacting." Even to herself, her words sound dull and dry. This poor man's pain goes well beyond anything Jude has ever seen, even her father's anguish at its worst.

Collum crawls over to his bag and pulls out a gleaming new double-bladed knife, which he unsheaths from a black leather case.

"What's that?" Jude says, beginning to panic. No one knows where she is. She could actually die here.

"Don't you recognize it? Your boys had brisses, didn't they, Davey? The other one, I forget his name, what was it? Moishe??"

"Joseph," she says quietly.

"Like my Lord's own dad, but I don't advise him taking the paternity test, cuz you never know what a lady's up to. Anyway. What was I saying. Ah yes, the blessed bris! Eight days to look like a sloppy goy, and then—zip! CLEAN!"

"*Shall* I cut it off for you?" he says. "Would that even *satisfy* you, you greedy little bitch?"

"Your—cut off your foreskin, you mean?"

"Shall I JEW myself for you, so that you'll love me all the way? Shall I 'whither thou goest,' or are you STILL NOT READY TO GO?"

"Collum, please! You're acting crazy—"

"I learned *Yiddish* for you," he peals, voice cracking, "and Hebrew; that's a damned hard language! I learned the Torah, I immersed myself in a *mikveh*—did you think that experience was nothing to me?

"I *wanted* to be like you and your dad and your people, to be baptized new and Jewish like David, the sweet singer of Israel, like your own lucky boy . . ."

He pauses. "This knife is called an *izmel*, by the way—"

"A what?"

"IZ-*MEL*! What's the difference what it's called anyway? It's time for action now, for the car chase! Time for the bang-bang and the cut-cut-cut! OK? I knew I wasn't good enough for you before, was I?"

"But I swear to God I will be now!"

"Collum, you were always good enough, that wasn't the—"

"Was I? Was I really? I was scum in my house, and scum in yours, that's what I know. But I want you to love me—so I'll cut it if it makes you happy, if it makes you accept me for once in this hellish life of mine."

"Where did you even get that knife? It looks dangerous!"

"It *is* dangerous. It's the big one they use for adults, like me. But I'll bleed for you. Because love, as we Christians know, is bloody bloody slaughter on the cross. I've done it before. I know what it feels like to shed my blood for the love of someone . . ."

"I never wanted that," says Jude quietly, remembering how his father had beaten him for her sake, on the last night of their youth.

"No pound of flesh for you today then, my love?"

Jude stands up abruptly. It is time to leave. She turns away from Collum, facing the door to their room, and takes a quick breath of resolve.

Even now, it is hard to go. Her life has long been humdrum, and here it is: the passion incarnate. She doesn't want it.

"Would you rather I use this for other holy quests?" he says to her back. "Like finding the truth in a false witness? Like rooting out the evil in my midst?"

"In your what? Collum—what are you doing!"

He's grabbed her with one strong arm, whipping her around to face him. With his free hand, Collum holds the circumcision blade against Jude's throat. Their bodies are close; their faces truly close, as though they will kiss. And they could. They both think of it; each feels the other think of it. It really could go either way, even then. They could try to make love again. A new beginning, after the storm. With forgiveness.

Instead, Collum lifts the knife and slices the air with it. He is careless with it. He thinks about killing his tormenting woman. He can't think of anything else but kissing or killing her.

"WHY??" he begs, sobbing, as though bottomless pain has an answer. "WHY DID YOU BETRAY ME, LITTLE JUDAS?"

"God, please be careful," she pleads. He is accidentally cutting his own hand with the double blade. Little rivulets of blood race down his wrists, his arms. "You're hurting yourself!"

"Nothing could hurt me like you hurt me that night."

Collum's voice has gone almost inaudible, but his grip is still there. His lips are pressed thin, and he pinches his eyes closed, tasting the bitter resentment in everything. She could have saved him. She could have saved him, and everything would have been different. He wouldn't be feeling this pain.

Her voice trembling, Jude tries to explain why she'd failed to run away with him so long ago. Her father had suffered a stroke that night. She had felt awful for contributing to it—going against his rules and falling in love with a forbidden boy. The one thing her father had asked her not to do. He was never the same after that. It took almost a year for him to walk and talk again— and he had never managed to walk or talk well. Less than five years later, he had had another massive stroke and died.

Collum listens intently. His breath becomes slower. He sighs, as though with relief. "And you thought you didn't need to tell me about any of this?"

"What do you mean? I *did* tell you! I told you every single detail! First I tried to call you, and your father answered, so I hung up. So then I wrote you a letter—a really long letter—and stuck it under your door! Your mother was in the house. She would have picked it up. Didn't you get it?"

"You know there was never any letter."

"It's the truth, Collum."

"What are you saying? Mum *would* have given it to me. She liked you."

"Maybe she tore it up. Maybe she didn't want to hurt you any more. Or maybe she did it to keep *your* dad from having a stroke."

Collum looks at Judy, softening. He does believe that. His mother Betty always protected Neil, the master of her world. They were planning to move to Australia; this letter might have stood in the way of her husband's wishes. Collum, she must have reasoned, did not need to hear from this girl anymore. What good would words have done him? He was soon flying to the other end of the world, and the fewer ties, the better, Betty would have thought. No need to stir up any more trouble. The world had enough trouble as it was. Let it lie.

Collum drops the knife and holds Jude to his chest.

"You're squeezing me so hard—"

"Oh, my love," he says, gripping her even more closely, "I never wanted to scare you. I'd never have harmed a hair on your head, don't you know that? I just felt so hurt. I believe you now. Please, Judy. I've come all this way for you. Come with me now. I've left my wife and my kids and even my career—"

Collum leans his head on Jude's shoulder. It feels heavy, like a bowling ball. Collum has acted insane, and the thought of him now makes Jude feel ill. Love is supposed to be unconditional, eternal, but she feels it alter in this very room. Now that she feels safe, she feels disgusted, an awful mix of pity and contempt.

The boy she'd loved had had the best and purest soul. A brave and loving boy, looking up at her through blackened eyes, through tears. But time has passed. It is too late. He is pathetic now; he seems as sick as his father had been. And now his tormented brain is on top of her, a dead weight she could never manage to lift. No one could. Jude thinks of the harsh word "skull," the end-point of all this passion. There is pain in the world; there is pain in some people's hearts that will never be salved on this earth. His father's. Her father's. Sometimes her own. But some people's pain becomes harsh and contagious and deadly.

"Where would we go?" she says, pulling away as though from a weaving tramp on the street. "The NYU dorms? To that cousin of mine who now commutes from Scarsdale?"

"I told you where. *Ta-heee-teeee!*"

He is making that dreamy place sound repulsive. That is the

oddest phenomenon, she thinks. How fast he's fading away, growing smaller. The last thing she wants is him.

"Why not the moon, huh? All we need is a space helmet and those special silver boots, right?" Jude is cruel because she is sad and disappointed. The Collum she knew has gone mad and dropped her. He thinks he is still clutching her, but he's already dropped her down to hell.

"*Judy.* You're the crazy one now! I actually have a house there. Privacy. My own island, for Christ's sake!"

"Yes, *I'm* crazy, Collum. You're just totally sane."

"That house is real as we are."

"But *we're* not real. This isn't me, anyway. Not right now. I don't feel normal at all. I'm feeling like I'm in some awful horror movie."

She hears herself say words that would destroy her, coming from him. She feels like a murderer—she needs no knife—but the truth is the truth.

"What happened to the sweet girl who took me in? What happened to your promise not to leave me?" he pleads, voice cracking.

"You always said—you made me believe you'd love me forever," he sobs, dropping down to his knees. Jude feels sorry for Collum. She feels pity for him and his dreams, and for herself and her own dreams.

Both of them fall silent. How beautifully stupid they once were, thinks Jude, to ever have believed that there was a "village" or a dorm, or even a South Sea island, where young and total love could last forever.

Still, she hesitates. She had loved Collum once, and a part of her still loves the deathless boy inside him. Maybe the love isn't gone—maybe it has been stunned for a moment, traumatized, and will rally again. She doesn't want it to be gone.

But what about his temper? Will that rally again? That boy had attacked his own father—there was no need to break his bones. And just now, Collum has held a blade to her throat. Does she want a life with this volatile man—a man who rages exactly as Neil Whitsun had, so many years ago? A man who, she knows, has left a family, a wife and children, down under—and could forget them there?

She could never forget her boys. They seem so old in her mind when she compares them to the cuddly children they once were. But in comparison to adults, they are still not fully formed. They need her, and love her as she loves them. Even the cavalier Joey had sent her a card at the start of term, saying he was fine. He did it because she had asked him to, to reassure her that she knows something, however little, about him. That he is fine, and that he will always tell her he is fine.

And what about Slam? Is he to become the male equivalent of Gingerean, valued only when useful, a bull that is milked for seed and then slaughtered? A racehorse that won't or can't race—and so, to the glue factory? Davey had told her about those poor horses at Angel-Fire, how close they had come to being sold by the pound for meat. Is that what we do with people who don't do precisely what we want?

"*Lust for me, Slam?*"

"*I care about you, but I don't lust for you. I can't force it.*"

"*Then die, you shit!*"

Is it that simple? For many married couples, it is. Divorce is an option. But she wants to go home now, she wants what is ordinary and customary. She wants this love racket to stop.

"Collum," she says, her voice almost prim. "Hear me out."

His deep blue eyes are full of tears, and he raises them to her. There is the gray, and there the flecks of orange, and none of it matters anymore.

"You're saying NO. That's what I hear. So I don't need your clever Talmudisms that make you right when you're so clearly, horribly WRONG!"

Collum's entire face, Jude notices, is as red as his nose veins. Especially when he screams at her.

"Talmudisms? Not that I'm proud of it, but unlike you, Rebbe Gipstein, I've never studied Talmud in my life! And what are you trying to imply with that particular word?"

He rises to her bait:

"That you're a wily Shylock, that's all. Worse. I actually offered you a pound of flesh, but it wasn't enough, was it?"

"You're right. I'm worse than Shylock. And I guess I'm personally responsible for all the world's wars," she adds, referring to a Neil Whitsun pamphlet. "Is that what you really think?"

"My dad *never* lied to me like you did," he repeats. "I won't waste my life on you. You're not worth it. This could have been epic! Something I know something about!"

He does; as Colm Eriksen, he has produced and starred in epics about the Basques, the ancient Aryans, and the Incas, each in the respective, dying tongue.

"But instead of an epic—instead of a story that will never die out—"

Collum bends down and reclaims his circumcision knife with a swoop. His words fly, spraying the air with furious spittle:

"GET OUT NOW! Run! That's all you know how to do anyway, you wandering—"

Jude knows he will say "Jew." She waits for her father's prophecy to come true, full force.

Instead Collum concludes with an epic bellow: "CUNT!!!"

Without a word, Jude gathers her things and walks out.

Now Collum throws himself on the bed, still warm from their bodies. He begins to stab at the mattress, pounding like a lover and a killer. He slices it down the middle, top to bottom. Tufts of batting fly in the air, a spark flies, and a little spring sproings. He stops.

The knife stays upright now, angry and unappeased. Collum stares at it as he opens the bottle of champagne he has brought, having anticipated that his Judy would say yes to him that night. They would have toasted their new lives together. She would have been everything to him. He would have worshipped her forever, with all his passion and all that is holy. He would have kept his oldest promises, and she would have kept hers.

Instead, he pops the cork and drinks the bubbly straight from the bottle. He drinks it all, then stumbles outside to his car.

You Can Touch This

Face on a beer mat, Collum sits at a bar, not far from where Jude S. Ewington still lives, safe and sound with her husband. Eating her cake of domesticity.

Ada sidles over again. She is there most nights.

"Aw, get lost, won't you, darling?" He carelessly smacks her face backhand, his fingers smearing with red lipstick. It looks like blood but smells like perfume. That's what love is, he thinks.

A part of Collum remembers this pub slag, how she'd wanted him before. The leotard, the heels, that whiny accent. *Aw keh.* She still finds him OK, even with the offhand blow she's just received. Come as you are, and he is coming drunk and angry. This time, though, he'll let her take him wherever she wants. This time, he has no particular plans, other than to kill himself slowly with drink and cigarettes. Which never seem to kill him, anyway.

"I live so close, now you will see," she says, efficiently spinning her steering wheel to and fro. Collum sits next to her in the tiny car, heavy as a package. Close or far, I'm coming with you, he thinks. And you—my bar-bag, my marzipan pig head—you'll be the first one I fuck after HER. Let's rub her out all night long.

257

Ada's lips are a deep, pinky red. He must have mentioned them, because she is explaining that the color is called "cherries in the snow." Movie stars wear this shade, she tells him with a wink of her spider mascara. Good luck to them, he thinks. I was a movie star myself. And then they arrive at her one-room flat.

How on earth did he get here, he wonders. For now he is sitting on a little stained sofa, and Ada is sitting at a baby grand that dominates the small space. Her hands are hoisted in the air, ready to go. She smiles confidingly.

"I will play theme from 'Mo Croi'—most wonderful movie you ever make, even with the subtitles for the Gaelic; I enjoyed it so much. Genius."

Ada plays with impressive hand motions, twisting her wrists to give karate chops to the piano, ending with both arms again held aloft, fingers curled like claws. The vibrations die out in the air, into blessed silence.

"Stand up; I will open sofa bed now," she says. Once she unfurls the flat surface he dives downward. Then, using similar Asian-combat hand motions, Ada gives Collum a massage, meant as foreplay. Annoyingly, he falls asleep, still murmuring about the last cherry blossom, now fallen in the dirt.

"You have your red cherry right here, stupit!" she spits out, her evening almost ruined. Her lips still hurt from the smack he'd given her.

Early the next morning, while Collum sleeps deeply, Ada calls the town caterer from the kitchen-wall phone.

"You'll never believe who I've got in my home, Heidi-Deidi."

Ada saves up to order Heidi-food on Sunday mornings, when she's often entertained a male guest or two. Despite the expense, she usually orders goat-butter scone-cakes and freshly squeezed "clumpies" (better than smoothies) with frothed and filtered ice.

"Think movie star. Big."

"Tom Hanks?"

"Eww."

"Tom Cruise."

"Don't insult me."

"Mel Gibson."

"Are you completely deranged?"

"Well, *I* was once obsessed with him. Probably still am. Who, then?"

"Colm Eriksen! The Viking Marauder!"

"Can I come and meet him? I'll give you three free mini jam-jars and my morning potage in a ramekin!"

"Yeah, OK. But don't flirt. You are married, remember."

"If you say so."

Heidi comes over as soon as she can, making sure that each part of the order is perfect. She clambers up the stairs of the condo development, so excited she nearly breaks an ankle. She is wearing four-inch platforms so that Colm Eriksen will know that she gladly suffers for beauty (and its sometime payoff, love). It takes guts to run in four-inch platforms.

As soon as the door opens, she sees him, rising up from Ada's open sofa bed. And he sees her, laden with food that smells wonderful.

"Breakfast," says Heidi, sailing in. "All fresh and home-made."

Ignoring Ada, she sits down next to the superstar and opens her bags. "See?" she says, flourishing a huge and savory muffin.

"I didn't order no sea-salt muffins and I'm not paying for no salty muffins," Ada grumbles, hand on hip.

"No, I'm throwing this one in for a treat. Here's your scone-cake," she adds, practically throwing it at Ada.

259

Collum chews his muffin gratefully. "You made this?" he says, looking up as he eats. "It tastes so familiar."

"It's got Marmite, kind of like your Vegemite," she says. She'd googled him and learned the famous story of how he'd met his wife, Gingerean. It had taken nearly an hour to find a place that sold the yeasty spread. She knew it would taste like home to him, not just Gingerean but the land down under.

"You're actually a goddess," he says, chewing. Heidi notices that he is fully dressed under the sheets, and smiles.

"It's nothing," she says. "I do this every single day."

"And now you can go," says Ada, rattled by the scene Heidi is creating.

"Not just yet—I want him to try my kiwi clumpy. It's got an incredible mouth feel," she adds, to Collum. She takes a tall flask out of the bag and brings it up to his lips. He tastes it.

"Good?"

"Mmm," he says, drinking as though at her breast.

"*Now is time!*" screams Ada, grabbing Heidi by the hand and pulling her off her opened sofa bed. "Really, this is not your boudoir!"

"Well, *you* are certainly off my client list," says Heidi, stomping to the door, then clambering down the staircase to the driveway. Collum, still clutching his muffin and his flask of clumpy, leaps out of bed and follows.

"No, *you* stay, my darling! I have better treats for you!" Ada shouts.

"I don't think you do," he says, racing down the stairs.

Heidi stands in the driveway, utterly shaken. Her light hair flutters in the breeze. Her manicured fingers grip the handle of her car. "I can't—I can't even open it."

"You just need the key, my pet."

"Oh yes, that's it. My hands are shaking. My legs are shaking.

And they never shake. I'd like you to know that I'm a competent, confident woman."

"I can see you're very sensitive, too. May I?" he adds, reaching into her neat white leather purse. He finds the key and plunges it into the door.

"I ran after you, you know?" he says, swinging it open it for Heidi. "Your food is—is so full of love. It satiates me."

She knows the significance of those words. Nothing ever fills her. But perhaps she can fill him.

"I can fill you up, too," he adds, getting in on the passenger side. It is as though he's read her mind. His generous words carry no trace of lewdness. "I can fill you like you've never been filled before. It's a question of your wanting to take me in all the way, with nary a flinch. Can you manage?"

Heidi stares at the road, her hands sweating more than they usually do.

"Drive away a few blocks and let's park somewhere. I don't want that loon to come after us," he says, turning around to see if Ada is chasing him. Fans sometimes did, particularly when he'd gotten too close to them for an hour or so.

"There's a little sports field near the tennis courts, is that OK?" she asks.

He nods. "And—the penny's dropped—you're the one who must have baked the magical oatcakes, too."

"You ate the—but did you know that they were horse food?"

"Of course I knew. And Clemmy and I often shared one."

"Clemmy?"

"Only the best gelding in the world. Seventeen hands high and a heart as big as a planet. Never been so close to the spirit of God. I held it in my mouth and he bit off the other end. Never seen a tamer beast."

Heidi is pensive.

"So you were Shy? The one my daughter thought was an odd-ball?"

"Oh," he says, laughing out loud for the first time in a long time. He is proud of his talent for changing from one persona to the next, all of them strange and new.

"Yes, I am quite an oddball, in and out of disguises."

"You were after Jude Ewington?"

"Operative word being 'was,'" he says, stiffening. "Glad to be quit of all that. Dead end, you could say."

"My daughter figured it all out. Wrangler *and* rabbi—impressive."

"She'll be all right, that one."

"Who? Jude?"

"No. Don't want *her* to be all right. Want her to suffer, want her to die suffering and begging for relief that never comes."

"Hmmmm. We're dear friends, but I never liked her all that much either. So who do you mean—Ada?"

"Ada the loon? *There's* a gang bang. Every night a different—"

"Then who?"

"Your daughter, Delaney. She'll be totally all right, you mark my words."

"I wonder," says Heidi, putting her car into park and exhaling the weight of the world. Marriage and motherhood in particular.

"She's so, so difficult," she says, an air of defeat in her voice. "So complicated. Lots of edges. She hurts me all the time."

"I've raised a pack of kids, seen the ups and downs. I know your girl. She's trouble right now, but she's a good'un. She's in love with that kid of Judy's—you know, David? And anyone who gets that boy's a lucky one. I'm thinking they should run away together. Wish I'd done that as a lad, but the fates were against me, I guess. But they fit very well, and it's a blessing when that actually happens."

"What can you possibly mean? That kid is a sophomore and

my daughter's a junior! She's got SAT practice, for God's sake!"

"With him, things'll always go slow. He's a gentle lad with a solid heart. I had a strong young heart myself once, but crikey, it feels bruised now."

"Mine does, too," Heidi admits. "We grow old, we grow scared, we make compromises. We grow long hair—if we're aging men, I mean."

"Not sure I follow, darling."

"Well, I didn't either, but you don't need to follow. I'll—I'll follow you." He seems strong to her, and maybe, with her, he is.

"You will? Bless your foolish heart, the only kind worth having."

"Where are you headed now? Malibu?" Heidi thinks of herself in a convertible Bentley, windblown by the sea. Periwinkle blue with cream interior?

"No, been thinking I'd leave all that dross behind and live out in the South Seas. Once bought an island in Tahiti, you know; never used it. Wasn't as expensive as you'd think. Everyone would do it if they could afford the access and the upkeep. You know who I am, right? By now, you must see it all."

"Well naturally, I can see that you're Colm Eriksen, the movie star."

"Full marks to you! But I'm done with that now. Done with all the waiting and the compromises. On all fronts. Time to raise anchor."

"But what happened with you and Jude? You found her, right? And then it didn't work out?"

"Finders keepers, losers weepers. She's changed, what else can I say?"

"I know, *quelle* hag. Cellulite alert. And you should see her kitchen—salmonella central."

"Yeah, well, on that score, my Gingerean was a good one for

cooking and cleaning. But wouldn't you know she turned on me as well."

"My husband changed, too. I hate people flipping on you. Where do they get the nerve? Life's hard enough with its awful tragedies, crashes and earthquakes and barrenness, cancer . . ."

"Who's Baroness Cancer? One of your posh gourmet clients?" he teases.

"No, I mean when someone says they'll take care of you and be your best friend forever, they should mean it. Right?"

"Yes! My point exactly! I mean I was an actor, it was legit to change. I was playing parts. But my real heart's still in here, and I never gave it away to anyone. Not even my wife, not all of it. I saved that for Judy. Just her, if you can believe it. But she really didn't take it. Ever. There's still a hole in it, you see, and no one to fill it."

"As *you* may see," Heidi retorts, "I have the exact same problem."

"Judy betrayed *you*?"

"The hole in the heart, silly."

Heidi realizes that Collum is trying to amuse her. It is rare that she laughs, and Heidi feels freed by the very movement of her chest and the funny bursts of her breath.

"I think you've got the sadness, too, luv," says Collum.

"No one else can tell."

"Yeah, we hide it well. But there is such pain—"

"And when someone turns on you—just, you know, breaks their promise to take care of you—"

"I won't do that to you. I'm not like Judy or the man who hurt you. I'm fair dinkum conscientious."

"Conscientious is my middle name. I mean, it's actually Dorcas, but—"

"Oh, darling girl," he says, laughing softly at her first attempt at humor. Collum feels warm with new hope; he wants only to take this woman in his arms.

"*Shall* we try?" he says tenderly. "All one can do is try, I always say. Just kindly show up for the main events, you know? Just climb onboard and take the journey, is all I'm asking."

"I can do that," she says. "If you can lead the way."

Valihona, Valhalla

Heidi gazes, as though for the last time, at her six-burner stove. Just last night, she had cooked pounds of Slam's special tube noodles, step number one of a cold pasta salad that would include succotash and mesquite-smoked trout.

"Can I still bake and cook out there?"

"You want to do your catering out in the middle of . . . ?"

"Just for you. Can I cater just to you?" (She likes the pun.)

"Of course you can," says Collum.

With a stab of sadness, he remembers the early days with Gingerean, when all she'd wanted to do was please him. He remembers her kind, eager expression, and how she'd showed him their first child. And Heidi remembers her husband, Daniel, when they had first met, and for years and years after, how she had been able to count on him for anything.

She finds these thoughts troubling, and shakes them off with a deft overview of her glowing future.

"I mean, do they have all the implements out there in—out in the South Seas? I want to do a good job. I want to heal the pain in your heart."

"Sweet of you to try. But to be honest, it's usually drink that does the trick."

"Nonsense. You don't need that anymore. Chocolate's going to be a big part of it. Full of endorphins. I'll stock up on Valrhona."

"Who's she?"

Heidi knows he is joking again and laughs. Her teeth, he notices, are pretty, with the luster of pearls.

"Oh, my girl. My girl," he murmurs, sinking his head into her halo of blond hair and sliding out the grosgrain band that holds it. It springs free like a Slinky and he noses it and kisses it. And then he kisses her mouth.

For a painful, undefended second, Collum compares Heidi's lips to Judy's (Heidi's are thinner and smell of buttered chives). But he pushes all comparisons out of his mind. He will pine no longer. He will settle now. That is the key to contentment. Settling. The old horses at the riding camp know that gentle surrender. Clemmy could show you all the grace of heaven in one long sigh.

"My girl." Heidi likes the sound of that. That she is "his," and that she can still be a girl and start over again. Jude has lost and she has won it all.

Love Is Not a Pogrom

The Kunst home is spinning off its axis. Heidi is gone—her best pots, knives, and spice racks are gone. Even her custom spatula. And Dante has cut his hair short and taken out both his earrings, which is almost as unsettling.

"Our families have gone insane, Delaney," says Davey, who'd told her about his own mother's weird rabbi friend.

"Do you know what that means?" says Delaney, as they lie sprawled on the bed in her immaculate room. "It means we are finally free! I wrote about this in a story, but never dreamed how soon it would actually come true."

"What do you mean, 'free'?"

"We don't have to meet anyone's expectations! We can start living our real, authentic lives!"

"What would that mean in practice?" he says, pulling her shirt up and trying to undo her bra.

"It means I can wear latex! I can get a nose chain! A tattooed ankle bracelet! I can do anything I want to!"

Delaney jumps up and paces her room excitedly. She undoes the curtain ties and throws them across the room. The curtains, released, sway together, obscuring what little light is left of that day. A row of handmade dolls with elaborate ethnic clothes and bisque faces arrayed on her dresser follow her every move, wondering how she dares defy the spirit of this house. It was Heidi who had built this home, selecting even them, her daughter's dolls, one by one. She had placed them on stands (alphabetical by country), had them dusted every other day.

Delaney now swipes at them with a large arm movement, causing Miss Spain and Miss Sweden to topple over. The rest of the dolls tilt and fall. It is a porcelain war, and petticoats fly.

"Delaney—don't make a mess out of the situation. Chill out. You must be upset—I mean, no one even knows where your mom went."

"I bet she went somewhere with Shy. I mean, he's gone, too, right?"

"I don't know," says Davey, who still has questions about that rabbi who knew so much about him. "And what about her catering business? Who's going to take care of all those clients?"

"Well, here's the funny thing, Davey. Mom left a bunch of her recipes, so I could just take over like that, if I wanted to. I could use them, I could market them, I could turn them into a real book that sold a million copies."

"Never saw it in her, I must say."

"Well, people change, right? I mean, my dad changed. It was her turn, I guess. And now it's mine, too. And yours."

"I'm hungry," says Davey. "Wanna go to my house for dinner? My mom is making my favorite—turkey burgers, fries, and peas."

"Sure," says Delaney. "Thank God I can eat normal food for a change."

Dinner is different that night at the Ewington table. For the first time, Davey mixes his peas and his fries, sipping water between bites of his food.

His mother stares at him in disbelief.

"I know what you're thinking, Ms. Ewington," says Delaney. "You're wondering whether Davey and I have 'done it,' but we haven't, not yet, but we want to and we're going to and nothing can stop us."

"Actually, that wasn't what I was thinking at all."

"What were you thinking?"

"Never mind. Don't you think Davey might be a little young?" She does not mean only that he is young, but that he is young for his age. Davey blushes all the way to the collar of his red-and-white rugby shirt.

"Oh, come on," says Delaney. "We're totally committed to each other. Surely you're no prude?" Delaney knows that many of her classmates in the creative writing class have written in great detail about their sex lives. Ms. Ewington has seen it all, she is sure.

"Plus," she continues eagerly, "you're my role model, did you know that? You have kids, and you teach, but you're even cool enough to have this thing with some crazy rabbi, which is beyond—"

"Davey, that was extremely private! Does the whole town know?"

"Delaney's not the whole town. She may have written about it in her online journal, but that's it."

"I did write about it extensively. I've often imagined your private life, Ms. E. Since I met you, I've wondered how a woman with your passions experienced the total loss of youth and beauty. I saw how you channeled those frustrations into being a gossipy and somewhat malicious wife who told on me to my mother— that's OK, I forgive you. But I knew that this life you led would not be enough for you. Your losses came from the soul, and a little fun making mommy-wars in the suburbs was not going to do it."

Jude is still mulling over the words "total loss of youth and beauty."

"It won't be so hard for me to get old," Delaney continues, "I'm not that pretty even now, but Davey showed me pictures of you from long, long ago, and you were drop-dead gorgeous. So how do you deal, I wondered."

"Well, I—"

"No, don't explain. I know the answer now," says the young girl. "You found an outlet for your deepest desires—and kept your female soul alive. Not to mention your sacred pubic flower. I'm just beginning that journey, and I can't tell you how inspiring you are."

"Well, thanks."

"You're welcome. May I ask you for your opinion, though?"

"Sure."

"As you know, Davey and I are in love. My mom is apparently gone-zo, and my dad's been orbiting earth for almost a year. It's a good thing we have money. My mother's family, the Dorcases? Loaded. She only made food for a pastime, you know? To keep herself from going crazy. She certainly did not want to sit around all the time with my father.

"But I want to be around Davey all the time. And I don't mean treated platonically, like so many of you middle-aged women seem to live. *Our* sex life is progressing really well. Davey is ready to be my mate in every sense of the word. So it might also be good timing for Davey and me to get our own little place somewhere. Don't worry about the money; I can pay. And Davey can make some extra at the ranch on weekends, if he wants to chip in on the utilities, right?"

"You mean a place here, nearby?"

"Anywhere. We'd still go to school, of course. But I'm just so sick of my perfect room and those creepy dolls I could never play

271

with and the idiotic outfits that hang in my closet on padded pink hangers. I mean, if I had my own place, I'd paint the walls a kind of indigo—what do you think, Davey?"

"Indigo—it's definitely a nice color," he replies. Delaney is going so fast, he thinks. He is only just beginning to enjoy the accidental taste of ketchup on his peas. Does he have to pack up all his things, too? Would he have to share a bathroom with her? He would hate that.

Jude says kindly to Delaney, "I don't want to be too bossy, like you think your mother was. But I do have one thing to say, with all my old-lady wisdom:

"*The time for running is over.*"

Davey and Delaney stare at her, he with relief, and she with the willingness to learn something new.

"Love doesn't come like a thief in the night," Jude continues. "A *pogrom* comes like a thief in the night." The lesson went quickly and well from there.

Delaney says: "What's a pogrom?"

Jude says: "Davey, tell her. Show her you know a little something."

Davey says: "*Pogrom?*"

Jude: "You know, when the people in the villages—"

Delaney: "The people? In the villages?"

Davey and Delaney giggle together. It sounds like Frankenstein and the mob with pitchforks.

Jude: "It's not a joke. There is real cruelty in this world."

Delaney: "And this is relevant, because . . . ?"

Davey: "Not sure. Mom?"

Jude: "This is relevant, because, as I am trying to say, love is not terroristic, and it does *not* come like a pogrom in the night and make you choose YES or NO and then make you run wildly amok. It is a kind of softer thing, and you feel it over time and you relax."

She isn't sure about the kids, but Jude herself is absorbing something new. "West, east, north, south. Over, under, inside, around—everywhere you go, it's the same thing, *see*, Davey?"

He can't, not really, but then again, he is very young.

Jude thinks back to her own blind youth. Could it ever have worked with Collum? Maybe, she thinks sadly. Maybe he'd have grown up working as an actor in the New York theater. Not so famous that he'd lost all idea of who he was. So much pain would have been avoided. Hers, his, Gingerean's, the children he abandoned. But that is not what had happened.

Delaney had thought that to be in love was to run and travel and move—the cowboy way that Shy had embodied. The way that Davey's restless ballads had described:

"Journeyin' nights in the flickerin' lights."
"Leavin' on a fast train, far far away."
"Lonely highway, skies so gray"—and so on.

But maybe, Ms. Ewington is saying, the true sign of love is not running. Maybe it is to stay where you are.

"Then why did my mother run?" Delaney asks her, after the baked apples are served. "Was she nuts or something?"

"I fear you're right," says Jude. "When a woman cannot stop cleaning and cooking and washing and wearing the outfits and the very uncomfortable heels, she may well be nuts, or something.

"At least your father, for all his hair issues, is a fine man and stayed put. When you come home tonight, you will find him waiting for you. He called me when I was in the kitchen, and wondered where you were."

"Really?" says Delaney. She sounds reassured.

Step by Step and Shlep by Shlep

As for Slam, the news of Heidi's flight with Collum came as welcome relief. Not only was he happy for Heidi, but his own life had been purged of a lingering woe. For decades, he'd had to hear his wife mope and wail about the man who got away. Whenever he, Slam, did not do exactly what she wanted (stand at attention, get an erection), Jude would bring up that blessed "boy" of hers, the perfect one, the one who turned into a huge movie star, the very icon of a hero.

Oh, only *he* knew how to love, how to feel, how to cry.

Their parting all those years ago was "tragic," Russian-novel sized, and Slam had been sick to death of hearing about it. But Jude now told him that she had had her chance to flee to Tahiti, and she'd passed. The fantasy was over.

Slam had forgiven his wife, who seemed calmer than she had ever been. And Jude had forgiven him. Not that he rubbed it in, but he couldn't let her think she was the first person to have invented extramarital dalliance. A few years ago, he confided, there had been a woman in Italy who released all his tensions (building a business, appeasing a wife, raising the son with bad grades, and the other a misfit) . . .

"Her hands could crack chestnuts," Slam said, and he and his wife laughed at the phrase, and the general oddness of life.

"So that's what *you* go for, huh?" she said.

"Not really," he replied, shuddering. He actually didn't like women very much at all. They were murky.

Jude spent the next few evenings up in the family attic, where, deep in the back, she kept an old milk crate as a "time capsule." It overflowed with her journals, homework, and letters, all written during the year of Collum Whitsun. She had not looked at it for decades. Now, among her papers, she found one of her father's poems, balled up at the bottom of the crate. He had written it in the hospital after his first stroke, and the penmanship was legible but shaky.

The poem was addressed to her:

No learning out of ordinary time,
in ordinary days,
as simple as a rhyming rhyme
our ordinary ways.
Day by day and step by step.
Heart by heart and shlep by shlep.
We roam.
To find our home.

Jude stroked the paper, as she would have stroked his hand, trying to release its kinks and wrinkles and woes. Her father was gone, but his words had remained, and now she began to understand them. He was trying to come to terms, she thought, with the ordinary rhythms of life, and how they were better than hysteria and excessive passion. The kind that she and Collum had brought to him like terror at the dinner table. The kind that so often possessed Aaron himself, causing him to suffer all his life, and to fall ill at the end of it.

"*Heart by heart and shlep by shlep/We roam/To find our home,*" Jude recited self-consciously to Slam. "I know it's sort of Dorothy's red shoes," she added, "but—"

"As in, 'there's no place like home'?"

"Yes," she acknowledged. "But it's also part Ulysses. My Dad is saying that you have to wander, but don't let yourself get lost. He never lived to see us married, but we did marry and we made a family. I think he would have been pleased with what we've built together."

A few days later, Jude S. Ewington sent this message to Collum Whitsun:

It may have been better if our lives had never gotten tangled together. We were charged ions that yanked each other. It felt so important, didn't it?

Time did stop, then and now. We stood outside ourselves. Our bodies soared and our souls, for a moment, were freed. It seemed so real, so much realer than anything else.

But you know what? It wasn't real at all.

Is mad love the epic adventure? Is ordinary life banal?

I think it is the other way around. Going on, moving forward.

The ordinary: That's epic enough.

I've never been able to be alone. It's painful not to have a soul mate. But however much the truth hurts, it's the truth, and what I need.

There was no answer. Later that day, Collum Whitsun's account was closed, and all anyone could reach was the fan page of Colm Eriksen, a man who didn't actually exist anymore.

Jude puts on the flannel nightgown that she loves, the kind with the ruffled neckline. Her husband wears a T-shirt and pajama bottoms that tie with a string. Each goes to bed with a good book made of paper and ink, their reading glasses perched on their noses. They put their books down and chat a bit. Joey was doing better at school, and Davey was still seeing Delaney, but had mentioned that another girl seemed to like him, and another boy, a senior, seemed to like her. Davey thought he might even want to go back to boarding school with Joey next year. It was good to get away sometimes, he told them. Both of them, mom and dad, are proud of him, relieved and optimistic.

Everything was fine, the two of them agreed. Satisfied, they kiss each other goodnight, a peck near the lips. Then they turn, yawn, and stretch, entering the depths of a good, untroubled sleep. Jude is more at peace than she has ever been before, even as a girl in her own parents' home.

After decades of roaming, she takes a well-deserved rest.

Just One More Step

nd after that restoring rest, she rises. The pillow-top king-size bed is cushy, and over the last few weeks Slam has even spoken of their moving to a larger house with bigger bedrooms, a real pool and stone decking. But Jude would stay where she was as her husband moved on and up. Something lived inside her now that she would not abandon.

Judy Pincus stands by the mirror and sees herself with honest, loving eyes. She looks at her changing face, the skin and bones that alter with each year. Time seemed to be moving faster now, and she was hurtling forward, just as she had when she'd met that lonely boy with the shaggy locks and blackened eye, when her heart had first opened. Even at this late date, even if she's scared, she will never give up on finding what she still needs. Down under, she senses the presence of someone she'd never been alone with, someone she now longed to know—the girl, no longer young, who'd never left her.

Acknowledgments

Afterword

Reader's Guide

About the Author

Acknowledgments

Once again I owe a heartfelt thank-you to my brilliant, elegant, and unassuming publisher, Ellie McGrath, and to her partner, husband, and cofounder of McWitty Press, Paul Witteman. After a valiant battle, Paul passed away on New Year's Day, 2013, leaving the world a legacy of boundless love and curiosity, and an extraordinary daughter, Kate. As with my previous two books, *In the King's Arms* and *The Watchmaker's Daughter*, I consider this one to have been godparented by both Ellie and Paul, and I am proud of this rare provenance.

Thanks again, too, to our visual dream team: Jenny Carrow and Abby Kagan, the cover and interior artists, respectively, who make these books so outrageously good-looking. The sensitive edits of Chris Peterson are also much appreciated.

A big hug to my dear friends Lynn Schwartz, Debra Berman, Anne Bookin, Bonni-Dara Michaels, Susan Weinstein, and Tammy Williams. My deep admiration to Jan Henrik Olofsen, who embodies the brave soul of the wounded child and is able to translate these wounds into travel, creativity, and love. While his own upbringing was sometimes jarring, Jan is the epitome of patient parenthood, which—like so much else—he turns into an art form. My brother, Emanuel, is also a maven in this field: gifted in the art of resilient living and a wonderful dad to his daughters, Jenny and Michelle.

As ever, I'm grateful to my husband, Paul, and our children, Emma, Gabriel, and Phoebe. They show me the true meaning of loyalty and love, and when I come out from "down under," their light guides me home.

Afterword

In describing this book, I've often alluded to a certain person in the "real world," an actor whose powerful work I've always adored and whose intelligence and integrity I've never doubted.

What I see in people like this is passion in its broadest sense. They show up, they struggle, they strive. They paint with broad, dripping strokes on great canvases. They love with all their hearts, sometimes to bursting. They create beauty and wreak havoc, often at the same time. Sometimes, of course, they crash—and when they do, the world rushes in to stare at the massive crater they've created. The spillage and the slowly drifting flotsam make fascinating front-page news. The press takes snaps, tapes rants, broadcasts the bald spot, and shows off the spittle-pelted lens. An entertained "public" stares at endless loops of degradation, appalled and tutting. But no one, I am sure, feels more appalled than these emotional kamikazes themselves, these brave hearts who send themselves into the world, naked and alone.

The troubles experienced by talented, complicated souls have inspired some aspects of this novel. I am attracted to ups and downs, to complex people who self-destruct. I am a willing witness to the brokenhearted child that often lies behind the rise and fall of such people. Not all of them fully self-destruct. Some rise to extraordinary heights (staying up there is the hard part; the air is thin). In the case of both Collum Eriksen and the star he may sometimes resemble, I have no doubt of resurrection, and wish for it. I love such people, fictional or real.

I'm the child of war-torn Holocaust survivors, and therefore bear a certain intergenerational legacy of trauma and pain. I probably went to law school to learn how to make the world "fairer," to heal it. Over the years, I've worked pro bono as an advocate for foster kids and have seen the lasting effects of abuse on young children. Fear begets fear, anger, and despair. At the same time, love—that elusive goal—can be an omnipotent healer. Like flowers, children turn to the light and grow toward it.

To understand is to forgive. I both understand and forgive the players in this novel—and I hope the reader comes to feel the same.

Reader's Guide

1. What do you think this book has to say about the quest for "true love"?

2. What truly sparks Jude's decision to reach out to her long-lost boyfriend?

3. One theme in the book is loyalty: to parents, to old flames, to one's own traditions. How is Jude loyal or disloyal? What challenges does she face?

4. The depiction of Collum Whitsun is complicated. How does his traumatic upbringing affect your opinion of him?

5. Do you see similarities between Jude's upbringing and Collum's?

6. How does the parallel story between Delaney and David add to the texture of the novel?

7. The author uses a lot of humor in the book. What do you think this says about the drama she describes? Can a book this entertaining also be serious? Can you think of other books that have used this combination of tones?

8. Apart from its association with Australia, what do you think is meant by the title, *Down Under*?

About the Author

SONIA TAITZ is an essayist, a playwright, and the critically acclaimed author of *The Watchmaker's Daughter*, *In the King's Arms*, and *Mothering Heights*. Her writing has been featured in *The New York Times*, *The New York Observer*, *O: The Oprah Magazine*, *More*, and *Psychology Today*, where she is a columnist on family trauma. She has been cited on ABC's *Nightline*, in a PBS special on love, and in countless quotation anthologies.

Sonia Taitz earned a J.D. from Yale Law School; she has a served as a law guardian for foster children and an ER advocate for victims of rape and domestic violence. She also holds an M.Phil. in nineteenth-century English literature from Oxford University, where she was awarded the Lord Bullock Prize for her fiction. She lives in New York City.